The
Shift
An Awakening

Gloria,

May your grandest dreams
for our planet become
reality for all of us.

John English

8/13/04

What people are saying about The Shift

"The Shift opens the door into assessing the power of individual and collective thoughts, an intriguing look into the world of mysticism and its powerful healing powers. Read and learn what you may think into reality."

> Tim Andrews
> Phoenix, Az

"John English has done a wonderful job of bringing to the surface some of the critical issues that we as a society are facing at this time. This story, although it is fiction, displays a great deal of truth about where we are headed as a civilization. It also invites us to explore new ideas and ways of life that could dramatically change the outcome of the path that we are presently on. One of the strongest points for me was the reminder that we are creating in our life time, the world that our children and our children's children will be inhabiting. WHAT ARE WE DOING?"

> Allan Mutschler
> Phoenix, Az

"John English has taken a dream and turned it into a tantalizing story about what might happen if the country suddenly decided to "shift" from the status quo into a new political system free of the current ties that bind us. I found his approach refreshing and even possible to redefine our political system."

> Judy Anderson
> Minneapolis, Mn

What people are saying about The Shift

"Beautiful in its intent, The Shift takes the reader on a mystical journey of transformation and planetary healing. English masterfully weaves a spiritually uplifting tale of a man's passionate struggle to make a difference in this world. An awakening has begun that will change the political landscape of our nation and the ultimate destiny of the planet. John English reminds us that we are all stewards of the earth and that a shared dream can heal our world."

Brad Fisher
Scottsdale, Az

"The Shift: An Awakening presents a powerful vision that shows humanity a way out of our current state of affairs. It accomplishes this by drawing the reader into a story that is both compelling and believable. Knowing John personally, I can attest that his passion for the message and its potential impact is both complete and authentic, and reveals his philosophy of dreaming the world into being. The only remaining question is, will the rest of us follow?"

Paul Schnabel
Speaker on achievement and co-author of
Give Stress a Rest

The
Shift

An Awakening

John English

Edited by
Rolf V. Lange

DREAMTIME
PUBLICATIONS, INC.

DREAMTIME
PUBLICATIONS, INC.
CAVE CREEK, ARIZONA
USA

TYPESETTING & LAYOUT BY COWLEY PUBLISHING
SALT LAKE CITY, UTAH
cowleypublishing@mac.com

ISBN 0-9727034-1-1
Library of Congress Control Number: 2003091138

Web address: www.dtpublications.com
Email Address: TheShift@dtpublications.com

Printed in the United States on recycled paper (30% post-consumer)

Acknowledgements

There are so many to thank that have been instrumental to the completion of this book. In particular I would like to thank my wife Laurie and our children Patrick, Kailee and Melissa for giving me the space to continually redefine who I am in this world. I would like to thank my teachers Alberto Villoldo, Arnold Rice and Harry Newberry. Thank you to my early editors Patricia English and Lori Stonebreaker. Thanks to all my friends I have met during my journey through the medicine wheel. Special thanks to Naomi Silverstone, Michael Cowley of Cowley Publishing, Jeff Carroll, Lindsey Favia, Lynn Berryhill, Jamee Curtice and Holly Wood. Thank you to all my friends who have put up with me over the last year and a half as I wrote this book: Scott Graves, Joy Stein Alder, Paul Schnabel, Brad Fischer, Allan Mutschler, Mitch Prager, Jane Rice, Bruce Zierk, Kirk Bogan, Terri Mitchell, and Judy Cottone.

Lastly, I owe a special debt of gratitude to my friend and editor Rolf Lange without whose camaraderie and ability to focus in on the minute details this book would not be pleasurable to read.

To my wife and children.

For my children's children and their children.

Table of Contents

Introduction

It has been suggested to me that I share a little bit about my journey while writing this book. This advice has come from someone that I trust and respect, so after careful consideration I have decided to do so. What happened in my life during the period that led up to and while writing this novel is a tale in and of itself. Therefore, I will simply try to provide the reader with some insight into my experience and how I was compelled to communicate it.

This journey began at a ceremony in May of 2001. During this ceremony I experienced myself as several different forms of life. As I walked back to my room I wondered what this experience could have meant and thought that perhaps the whole thing was just in my imagination, something I've been accused of having an overabundance of. After returning to my room I decided to meditate on what had happened, so I put a chair in front of the window and stared out at the mountains and the stars. During my meditation I had the realization that the One Spirit that many of us call God is not separate from any part of creation. I understood that the reason I had the experience during the ceremony was because I am a part of this spirit that animates and flows through the entirety of creation

Then a picture unfolded before me and I directly perceived that there is a necessary energetic balance between human beings and all other forms of life on earth that is both delicate and in jeopardy. I had the realization that we are connected through Spirit to every living thing on this planet and as we continue to crowd out other life we are slowly killing a vital part of ourselves.

Then the understanding that the earth would not allow us to continue in this way overcame me. It was at this point that I was given the dream that became the novel you are about to read. It is a dream about how things could change dramatically and quickly through the power of our intent. It is a dream about the possible, not the probable.

After receiving this dream I was told to write it down in the form of a book. Now I had a problem on my hands. Don't get me wrong I loved the thought of becoming a writer, but I was afraid: I had never written anything more complicated than a high school paper!

I delayed starting this book for about two months. This is when Spirit began to apply the pressure. One day I went for a hike in the Sacred Canyon. During the hike Spirit began chattering in my ear about how I promised to write this dream down and that I was not following through. The canyon walls and all the plants seemed to be crying to me about how I had made a promise that I wasn't keeping. That day, when I got home, I began writing.

At first I recorded the book hoping that I could get a ghost writer to write it for me. This seemed perfectly logical, after all what did I know about writing a book? The first person I approached flat out refused, three or four times (thank you Joy). The second person found the idea appealing and agreed to my plan. However, she would never find the time to proceed at a pace that was congruent with the pressure Spirit was putting on me. Later the computer file that contained her writing would be lost. In the meantime I got the message that I was supposed to write this book by myself and that the necessary help would be sent to me.

Over the last year and a half my business went south with the rest of the economy. At times during this period I actually didn't have any work, so I continued to plod along with this novel. At one point I was so broke that I was a couple of weeks away from having to borrow money just to pay my family's bills. One day I took a break from my writing to pour a cup of coffee and Spirit spoke to me saying, "We are going to let up on the financial pressure, but remember you promised to finish this book. It must remain your top priority." That afternoon I got an unexpected phone call, unexpected because despite my best efforts there were no prospects for any work. That phone call resulted in a contract for my company and the next day another contract came in. Since then I have received just enough work to keep my household afloat while I continued to focus on learning to write.

After this experience I worked six to eight hours a day at my job so I could pay my family's bills and three to four hours a day writing this book. With the exception of an occasional mountain bike ride my entire weekends were devoted to writing down this dream. One weekend I was taking a break from writing and enjoying a mountain bike ride. While riding I heard a squeaky noise, so I stopped to investigate. What I found was that the frame on my mountain bike had cracked. This does happen on occasion, but what happened next got my attention. I proceeded to crack the frame on the next two bikes that were provided under warranty to replace my original one. Mountain biking was taking four to six hours a week, this was four to six hours a week that could be spent recording the dream I was given. About a month or so later (while I was waiting for frame number three to arrive) I asked my friend if I could borrow his mountain bike that he had left at my house. I went for short ride of about half an hour in the desert behind my home and…I broke his bike! Not the frame, but it was broken nonetheless. After this, I completely got the picture. When my new bike arrived, it sat there waiting for me until I finished what I agreed to do.

Too many people have shown up in my life at precisely the right time to help me in the journey of writing this book, thereby eliminating the possibility of their appearances being coincidence. There are many things written in this book about life, about spirituality and about the importance of the times we live in right now. Of all the things written, one bears repeating here. I believe it is the key that leads to all of the experiences had by the characters in this novel.

A character is asked, if his party accomplishes but one thing what would that one thing be? He replies that it would be for people to get in touch with the spirit of the earth and become caretakers of the planet.

To the possible, instead of the probable.

John English

January 2003

"What is the force that binds the stars?
I've worn this mask to hide my scars.
What is the power that pulls the tide?
That never could find a place to hide.
What moves the Earth around the Sun?
What could I do but run and run and run."

Sting

Chapter 1—The Spark

Jack and Ben spent the day fasting in prayer and meditation to prepare themselves for their ceremony that evening. They passed the time walking along the Mogollon Rim overlooking the forest below. There was a cold November wind blowing and weaving its way through the trees, it carried a lot of information with it. To those who had ears to hear, the wind spoke from the heart of the earth. The two men spent the day listening to the wind talk of things to come.

Days earlier in Phoenix, Scott sat tensely on the edge of his couch, gripping the cushion with both hands as he glared in disbelief at the evening's top news story. His passion for politics and his great love of country were about to get the best of him. Andrew Knight, the democratic candidate was announcing he would contest the presidential election in Florida.

He turned to his wife seated next to him. "I can't believe he's going to do this! Don't they see this country is teetering on the edge of recession, and we need a quick resolution to this mess?" No longer seated on the couple's couch, Scott was pacing the family room as Andrew Knight did his best to appeal to the American public.

After 25 years of marriage Scott's wife Elizabeth was accustomed to his passionate outbursts. "Relax honey. Did you really believe he would do any differently?"

"I did. He said if the election was certified he wouldn't contest it. I wonder if anyone keeps track of how often politicians say one thing and do another," Scott said.

"A lot of people believe he should contest the election. Besides, reporters cornered him into answering that question a week ago. Much has happened since then," Elizabeth said.

"I'm so sick of this. I just can't stand it any longer," Scott said.

Scott had long pondered the consequences of our elected official's short-term thinking. He believed as long as they continued to protect the status quo and those who profited from it, that the American way of life would be unsustainable. He saw no hope for our planet if the American model of consumerism were to spread to the over six billion people on Earth. From the research he had done he didn't believe the earth could sustain even a third of its current population consuming the way America does.

"We've been watching this for over a week now. What has got you so excited all of a sudden?" Elizabeth asked.

"I've been waiting for twenty years for a leader with vision to step forward and put it all together. Why does the environment have to suffer at the expense of the economy? Why can't we have lower taxes and still address the social issues of our country?" Scott said.

Elizabeth looked at Scott and shrugged her shoulders and then went back to her book. Scott took a deep breath and tried to return to a state of apathy but he just couldn't seem to get the job done.

"I don't think either one of these guys," Scott said referring to both candidates, "gives a rat's ass about this country or any of the people in it. All they care about is power."

"Well you know that's true," Elizabeth commented without looking up from her book. Scott continued talking to himself and Elizabeth noticed his voice was growing fainter as he climbed the stairs and disappeared into his office.

Scott sat down at his desk in front of the computer and let out a deep sigh. He felt helpless but he wanted to do something. What could he do? Suddenly he got a spark of inspiration and decided to fire off an email to the senator from Arizona, Patrick Kincaid the sponsor for campaign finance reform legislation in the Senate. He found the senator's web site, linked to his email address and began writing an email entitled:

"Don't give up."

Dear Senator,

I am appalled by what I see in the American political scene today. The effects and influence of big money and what it has done to our country and our political system anger me. I just don't believe that this is what our forefathers had in mind. I know that this is a subject that is near and dear to your heart also, and you promised that after this election there would be blood on the senate floor if campaign finance reform weren't passed. The influence of the political power brokers is one of the reasons why this election hasn't come to a close yet. Neither one of these men could step down at this point if they wanted to, because they sold their freedom to those who bank rolled their campaigns. I don't believe for a minute it has anything to do with the best interests of this country. The election has been certified, and Andrew Knight should step down. In my opinion, he can't do that however, because he's trapped by the very friends that helped him get this far in the first place. Something must be done! I hope that you will stick to your guns and get campaign finance reform through congress. I am behind you 100%. I don't know anyone who isn't.

Good luck and thank you.

Scott Stahl, Phoenix, Arizona

After emailing Patrick Kincaid Scott fired off a similar email to his own senator, the other senator from Arizona, and to his congressman. This activity brought him a bit of temporary relief, but somehow deep inside he knew that he was supposed to do more.

Unfortunately, he had no idea what that was.

Scott believed that fear; power and the lack of integrity characterized this campaign on both sides and at every level. Neither one of the candidates seemed to have the combination of qualities that were necessary to bring about the kind of change that was needed in this country. Both candidates used fear rather effectively to sway the voters not to vote for their opponent.

What did this say about their ability to be true leaders? He wondered.

The republican candidate Robert Kelton, played on people's fears of big government. Andrew Knight played on the fears of the elderly in regards to social security, and did his best to pit one class of people against the other. The message that Scott got from the election results was that most Americans wanted neither candidate to become the country's leader.

"Maybe we should declare a do over," Scott said aloud, "or they should put in a spot on the ballot to vote for none of the above. If none of the above wins they toss these two guys out and two new candidates give it a shot."

Scott believed that Americans know consciously or unconsciously that our current course cannot be maintained.

He thought about how so much of what we're doing doesn't make any sense at all, how we can't continue to consume the earth's resources at this pace, expecting the rest of the world to join us and bury our heads in the sand pretending we aren't courting environmental disaster. Even if we could burn fossil fuels indefinitely our atmosphere would become unable to sustain life. Neither candidate's behavior demonstrated they had what it took to guide Americans away from their fear and apathy into consciously changing their impact on this planet. Probably, neither one of their parties has the capability to provide the kind of leadership that is necessary to accomplish this change.

Scott thought about how the majority of Americans were not on the left or the right politically, they were right down the center. The hair on the back of Scott's neck stood up when it occurred to him, what we really need is another political party. One that is funded exclusively by ordinary Americans and therefore free to make policy that benefits the majority instead of the powerful.

There was no way Scott could have known at this time how that simple notion would affect the rest of his life.

He shut off the light to his office, and walked back downstairs to join his wife who had already gone into their bedroom. "What have you been doing up there?" Elizabeth asked. "I thought you were never going to come down."

"I sent an email to our senator and one to our congressman. I am tired of feeling helpless and frustrated so I decided to make my voice heard."

The couple discussed what Scott had thought about in his office. Elizabeth agreed that another political party would surely shake things up. They kissed and shut off the lights and went to sleep.

Shortly after drifting off to sleep Scott began to dream. In his dream there was a man standing at a podium with a red tailed hawk circling above him. It was a lucid dream and Scott began to ask questions.

"Who is this man?"

A voice that seemed to come from all around him answered, "Who he is does not matter now. What is of importance is that he is there. Try not to forget this."

Scott felt that he knew the man, but could not quite remember from where. He asked another question. "What does the red tailed hawk mean?"

"The hawk brings the vision from above where everything can be seen without losing the ability to focus in on the smallest detail. The hawk judges the winds flawlessly and soars accordingly."

Scott wanted to ask another question but he awoke immediately. It was 2:30 a.m. He was thirsty, so he got out of bed and went into the kitchen to get a drink of water. He was standing in the kitchen holding a glass of water when a voice from behind him sent a jolt of adrenaline through his body.

"Scott my son, you are the one who will be the founder of a new political party."

Scott was shocked and wheeled around to see who was standing behind him, almost dropping his glass of water in the process. There was no one standing there, but he had heard that voice. Goose bumps appeared all over his body, and a chill ran up his spine. He had the sense of a presence very close to him

He regained his composure, finished his glass of water, and put the glass down on the counter. On the way back to bed he laughed at himself thinking he must still be dreaming. He crawled back into bed with his wife and snuggled up next to her.

@

That evening was full of dreams but none were more important than the one experienced by Patrick Kincaid. He was enveloped in a white light that radiated warmth throughout his entire body, and he had a feeling of peace unlike anything he had ever experienced.

A voice that seemed to come from everywhere said, "I am…the voice of the one you spoke with so long ago when you were imprisoned during the war. I held your hand for five years. I am the one who gave you the strength and passion to pursue the life you have lived since you left that place, the one you pray to every day."

Patrick began to feel uneasy being in this presence, because he felt unworthy. As soon as this feeling appeared in his dream the voice spoke again saying,

"Do not fret my son; all men and women are worthy. You made a promise when you were in prison. Do you remember?" He remembered immediately, and nodded. He had promised God that if he ever got out of that prison he would do whatever was asked of him.

"That is correct my son," the voice said. "The time has come for you to fulfill your promise. You will be asked to make a couple of very important phone calls. You will be told at precisely the right time to make them. Patrick, timing is very important! Do you understand this?"

Patrick nodded. He was then told the names and phone numbers of two people. He recognized one, but not the other. He was told to write them down immediately upon waking.

Patrick jolted awake.

He was covered in sweat, and he quickly scanned the room. There was only his wife lying next to him fast asleep. He swung around and put his feet on the floor and sat on the edge of the bed, trying to come to grips with what had just happened.

He knew he was dreaming, but it seemed that God himself was speaking to him. *Could this be real?*

The voice answered his thought saying. "Yes, it is real. Do not be afraid, write down the names and numbers and go back to sleep." He grabbed his wallet off the nightstand and wrote down the information on the back of a business card, put the card back in his wallet and despite what just happened, the senator lay his head back down and immediately fell back asleep.

After waking the next morning he walked into the bathroom and looked long and hard at himself in the mirror. He shook his head and wondered if it all had really happened. Was it just some strange dream? On the way into the office his mind kept playing the dream over and over again in his head. He then flashed back to the time he spent imprisoned during the Vietnam War and the torture and indignities he suffered at the hands of his captors. One day was extremely horrible and he was at the point of giving up on life. He sensed that all he had to do was give up his will to live and he would perish and his suffering would end, it was on this day that he made the promise that the voice in the dream reminded him of last night. Again and again he thought about hearing that voice as he sat on the edge of his bed, and how easily he fell back asleep after the whole experience. His rational mind was having trouble with the fact that there were two names and phone numbers written down on a card in his wallet.

That same morning Scott awoke at 5:15 a.m., his usual time. While he lay awake in bed he remembered dreaming earlier that morning. In his mind he associated what had happened in the kitchen with the dream.

When he made the coffee that morning he didn't even notice the empty glass on the counter. Perhaps he wasn't supposed to. After his coffee was finished brewing, he made his way upstairs to start his work day. Scott's company provided engineering services for the manufacturing sector. He had been working from his own home since moving to Arizona from the Midwest ten years ago.

The night before when he was writing the senators and his congressman, he made some notes on a yellow legal pad. He had detailed some common-sense solutions to the issues facing America today. This morning he took these thoughts a little further by writing down why he believed America needed a new political party and what that party's vision might be. He smiled at himself and put the legal pad to the side.

He thought again about his dream, particularly the part where he was standing in the kitchen and the voice spoke to him telling him that he would start another party. Just for grins he got up out of his chair, exited his office, and looked down in the kitchen where he saw a lone empty glass sitting on the counter. He stood there staring at it for a long minute, feeling uneasy, and then dismissed the whole thing telling himself that he must have dreamed about the voice after he got up to get a drink.

"Enough of this nonsense!" He said aloud after sitting back down at his desk. "I've got work to do."

Scott set about his normal routine; he checked on the stock market, and then began his engineering work. All day long he couldn't shake the feeling that something big was going to happen. He mentioned this feeling to his wife after she got back from attending classes that afternoon.

"Well you know how that is," she said. "You've had these feelings before, and you just can't put your finger on what they're about. But in time, you always seem to find an answer. Just be patient."

Scott knew she was right. He had had intuitions before. In the end he always found out what they were about.

Scott thought about how early in the race Robert Kelton was very far ahead in the polls. A few good moves would have salted Andrew Knight away, but Kelton just couldn't seem to clearly present his case.

Scott also saw how Andrew Knight, after gaining momentum, could have clearly overtaken Kelton's lead. However, he would have had to drop the class rhetoric, and ease up on the campaign of fear and resentment. Couldn't they see their missed opportunities? Scott wondered who wrote their speeches, and prepared their campaign strategy. What was going on in their minds? He asked himself.

"No wonder neither one of them could get elected!" he said.

"What's that?" Elizabeth asked.

"Oh nothing. I was just thinking out loud."

Jack and Susan Anderson stood in the dairy section of their local supermarket in Phoenix. Jack normally wouldn't accompany Susan to the market on a weekday, but he had taken the day off from work, and he had nothing better to do.

Susan was milling around in front of the dairy section, and Jack was not paying attention to anything in particular when Susan said. "Huh, that's funny, there are no organic eggs left." Susan insisted on buying eggs from cage-free hens. She was very conscious of everything she puts into her body; believing that the way an animal is treated affects its essential energy as well as that of the person who consumes it.

Just then a clerk walked by and asked. "May I help you find something?"

"Yes you may, I am looking for eggs that are laid by cage-free hens."

"I'm sorry we're all out," the clerk said, "its the strangest thing; those eggs cost twice as much as the other ones and lately we just can't seem to keep them in stock."

"It doesn't surprise me," Susan said.

"Well then you'll be glad to hear that our manager says we're going to be getting a whole new section dedicated to organic foods."

At that moment Jack awoke from his daydreaming. First he looked over at his wife, and then at the clerk. He glanced around at the other people in the market and the air became electric. His eyes came back to his wife and the clerk standing in front of the refrigerator it was a moment suspended in time and then a voice said to him,

"Jack, it's starting!"

Unlike Scott, Jack was accustomed to hearing the voice of Spirit and acting upon it. He knew exactly what was starting; his shamanic training had prepared him for this.

Jack's destiny was beginning to unfold.

He finished helping his wife with the grocery shopping, loaded their groceries into the Jeep, and headed home. After they had unloaded the groceries he had a strong urge to turn on the television. He turned the channel to CNN where they had 24 hour a day coverage of the election debacle. Susan thought this was kind of unusual because Jack did not care much for television and rarely ever watched it.

He laughed aloud as a member of the republican campaign team said with a straight face that they were not trying to stall the vote counting in Florida.

Neither one of these candidates has the kind of power to bring about the changes that are needed. Jack realized that this thought did not come from him because, up until now, he hadn't paid too much attention to what was going on in Florida, nor had he cared.

He knew that after the message he received in the supermarket he would have to be vigilant, especially about the clarity of his awareness. It wasn't a coincidence that he had a sudden interest in the political mess that he saw on the television before him.

"Susan is there anything else you need me for?"

"Not that I can think of off hand, but I'm sure if you give me some time—

"Well then before you give it too much thought I'm going to head off to my room to do some work," Jack said.

After entering the room that he used for his shamanic work, Jack called upon the archetypal energies of the south, west, north, east, earth, and heaven and connected with them to create sacred space.

To the shaman sacred space is where the veil between man and Spirit is at its thinnest, sometimes disappearing entirely. In sacred space the shaman works with the energy that is created by the universe and informs all life. The Chinese call it chi, the Hindu call it prana; in the mystical tradition that Jack is a part of it is called kausai.

Jack sat down on a pillow in the middle of the room and began to meditate using rhythmic breathing. He went deeper and deeper into his meditation until he reached a place where there was no thought, and no time.

Then he asked. "I am here, how can I be of service?"

It had taken him years of practice to become available to the voice of the other world that was about to inform him. Jack learned that a man named Scott, whom he saw in a vision three years ago, was to start a new political party, although he was not yet aware of it.

The voice of Spirit spoke directly to Jack saying, "This man's calling in this life is a tall order. He needs your help. He is not as strong as you, and his faith is going to be completely and thoroughly tested. His heart is full of a great love for his country, the earth and its environment."

In this deep trance state Jack could only hear the constant vibration of kausai and the voice of Spirit. He was told that Scott Stahl is the person who would catalyze a great change in awareness as a public figure.

"He will be the first; the spark that ignites the flame. Your destiny, Jack, is to stand behind this man, and do everything in your power to make sure that he doesn't give up."

"Your destiny is to make certain that he fulfills his destiny!"

While still in his trance Jack perceived a vast source of kausai energy that seemed to be everywhere and nowhere all at once. As he bathed in its undulating flow, he gathered strands of this energy and directed them towards Scott, a man he had never met, but who's destiny was apparently intertwined with his own. As he began to emerge from the trance the voice that came from all around him repeated the words,

"He must not fail!… He must not fail!… He must not fail!…"

Susan knocked on the door as Jack was coming out of his trance.

"Jack its almost time for dinner. It's been over two hours already."

"Thanks sweetheart I'll be out in a few. I've just got to close the space."

It never ceased to amaze Jack how time stood still in the presence of Spirit.

In keeping with the ritual practice he had learned long ago he closed the sacred space, releasing the powers of the south, west, north, east, heaven and earth, and stood up feeling renewed. Jack was filled with love at that moment and it exuded from every pore of his being.

Jack was beaming as he sat down to dinner. "Wow! You're awful bright," his wife said.

"Oh, yeah," he said, and shot her a wink.

Scott and Elizabeth were relaxing after eating dinner when Elizabeth asked.

"I have to go to the mall to pick up a couple of things. Would you like to come with me?"

"I would," Scott replied, "I've been wanting to buy some software to design a website for my company."

As they drove, Scott put on some of their favorite music. *Maybe this will help me get my mind off the mess we're all in now. We still don't have a president elect, the stock market is diving, and even worse some people are predicting a recession. I wonder how this will affect my business—*

"Earth to Scott...Earth to Scott," Elizabeth said. "Where are you?"

"I'm driving to the mall," Scott said. He turned and smiled at her.

"No you're not."

"I know," Scott sighed. "I was thinking about the stupid election fiasco."

"Oh, not that again."

"What we really need is another political party," he said. "One that combines what little common sense is left in the other two, and supports the interests of the majority. I mean, how come so many of us can see clearly what needs to be done and still all we get is politicians arguing over who gets to take credit for inadequate results?"

"Are you sure you can drive and talk about politics at the same time?" She smiled. "Maybe you should pull over and let me drive."

"No really Elizabeth, I'm serious, this is really bothering me."

"I'm sorry, I know it is, I just can't resist the urge to tease you. You're right, what we need is a political party that is not afraid to tell the truth, about everything, especially when it comes to the environment. Who knows, maybe someday we can vote for a party like that."

After Elizabeth said this, Scott got a strange feeling in the pit of his stomach.

As the couple walked into the mall he was thinking about the dream he had last night and wondered again what it could have meant. The couple split up to save time. Elizabeth went off to do her shopping, and Scott headed for the computer store.

Scott walked straight to the software section. He had been toying with the idea of a company web site for quite some time now. After getting quotations on the price however, he decided against it until he had a conversation with one of his friends about doing it himself. A young man who seemed to know more about computers and software than was healthy helped Scott pick out software he could use for his own web site design.

He met up with Elizabeth after she finished her shopping and they drove home talking about politics and their children. The couple wondered what kind of world their son and daughter would be living in when they were their age. Their son was in his third year of college and had a serious relationship with a young woman he met there. Scott and Elizabeth talked about the likelihood that they would become grandparents in the next five to ten years. They wondered what kind of world their grandchildren would inherit?

The next morning began normally for Scott. The phone rang at around 8:30; it was the customer he was currently working for. The customer indicated that the contract Scott was working on, was being put on hold indefinitely. Suddenly, Scott found himself with nothing to do.

After milling around his house and office for a couple of hours. He decided to take a look at the web design software he had purchased last night. The urge came over him to load the software and see how it worked. This was kind of unusual behavior for Scott because he worked in front of a computer eight to ten hours a day and had been doing so for the last eight years. He usually waited until the last minute to accomplish anything that had to do with the computer that didn't result in invoicing a customer.

Scott, a whiz with software and computing, worked his way through the software tutorial in no time. Out of the blue he had the idea that maybe he should design a practice web page first before designing one for his company. This seemed to make good sense to him. He could get to know the ins and outs of the program while designing a dummy web site. He laughed out loud as the thought crossed his mind of creating a web site about the insanity of current politics. At first he thought about a site where he could voice his opinions with a web page allowing others to do the same. The appeal of this idea faded when he considered that it might just make him angry.

What to do? What to do?

Then, in a flash of what would later be referred to as divine inspiration, he said aloud, "I know. I'll design a web site for a completely new political party."

It'll be fun and besides, I don't have anything else to do.

He grabbed the legal pad on his desk and began to write down some ideas. *What to call it?* He asked himself.

Hmm.... How about the Centrist party? Americans are definitely split right down the center when it comes to which way they lean politically. Centrist is a word that he had heard a lot of lately, but for some reason it just didn't seem to have enough appeal.

Scott played with that word in his mind for a minute or two, and then wrote down the Centrust Party. *Yeah that's it, a party in the center politically worthy of Americans trust.* It had a ring to it. It had two syllables unlike democrat or republican.

What could be their motto?... What leads to trust? He asked himself.

The consequences of many of our collective actions are not always clear, but if our elected officials allowed everything to be seen, then Americans could be better informed about the impact of

their decisions on this world.

He wrote down The Centrust Party, the party of visibility. When all things are brought to the light there can be nothing but trust. He continued telling himself that all he was doing was practicing for his own web site so he wouldn't feel silly, as he played with these ideas.

He grabbed the legal pad that he had, for some reason a couple of nights earlier, jotted down his dreams for political reform in America and in bold gold letters on the top of the page he put THE CENTRUST PARTY. Underneath it he wrote, "The party of visibility, a new political party for America." Below this he listed the ten items of the party's mission statement.

1) The Centrust Party's goal is to make the American governmental system visible. All Americans will then be able to make informed decisions about issues important to them. This can only be accomplished through complete campaign finance reform. The Centrust Party will not accept soft money. Political contributions will only be accepted from individuals within the legal limits of campaign finance law.

2) The Centrust Party is committed to finding practical solutions to the social issues that face our country. This can, and must be done with less of a tax burden than Americans carry today. A government that operates even close to the efficiency of one of our successful American companies, along with lower taxes will foster the majority's cooperation.

3) The Centrust Party is the true conservative party, as it views everyone as a part of nature, not apart from it. We will make known in a clear and concise fashion all of the facts that our government currently has about our environment and the effects we have on it. We will then enlist Americans help in consciously changing our

impact on this planet to preserve a natural heritage worthy of our legacy.

4) The Centrust Party, in conjunction with American business, will move quickly towards building an economy that is environmentally sustainable for generations to come. Using tax incentives that encourage the business community to lead us in reducing our environmental impact and closing corporate loopholes that allow environmental destruction to continue will help to accomplish this. Accelerating our use of alternative fuels and energy sources along with increasing the funding for energy and the environment are among the first steps that we propose to move our economy in the right direction.

5) The Centrust Party will abolish the IRS and establish a progressive flat tax with no deductions. Implementing a progressive flat tax will result in a substantial tax savings for all Americans. It is time to eliminate the influence of special interests through our tax code. It is time we usher in a new era, an era during which our government informs consumers about the impact of their decisions rather than trying to control them using the tax code.

6) The Centrust Party supports increasing teacher's salaries until their pay is commensurate with other professionals. This will encourage our greatest minds to enter one of our most important fields, educating the youth of our country. Teachers who no longer produce the results necessary for this transformation in our educational system, or no longer have the passion needed to bring about this transformation will be eliminated from the system.

7) The Centrust Party will not bandy about social security as a political issue and something will be done about its impending crisis. Private accounts that earn a rate of interest comparable with treasury notes are an excellent

idea. Individuals that don't consume their social security account during their retirement can leave the leftover funds to their children's social security accounts. Social security should provide social security, currently it doesn't.

8) The Centrust Party believes industrial hemp needs to be legalized for use as paper, and the many other products it is suited for. Farmers deserve the opportunity to grow this profitable crop. What is left of our country's forests can start the process of regenerating naturally under our care and supervision.

9) The Centrust Party will promote forgiveness in America. The spirit of forgiveness can heal the American soul. Forgiveness promotes unity instead of separation. Each of us needs to wipe the slate clean and let all people be judged on their present actions, not the actions of their past, nor their ancestral past. In doing this we can all move forward with the wisdom obtained by our mistakes in the past without being encumbered by them.

10) The Centrust Party encourages republicans and democrats who are fed up with self-serving politics to join us. Join us in building a party that is founded on visibility and trust. Together we can begin to bring common sense back into American government.

Scott looked back over everything he had written and took a minute to admire what he had created. He scanned through the software manual section that covered customization and because he had experience in programming for his engineering software he understood what he was reading.

He added email links next to each of the ten items in the mission statement that would allow people to respond and express their opinions regarding the issues. Since he was just playing with the software he put in his company email address just to see how it would work. Scott programmed in different keywords into the header of his home page that would be recognized by the major Internet browsers. Scott concluded that his company web page wouldn't be any more complicated, or require any more space than the one he had just created. He called his Internet Service Provider to reserve the space on the server he would use. The service explained how to load his web page once he had obtained his domain name.

After the voice of Spirit spoke to Jack in the supermarket and during his meditation later that day, he contacted his mentor Ben and brought him up to speed.

The two men decided a trip to their ceremonial place on the Mogollon Rim was in order.

Jack finished packing up his jeep with his camping gear and came back into the house.

"Okay sweetheart I'm ready to go. I'll see you in a couple of days."

"I love you honey. Have a safe trip," Susan said.

Jack kissed her and the couple enjoyed a long embrace.

"I love you too," he said.

Susan reminisced for a few minutes after Jack's departure. She had been concerned at first when Jack decided to, as he put it "walk the medicine way." She had some fears about him adopting such an unconventional spiritual path. Instead what followed was a complete transformation of Jack, and he became a complete person unlike anyone else she had ever met.

She thought about how her husband no longer considered himself separate from anything or anyone, and he did his best to live his life in this state of being. One of the shaman's obligations, he told her, was to become the luminous warrior and practice peace and non-engagement.

Another obligation was to become a servant, and fulfill his highest destiny. Every time Jack left on one of his trips, she wondered if it would end up having something to do with his destiny. She also understood that this would have an impact on their marriage and her life. Before he committed to this high destiny long ago, (without even knowing what it was, or what it entailed), he asked her permission to do so.

Meanwhile, on the drive over to Ben's house Jack thought back to a conversation he had with Susan a couple of years ago. In this conversation he told her about a vision he had regarding a major change in planetary consciousness that would begin in America. He explained to Susan that contributing to what the voice of Spirit called *the Shift* was to be his high destiny. He hoped after this weekend with Ben, the time would be right to tell her that the shift had started.

Jack's thoughts then turned to his friend Ben. A chance meeting between the two had led Jack to adopting the experiential path of shamanism. He laughed aloud as he thought back to how Ben had patiently answered the thousand and one questions Jack had about being a shaman. Early on Ben explained to him that the path of the shaman was a beautiful path, but it was very difficult and humbling also. Jack didn't understand this in the beginning, but he has returned to those words and that conversation many times during the last ten years.

The humility his friend spoke of comes from the shaman's relationship with power and being. There is an awesome amount of responsibility that comes when one works with and directs the power that created our universe.

Ben was ready to go when Jack arrived at his house, and after a goodbye to his wife Patricia the two men went on their way. The drive would take about four hours, and the two friends enjoyed every moment of it. Their conversation on their drive included every subject they could think of except for the current political situation, and the reason for their trip. These two things would be dealt with in their ceremony, and both men knew that bringing them up now would be fruitless.

Jack and Ben laughed a lot that evening on the way to the Mogollon Rim. The funniest moments however, came as the two men stumbled around in the dark setting up their campsite. The November wind was howling and their first two attempts to set up their tent were unsuccessful. The Mogollon Rim is essentially one half of a canyon. It is a sudden elevation change of several hundred feet that runs for hundreds of miles in central Arizona. The wind that evening was whipping through the forest below them hitting the cliff wall, rising to meet the wind at their elevation and crashing down upon them where they were attempting to set up camp fifty feet from the rim's edge. On their second attempt to set up the tent, Ben was holding the flashlight while Jack attempted to get a couple of stakes in the ground. Before he could get the first stake in the wind picked up speed and in a swirling motion lifted the tent from Jack's grasp. It disappeared in an instant and Jack looked up at Ben, "That couldn't be good."

As they ran after the tent Ben said in between bursts of laughter, "Spirit sure isn't making it easy on us so far."

A ponderosa pine about three hundred feet into the forest caught their tent for them. Jack thanked the tree and then said to Ben as they walked back to the rest of their gear. "Perhaps an offering to the wind is in order."

"I was just thinking that exact same thing," Ben said.

Jack pulled some tobacco from his pouch while Ben connected with the wind several miles away from them in the forest below. Jack made the offering of tobacco and shortly thereafter it began to slow down until it resembled more of a breeze. Both men gave thanks.

After their camp had been set up they sat on the edge of the rim and looked down at the forest below bathing in the light of the moon and the stars. The beauty and peace of this place needed no words and each man was silent.

Back in Washington D.C. Patrick Kinkaid lay awake in bed. He had not been sleeping well the past couple of nights and even though he was exhausted when he went to bed he was still not asleep a couple of hours later. Despite his rational mind kicking and screaming he had not disposed of the names and phone numbers in his wallet.

I am a United States senator! I can't be calling people, because of some dream I've had. What will I tell them? That I made a promise to God years ago and recently in a dream he gave me instructions to contact them?....I don't think so!

Immediately after this thought he fell fast asleep. In a dream he found himself alone in a magnificent forest. He could feel the life force pulsing through everything around him and this made him feel very happy. Slowly a presence approached him and he felt his happiness begin to increase immeasurably. He turned to his left and he noticed a flowing luminous milky colored substance about the size of a human being next to him.

"Who are you?" he asked.

"I am the helper," the presence replied. "I have been sent to give you a message."

"What message?"

"There is a new paradigm in American politics trying to be born at this very moment in the western part of the United States."

"What do you mean trying to be born?"

"It is up to you and everyone else involved to do what is necessary to bring this shift about because you have free will and you can decide to follow through or not. Can I show you something?"

The next thing Patrick knew, he and the helper were floating in space miles above the earth. Below Patrick could see the entire western hemisphere.

"Patrick this is what will happen if people follow their hearts," the helper said.

Slowly at first, starting in what appeared to be central Arizona, and then picking up momentum as it continued the color green began spreading across the United States, into Canada and South America until it covered the entire planet. After this Patrick became elated.

"Green is the color of the heart. Suddenly making a couple of phone calls doesn't seem like a very big deal, does it Patrick?"

"No, I guess not," he replied.

"This is what will happen if no one follows through."

As he continued to look, he saw explosions happening simultaneously at different points on the earth. Fires broke out as a result of these explosions leaving behind scorched gray areas that began to grow. Their growth accelerated and as they did Patrick's dream turned into a nightmare. When they covered over sixty percent of the earth's surface there was a flash of red light and an explosion happened that jarred Patrick awake.

He laid there in bed with eyes as wide as saucers trying to make sense of what he just saw in his dream. He got out of bed and put on his robe and went into the living room to try and calm down. There would be no falling back to sleep peacefully this time, his rational mind however, was absolutely silent for the first time that he could remember.

Jack and Ben spent the following day fasting and meditating to prepare for their ceremony that evening. At the end of the day the two men split up to gather wood for their fire. Not one piece of wood was gathered unconsciously. Both Jack and Ben had a feeling that this ceremony would be very powerful, but neither man could imagine its importance, nor that it would be the last one they would have together for quite some time.

The two prepared the area for their fire. They placed the wood and its kindling in the manner taught to them by their teacher, as their teacher was taught by his teacher before him and so on back it went for thousands of years. They purified each other with the smoke from sage and waited for the sun to go down. Shortly after the sun went down the moon made her appearance in the nighttime sky. Ben opened up sacred space calling in the forces of nature from the four directions, the earth and heaven, and then the two friends began their ceremony.

There was an incredible amount of kausai energy present from the very beginning of the ceremony and it permeated every aspect of their beings, increasing their awareness and connection to all that is. The ceremony continued and the two men consciously drew more and more kausai to their circle. The two shamans stepped beyond the curtain of time into the land of mystery and began to experience the same vision together.

It was then that they both saw Scott. For the first time Ben became aware of what Jack knew. This man was going to start a new political party in America.

They saw Scott's great love for his country and his fellow man. They saw that Scott carried with him the power to make the winds of change blow at a gale's force. It was his life's destiny. He just wasn't aware of it yet. As they focused the flow of kausai to Scott in their vision he became illuminated.

The power in their sacred space was growing stronger and stronger, until the forest around them basked in its glow. Neither shaman had experienced anything like it before. Their vision became clearer and they saw that Scott had no idea how far-reaching the efforts of his passion would be. At that point they were both reminded of the importance of supporting this man. They saw many others coming to help him and then the winds of change blew harder.

Next they saw a man standing at a podium with a hawk flying overhead. At this point their attention was diverted from the man at the podium to something in the sky. They looked up, deeper, and deeper into the distant darkness where they saw an enormous red ball of fire hurling through space.

Their vision quickly faded and without a word they both knew it was time to make their offerings to the fire. Jack lit the fire so he went first. He moved closer and crouched down in front of it. Ben took his place standing behind Jack with his arms outstretched enveloping him in a ball of light, holding sacred space so that Jack could concentrate on his offering.

First Jack took his offering, a little twig, and held it to his heart, and then to his forehead. He blew his intent to be of service into his offering and placed it into the fire. Ben saw Jack's aura turn bright bluish white and then it merged with the fire.

What Ben saw next almost knocked him off his feet! It was a glimpse of Jack's future. He nearly lost his composure, and had to concentrate to hold the space for Jack who was still in front of the fire. His friend stood up with that great big grin on his face that Ben had grown so fond of and motioned for him to approach the fire.

Ben took his turn in front of the fire. He could feel the presence of his best friend behind him. The bond between the two men at this moment was something that most people wouldn't understand, and few would ever experience.

After Ben made his offerings to the fire, the two men prayed for the earth, her healing, and all her people. They prayed for Scott and that his life's work would be successful. After completing their prayers, the two men stared into the fire and began to journey in the same vision again.

They saw thousands and thousands of people longing for something that wasn't available. They saw millions of people awakening to a new power, and using that power to heal the earth and its inhabitants.

The fire was dying down now and Jack closed the sacred space releasing the forces of the four directions, heaven and earth. The two men stood in front of the fire as it burned down. They began to talk.

"I knew capitalism could be a good thing," Ben said. He smiled and shook his head slowly back and forth. "But I had no idea people would be able to use it to reverse the destruction of the planet."

Jack smiled and said, "When that happens it's going to surprise a lot of people."

"After we saw the man at the podium, did you see the ball of fire blazing through space?" Jack asked.

Ben raised his eyebrows and nodded. "Oh yeah, I saw it."

After an uncomfortable silence Jack looked at Ben.

"I got the distinct impression that it was headed for the—

"That is not information you and I are to bring forward. I got the distinct sense that someone else is going to call people's attention to it. I believe it falls under the kind of thing that we probably shouldn't even talk about. Information that we should even keep secret even from ourselves," Ben said.

"No argument here," Jack said. "Boy, that fella Scott has no idea what he's in for. Sometimes Spirit just takes a man's life, shakes the hell out of it, and turns it upside down," Jack said, and then began graphically illustrating a shaking motion like some Dads shake their teenage sons.

Ben laughed at his friend's animated gestures, and added. "He's going to need your help, and I got the feeling it's gonna to be soon."

"Yeah, I know," Jack said.

As the two headed back to the tent Jack got the sense that Ben was holding something back from him. He knew better than to look into it, for two reasons. First, using one's vision to see something that is none of your business causes pain. He had learned that lesson the hard way. Second, if his friend wanted him to know he would tell him. By the time they made it back to their tent he had let it go.

After crawling into their sleeping bags and saying good-night, Jack drifted asleep quickly while thinking about his new friend Scott who he had yet to meet. Ben lay awake staring at the stars through the screen in the top of their tent.

He could tell by Jack's breathing that he was asleep, so he let his mind drift back to when Jack became one with the fire earlier. He was told in a vision so many years ago that he would meet someone special after he moved from Maryland to Phoenix. He was told that he would introduce this person to the shamanic path, and that this person had a very important life mission to fulfill.

Ben hadn't known for sure until tonight that that person was Jack. His thoughts drifted back to when Jack's aura became one with the fire. He saw a glimpse of Jack's destiny and he no longer felt the need to hold back the tears so he let them flow freely as he stared up into the stars through the window in the top of the tent, and asked God.

"How could one man love so much?"

"There's something wrong with the world today
I don't know what it is.
Something's wrong with our eyes.
We're seeing things in a different way and
God knows it ain't his. It sure ain't no surprise.
Were livin on the edge."

Aerosmith

Chapter 2—The Flame

Scott spent the morning talking with his customers trying to drum up some business to replace the work he had lost the day before. After lunch he considered what to do next. He thought perhaps he should start working on the web site for his company, but he just couldn't seem to work up the motivation. He opted instead to finish reading a book he had started a while back entitled "Conscious Evolution" by Barbara Marx Hubbard.

The author dedicated her life to awakening the power of our social potential and the importance of having a plan to consciously evolve our way out of the current state of crisis we find ourselves in. She pointed out rather eloquently that what was once used to serve us has grown to the point where it may consume us.

He was daydreaming about the potential of the human race when Elizabeth entered the office and told him it was time to attend their sixteen-year-old daughter's basketball game. The couple got ready and left for Michelle's high school.

They thoroughly enjoyed watching Michelle's basketball game, and Scott even managed to forget about his current lack of work.

After the game the parents gathered around in front of the gymnasium savoring their daughters' victory. Unfortunately, after a few minutes the topic of conversation switched to the election in Florida. It seemed that no matter where he went Scott couldn't get away from it. However, the family arrived at home in good spirits. Michelle went upstairs to her room to get ready for bed. Elizabeth decided to study for school, and Scott figured he would use the time for some more reading.

He sat down on the couch and cracked a new book he had been waiting to read. After several minutes of trying to focus on the book he realized it was useless. Against what he thought was better judgment, he decided to turn on the television and see what was the latest news in Florida.

After scanning the channels he decided to watch one of the political programs that had been prerecorded earlier that evening. Scott watched sadly, as proponents of each side shot accusations back and forth. There seemed to be a genuine hatred among the show's guests.

One of the show's guests, a very opinionated Reverend, was doing his best to turn what was going on in Florida into a race issue. He seemed to be insinuating that the republican, Robert Kelton, was trying to stop the recounting of African American's votes in the disputed counties.

"Of course he's trying to stop the recounting of these counties, but it's because they favor Knight. It has nothing to do with race!" Scott said.

"You know Scott I'm trying to study. If you continue to interrupt me by talking to yourself and yelling at the television set I'll never become a teacher," Elizabeth said.

Scott thought that perhaps the Reverend was unconsciously becoming part of the problem, and he wondered if the Reverend thought the candidate that he supported would have done any differently if the situation was reversed.

As far as Scott could tell, this election, or lack thereof, had nothing to do with race relations in this country. It had nothing to do with chads, swinging or dimpled. What was going on had nothing to do with how many votes were recounted or where. Florida's election results were about money and power, and how far people will go to achieve them.

The Reverend continued hammering on Robert Kelton. Interrupting the other guests of the show, and fanning the flames of racial tension by claiming that the republican didn't want their votes to count.

Something inside of Scott snapped. This was the last straw!

He quietly turned off the television, and turned to Elizabeth who was seated at the kitchen table and said. "I'm going to do some work on the Internet for a while."

"Are you all right?" Elizabeth looked at him and smiled. "I wondered if turning on that television was a good idea."

"I'm fine," he mumbled and walked upstairs to his office.

Scott started his web page design software and loaded the Centrust Party web page into it. At the bottom of the ten items on the mission statement he added a closing comment:

The Centrust Party is a bridge, and Americans who no longer want to stand still and argue about which direction their country should move in will build this bridge. The bridge will allow Americans of consciousness to cross over to a new era in which their hopes and highest ideals for the country can be realized. As they do so, the political structure will have to be reformed to accommodate this new consciousness.

Scott logged on to the Internet and went to a web site to obtain a domain name. He conducted a search for the centrustparty.com and he wasn't surprised to find that the domain name was available. He used his personal credit card to pay for it.

Suddenly the air in his office became electric. Scott could feel the energy coursing through every atom in his body. Sometimes a man feels that he was born to live a particular moment in time and for Scott Stahl this was it. After the domain name was transferred to the new hosting address, Scott uploaded the Centrust Party web page onto the server and it was now on the Internet. That evening in late November Scott Stahl took his first public step towards what others would refer to later as *The Shift*.

That night Patrick Kinkaid had a difficult time finding sleep again. He couldn't get his mind off of the dream he had a couple of nights earlier. He tossed and turned next to his wife. He got up and tried reading for while. He even tried a late night snack. Nothing seemed to work.

Finally at around 1:30 am when he had given up hope he drifted off, only to awaken a few hours later. He decided to forget about sleeping so he got up, put on his robe and went into the living room to think. His thoughts drifted back to the dark gray areas that almost consumed the earth in his dream. He shuddered as a chill came over him. He thought about how neither Robert Kelton nor Andrew Knight had provided a vision for America during their campaigns and as result neither one of them could get elected. He wondered if the day would ever come when the majority of his colleagues would address the long-term social and environmental problems facing this country.

His wife found him alone and in the dark staring out the window.

"What's going on Patrick?" She asked.

"Nothing more than usual."

"Is everything alright?"

"Let's hope so," he said.

The 55-year-old priest stood in the middle of his living quarters above his church in San Vincente, El Salvador. Father Morales scanned the room to see if there was anything else he needed to pack.

Long ago he had been given the gift of prophecy. Shortly thereafter the church confirmed his gift and he became one of the few prophets in their service. He reported the visions and prophecies he received directly to a council of cardinals in Rome. The Council of Cardinals would review what he and the others sent them and determine what course of action, if any, was to be taken by the Church.

Over the last year Father Morales received a prophecy of biblical proportion. He finished recording the prophecy a week earlier and yesterday Spirit told him to do two things he had never been told do before. First, he would mail the prophecy to Rome and not call beforehand, which was customary. Second, the priest was told to pack for a trip immediately. This trip might mean that he could never return to El Salvador, nevertheless he packed his clothing and only his most treasured belongings.

Of the mystics and prophets who belonged to the Church of Rome, Father Morales was hands down the most accurate. The veil between him and Spirit was very thin. After packing he placed his suitcase in the closet of his bedroom and decided to pass the time watching children play from the balcony.

As he watched the children play he thought about how much El Salvador and the rest of Central America had changed over the last 30 to 40 years. Gone was much of the rain forest and jungle that once made his country feel so alive. They were replaced with huge farms and land to graze cattle for the American fast food companies.

The majority of his countrymen once lived in close-knit village communities. Thanks to the influx of large multinational corporations, the majority of his fellow citizens now found themselves on the lowest rung of the new world economic order. His heart filled with sadness as he thought about the possibility that in one more generation the colorful life style of El Salvador's villages could be forgotten.

Father Morales thought about how what is happening in El Salvador is also happening all over Central and South America. He knew that today 72% of all Salvadoran infants are underfed. A typical acre of land in Central America can produce 1200 pounds of grain. The same acre of land only produces 50 lbs. of beef. While Salvadoran youth go hungry over 50% of Central America's beef is exported. These unconscious actions challenged his faith in his fellow man.

Hopefully the prophecy he was waiting to deliver would wake mankind up to the consequences of its unconscious actions. He hoped Rome would recognize its authenticity. He made a conscious decision to no longer follow this train of thought, and came back into the present moment to enjoy the children playing below him.

Scott was in no particular hurry to get out of bed the following morning because he had no pressing matters to attend to. He had forgotten completely about the web site. After Elizabeth got up he made the coffee. The couple sat down to enjoy their morning time together. After chatting for about 45 minutes it was time for Elizabeth to get ready to leave for school. After Elizabeth left he took his time getting into the shower and getting dressed for the day. Finally, at around 10:00 AM he made his way upstairs and into his office. He turned on his computer monitor and started his email program to see if he had any messages. Scott grabbed the remote to turn on the television. He turned back to his computer monitor and noticed that his email program was still receiving mail.

He didn't give it much thought and turned back to watching the television. A few more minutes passed and the program was still loading mail. He figured this must be a mistake so he closed the program and reloaded it. A couple of minutes later the program was still receiving mail. Now, whatever was going on had his attention. He hoped it wasn't a computer virus.

Suddenly, he remembered that the Centrust Party web site he loaded the night before had his company's email address attached to it. Could it be? He wondered. After about five minutes the tone that let him know the program was done loading went off.

"257 emails!" He said as he stood up from his chair. "Oh my God, this is unbelievable!"

His mind was reeling as he scanned the messages. Among the titles were, Way to Go!, It's about time, How can we help? There seemed to be emails addressing every item on the Centrust Party mission statement.

The first email he focused on was entitled Where do we send the money?

"Oh no, what have I gotten myself into?" He said under his breath.

At that moment the phone rang.

"I need to speak to Scott Stahl please."

"This is Scott."

"This is Robert Benson calling from Phoenix Web Servers Inc."

"Yes how can I help you?" Scott asked.

"The web site you started last night is presenting some problems."

"Uh huh."

"You haven't contracted enough email space and bandwidth to handle this kind of traffic," the man said. "As a matter of fact until you make other arrangements your web site will continue to crash—

"Wait a second. My web site is crashing?" Scott said.

"Oh yeah, there is simply too much traffic. We already have over 3000 emails waiting for you on our server."

Scott's heart began to race.

"Hello! Are you still there?" the man asked.

Scott cleared his throat and replied.

"Yes I'm still here, this whole thing has kind of taken me by surprise."

"Well, you're going to have to contact our sales department and arrange to purchase more email space and bandwidth if possible."

"OK, well that's exactly what I'm going to do," Scott replied without thinking, and hung up the phone.

Scott took a few minutes to regain his composure and get his arms around what was happening. He began to scroll back through the email messages and stopped at one that was entitled Great idea/Lame web site. So he opened it.

My name is Jeff Kline I own a web design company located in Tempe, Arizona. I don't know where you came up with the idea for the Centrust Party, but I am thrilled that someone has stepped forward to do so. Like so many other small businessmen in this country, I have become disillusioned with American politics. Please do not give up on your quest without seeing it through. I am sure there are many Americans who will help you and I would like to be one of them.

Please do not take offense, but your web site is pretty unprofessional and I also had trouble logging on to it. I suppose this is because of the amount of traffic it is receiving at this time. You need a web site that can handle the traffic with graphics that complement this most important cause. I can help you with these things. My company has designed web sites for several Fortune 500 companies and I would be honored to help you. My phone number is (480) 555-2012.

Thank you and good luck, Jeff Kline.

Scott printed the email and set it on his desk. He sat there wondering what to do next, when his phone rang again. It was a manager at Phoenix Web Servers Inc.

"We've got a problem brewing here, our server just doesn't have enough space to handle your web site. When we take on a corporate customer whose web site we anticipate will have this kind of volume we purchase a server or a series of servers specifically for that account—

"How much is this going to cost?" Scott asked.

"I couldn't really tell you that right now. I've contacted our sales department and they are preparing a quote. I would estimate that it is probably going to be somewhere in the neighborhood of $500.00 a month."

$500.00 a month, Scott thought, that's going to be a problem.

The manager assured Scott that they would do their best to make the web site as stable as possible under its current limitations and said goodbye. Scott hung up and without even thinking dialed the phone number for Jeff Kline at New World Web Design.

While he was on hold, Scott did his best to calm himself down. Suddenly he realized that what he was experiencing was excitement and not fear.

"Hello Jeff," Scott began. "My name is Scott Stahl, and I am the one who put up the Centrust Party web site."

"Hello Scott, first I want to tell you that what you are doing is incredible!" Jeff said, "and by the way your web site is down."

"Yeah, I know," Scott said. "Apparently my account is not set up to handle the kind of traffic it's receiving."

"Who are you using?" Jeff asked.

"Phoenix Web Servers," Scott replied.

"Oh yeah. They tend to service a large number of small individual clients. To my knowledge they only have a couple of corporate customers. I would recommend that you use the same service that I use. They have a ton of capacity."

"I've already received 3000 emails and I only put the site up last night," Scott said.

"That's fantastic! What we've got to do is get together as soon as possible to bring this under control."

Scott noticed that Jeff had used the word we. Suddenly he had a partner and he never felt alone again in this momentous journey. In that moment, one person became two people and this was the beginning of a series of coincidences that was to become the Centrust Party.

Jeff's company was less than an hour away from Scott's home so the two made plans to meet for lunch that afternoon.

Scott scanned through the emails he received. They were from people in all walks of life; farmers, teachers, small businessmen and housewives. The common thread linking them was that they all wanted to make a difference, but they lacked an avenue for change.

After scanning the emails he spent the rest of the morning gathering up all the information on the environment, campaign finance reform, industrial hemp and many other issues he had been keeping track of over the last several years.

At his office in Washington Patrick Kinkaid sat at his desk with his head in his hands completely exhausted. The dreams and his lack of sleep over the last several nights were beginning to wear on him. He was feeling completely disgusted with the events in Florida and after his dream about the earth he couldn't help but think that what was happening in Florida was just another enormous distraction. He was looking ahead and thinking that perhaps he wouldn't seek another term in the Senate when the urge overcame him to scan through the emails he received from his web site. This was a job that he usually reserved for his staff but he went ahead and did it anyway.

Scanning through the emails he spotted one that was entitled "Don't give up."

How appropriate, he thought, so he decided to read it. The email's author pledged his support to Patrick's campaign finance reform legislation and indicated that he didn't know anyone who wasn't in support of it. When he read the author's name he almost fell out of his chair. It was Scott Stahl the second name on the business card in his wallet.

Just then the voice returned. "Patrick call the first name that you wrote down on the card. Remember timing is very important, so do it now." He was then told what message to relay in the first of the two phone calls.

Back in Florida Kate Seymore, the newly appointed Washington correspondent for CNN, was getting ready to do yet another meaningless interview in Florida while the election mess was being sorted out. She was conscious of being involved in a historic event, but she was growing tired of living out of her motel room and rental car. It was unfortunate, but for her the time for really caring who came out on top of this election had long since passed. She was not unlike so many other Americans who had become disillusioned with the status quo in American politics.

Her cameraman called her aside. "Kate it appears someone has started a new party and it's posted on the Internet. It's called the Centrust Party."

She looked around at the commotion surrounding them. "Well if they had started this party two years ago we might have a story. There are thousands of political web sites out there. I don't see how the one you're talking about has any relevance at this late date."

"Ok...I thought perhaps you would want to know about it," he said.

Her cell phone rang at that exact moment.

"Hello this is Kate Seymore."

"Good morning Kate this is Patrick Kinkaid."

The phone call took her completely by surprise and she was speechless.

"Hello...are you still there?" Patrick said.

"Yes Senator. What can I do for you?"

"Well it's not what you can do for me. It's more a matter of what I can do for you," he said.

"Yesss?"

"I'm calling to tell you that at this moment there is something very special and very important getting underway in the western part of the country."

"What is it?" Kate said.

"There is a new party that is going to usher in a fresh paradigm of great political importance." As the senator was saying this Kate turned to watch her cameraman walking back to the truck to get his camera to prepare for their shot.

"How do you know this?"

"How I came upon this information is not important. What is important is that this is going to be a huge story for quite some time and if I were you I would find a way to be the first one in on it. It could quite possibly be the biggest break of your career. Oh yes, by the way, we never had this phone conversation. Have a good day."

"Wait, wait! How am I supposed to find..." It was too late; the senator had already hung up the phone. Thinking that perhaps the senator's phone call and her cameraman's comment were related in some way she caught up with him at the truck.

"Bob, how did you hear about this web site?" Kate said.

"I just talked to a friend of mine. He was wondering if we knew anything about it!"

"That phone call I just received was from one of our senators who told me about a new political party making waves in the western part of the country. He told me that this was going to be a huge story for some time to come. I'm thinking perhaps he was referring to what you were talking about."

"I suppose it's possible," he said.

"Do you know who started the web site?" Kate asked.

"My friend told me that the web site doesn't give any information about who started it." Kate frowned when he told her this. " But", he said as he took a piece of paper out of his pocket, "the responses solicited from the web site are going to this email address."

"Great work," she replied.

She took the email address from her cameraman and called a private investigator she worked with. She explained the situation to the private investigator, leaving out the part about the phone call from the senator, and asked him to find out the name and phone number of the individual who owned the Centrust Party website. "I'm sure I don't have to remind you to keep this quiet," she said before hanging up.

On the drive down to meet with Jeff Kline at New World Web Design, Scott began to accept that the dream he had a few nights earlier was actually a premonition.

The whole morning he felt like he was living someone else's life. He found the address with no difficulty, gathered the information he brought with him and went inside.

He told the receptionist he was there to see Jeff Kline.

"Oh yes Mr. Stahl, he's expecting you. Please follow me." The receptionist led Scott through a maze of cubicles back to where a woman was working in front of a large monitor. A rather large man was standing behind her with his chin in his hand.

"Mr. Kline," the receptionist said to the man. "Mr. Stahl is here." This large man wheeled around and darted over to Scott and introduced himself enthusiastically.

"Hello Scott. It's a pleasure to meet you. If you come over here", he said as he motioned to the woman's workstation, "you can see we've already started on the new web design. I can't explain it, but I just couldn't seem to get it off my mind. I hope you don't mind that we started working on it immediately after our phone conversation this morning."

"I don't mind at all. Actually I'm thrilled," Scott said.

He introduced Scott to his assistant, Paula, who would be the lead designer of the web site. They explained to Scott that what they were stressing was a completely interactive experience.

"People will be able to navigate effortlessly to the issues that are of greatest importance to them. Their responses will be organized by keywords in their email titles." Scott noticed that Jeff's eyes came alive as he talked about the web site.

Jeff showed Scott what they had completed so far, which included Scott's comments and the Centrust Party's mission statement. "Wow! You've accomplished a lot in just a couple of hours," Scott said.

"We get things done pretty quickly around here," Jeff said. "Time is of the essence, and we need to strike while the iron is hot. Everybody and their brother across the country are talking about the election. I believe we need to use this to our advantage. Also Paula is in between projects right now, and soon I will need her to work on something that is going to pay the bills. Oh, by the way, in case you're wondering completing this web design is my first donation to the Centrust Party."

"Thank you so much," Scott replied.

Jeff looked up from the computer monitor and his eyes met Scott's with intensity. "No, thank you so much."

Scott and Jeff got into Jeff's car and left for lunch. On the drive over Jeff never seemed to stop talking about the Centrust Party and its possibilities. Scott wondered if he would be able to get a word in edgewise and also where this man got his incredible energy. Jeff had an aura of natural charisma about him and Scott liked him immediately.

Scott and Jeff pulled into the restaurant's parking lot. Scott smiled as he noticed it was a rib joint.

While ordering their lunch Jeff noticed that Scott had not ordered any meat, so after the waiter left the table he asked Scott if he ate meat. Scott replied that he was a vegetarian, but Jeff wanted to know more, and why. So as best he could without sounding preachy Scott explained the effects America's beef habit has on the environment, and our health.

"As a matter of fact the governmental agency that is responsible for educating Americans about their food choices, is the same agency that promotes agricultural and ranching concerns," Scott said.

"That sounds like an obvious conflict of interest to me," Jeff replied.

Jeff was like so many other people whom Scott had met and talked with. They had a strong desire to change the world they live in, but they lacked a vehicle for change. Scott believed that if Americans knew what the environmental consequences were as a result of the food that they eat, the majority of them would alter their eating habits.

In between bites of his barbeque sandwich Jeff asked. "I was wondering, what do you believe is the biggest problem we face in making the changes that are necessary?"

"Fear," Scott replied without hesitation.

"Fear? What exactly do you mean?"

"Most people are terrified of change. However, changes are coming whether we want them or not. Now we have the choice of embracing these changes with as little impact on our lives as possible or waiting until these changes are forced upon us, drastically altering our lives."

Scott thought for a moment and continued; "Our fear of change is particularly evident in industries that must change their business practices. Let's say, for example, because of their environmental impact. The leaders of these industries will have to find new ways of doing things, which might result in job losses. Perhaps many of their employees will have to move on to another line of work. In fact, many industries are going to have to change or be eliminated sooner or later because of our need to preserve the environment that supports us. Our fear of economic insecurity prevents us from making transitions easily in our lives, even if we see the need to do so for the common good. Then we say to hell with everyone else I've got to look out for myself."

"That's true," Jeff said.

"People need to be encouraged to step outside of their fear, and together we can build a sustainable economy that won't destroy our environment."

Scott paused for a moment, and then added. "I would venture to say, Jeff, that if you were to ask individual people within these industries if they would move on to a job in another industry for the good of our environment, many of them would say yes. They would probably be afraid of having to change jobs, but the majority of them would do it anyway to leave a better world to their children. We are the most prosperous country in the world. There is plenty of work for everyone who wants to work. The U.S. is also the leader of the free world. Now is the time to make these changes with as little pain as possible, before they are forced upon us."

"You ought to be a politician," Jeff said. "Yeah I know." Scott sighed. "My wife has told me a million times that I missed my calling. Well, enough of politics for now. Let's get down to the details about the web site. Besides, you've almost finished your lunch. It's your turn to talk so I can have a chance to eat mine," Scott said.

"I have a dream about the internet creating a well informed society," Jeff said.

"That's interesting," Scott said.

"A society that is well informed would naturally want to be more involved in the decisions that their government is making on their behalf. The internet can make this possible," Jeff said. His eyes lit up as he talked about this possibility.

"This gives me another idea for the web site," Jeff said.

"Oh yeah, what's that?"

"Each subject page could have links to other web sites pertaining to that subject. We will be encouraging people to investigate for themselves what is happening rather than relying on our viewpoint for the information we present to them," Jeff said.

"That's an excellent idea," Scott said.

"Thank you. I also thought it would be nice to have a page for voicing their opinions and encouraging open dialogue."

"How much do you think it's going to cost to run the web site?" Scott asked.

"Well, like I said before my company will not charge anything for the web page design—

"And I appreciate that," Scott said.

"Hey, I'm just thrilled about having a chance to be involved in this project with you. It's about time we did something about politics in America, because so much of what we're doing doesn't make any sense at all. I have contacted the server company that I think would be perfect to host our web site. I've talked him down to about two hundred dollars a month to start," Jeff said.

Scott let out a deep sigh to which Jeff replied. "I'll tell you what, until things get off the ground I'll split the cost with you."

"Wow, that would be great," Scott said. "It's a deal."

Scott wondered how he would explain all of this to Elizabeth and realized he had an interesting evening ahead of him.

"How long do you think it will be until we're up and running?" Scott asked.

"48 hours."

"That's really fast," Scott said. He had a look of amazement on his face.

"In the meantime continue to work with your current server. Their web site will probably crash again and again, but at least you'll still be on the web. If you give us 48 hours we can come up with a great web site."

"I can't tell you how much I appreciate this Jeff," Scott said.

"It's my pleasure," Jeff replied.

"This is absolutely amazing! I put the web site up only 24 hours ago, and in two more days you will have turned it into a first class site. Over 3000 people have e-mailed us already. Some of them are asking where to send political contributions," Scott said.

Scott sat back in his chair and, and took a deep breath.

"This is almost moving too fast, even for me."

"Well you're not in it alone anymore," Jeff said. A reassuring smile appeared on his face and Scott felt confident again.

The two men finished their lunch and then got back into Jeff's car for the ride back to his office. They had hit it off immediately and this day would prove to be the beginning of a long relationship. They shook hands before parting company on the sidewalk in front of Jeff's office.

Scott jumped into his car and started the drive back to north Phoenix. On the way home, his mind was going a mile a minute thinking about all the different issues that currently face this country and the world. For some reason he felt an incredible amount of power in being able to do something about them. The ideas kept coming so fast he decided he had better write them down.

He pulled off the freeway onto the shoulder and began rummaging through the material he had looking for something to write on. All his papers had printing on both sides because he felt it was important to conserve paper. However, he was able to find an empty deposit envelope in his glove compartment. This will have to do, he thought.

He spent the 45-minute drive home thinking about America's potential to reverse the current course of environmental destruction. He thought about all that had taken place in the last twenty-four hours and he had a sudden and clear inspiration that told him that this reversal could start with just one person. He wrote down every idea that came to him on the drive home on the empty deposit envelope.

As he pulled into the driveway he hit the garage door opener and he could see as the door opened that Elizabeth was home.

This is going to be interesting, he thought.

He pulled into the garage, turned off his car, and gathered up his things. He looked at everything he had written on the deposit envelope and realized that it captured his dreams for this country and the world. He folded it up and put it into his wallet. After sitting in the car for a couple of minutes trying to figure out how to explain everything to Elizabeth, he realized he couldn't even explain it to himself. He got out of his car and walked into the house. In an instant the exhilaration and confidence of just a couple of short minutes ago shifted to confusion and trepidation.

What would he say to Elizabeth?

Hi honey, you'll never guess what I did today. I started another political party. I know you had no idea I was up to this, but it just seemed like a good thing to do.

The tone of sarcasm in his head brought with it a feeling of inadequacy about following through with the whole thing.

Scott walked down the hall and turned into the kitchen to see his wife sitting at the kitchen table studying. She looked up from her books and smiled at him. Her smile warmed his heart and the fear left him. That smile had always made him feel that he could accomplish anything.

"Hey, hon, how was your day?" She asked.

"Well, it was interesting, to say the least," Scott said. His answer sparked her curiosity and she asked with a combination of enthusiasm and intuition.

"So you picked up a new client today?"

"Yeah, I guess you could say that I do have a new client," Scott replied.

Scott paused for a moment and took a deep breath before explaining the events of his day. Just as he was about to start speaking the phone rang on his business line upstairs.

"I better grab that," he said and darted off upstairs.

It had been a long day for Patrick Kinkaid. He spent some of this time on the hill, but the majority of his time was spent politicking to gain support for his campaign finance reform initiative. There was a lot of negotiating going on and he was concerned that it might lead to a bill that was less than what he would consider adequate reform.

Some people were questioning his future with the Republican Party, while others were questioning whether he would even remain a politician. He tried to use this publicity to further point the spotlight on the need for campaign finance reform.

He believed that what was going on in Florida had the seeds of change in it. He hoped these events would wake Americans up to the overwhelming influence that the special interests have in Washington. He thought that neither the republicans nor the democrats could back down from the deadlock in Florida even for the good of the country, because of all the special interest money that was behind them.

When he got back to his office he was very tired. He closed his office door and sat down at his desk to ponder his next move. He decided to lay his head down for a couple of minutes and the next thing he knew he was asleep and dreaming.

The voice returned, "Patrick, the time has come to make the second phone call. You will speak to a man who has no idea that what he has started is of grave importance to the whole human race. Your task will be to encourage him to continue his efforts at all costs. Tell him that the path he has started on is what he was born to do. Tell him that he chose this path before he was even born! He will remember. Let him know that there will be times where he will want, more than anything to give up, but he must not. I have sent much help to him. More than he could ever know. Tell this man that even now there are many others who know and have known for some time about what he is trying to do. Add a note of levity and tell him to fasten his safety belt and put his seat in the upright position because the next two weeks are going to be a ride unlike anything he has ever experienced."

"There's something else Patrick," the voice continued. "You will receive a FedEx letter from El Salvador in the next week. Inside it will be an envelope addressed to someone you know. Keep this envelope in a safe place until the time is right to mail it. You will know when this time is. As soon as you wake up Patrick, make the phone call. Do it now!"

The senator jolted his head up off the desk. He wondered how long he had been asleep. When he looked at the clock he was amazed to find out that it had been less than a minute. He stood up, got the telephone number out of his wallet and dialed the phone number. A man answered on the other end.

Somewhat out of breath Scott answered, "Precision Engineering."

"Hello, this is Senator Patrick Kincaid."

Scott wondered if this was some kind of joke, but when the man spoke again there was no mistaking the senator's voice.

"I would appreciate it if you wouldn't divulge this conversation to anyone. I have a message for you and as strange as this may sound, this message has come to me in a series of dreams."

"What, how did you get this number?" Scott said.

The senator chuckled and said, "Your number came to me in the dream also. What I have been told to tell you is that the journey you have embarked upon is of great importance. There will be several times that you will want to give up, but you must not do so. I have been informed in these dreams that this is the job you were born to do, and that you knew of it before you were born."

On the other end of the line Scott's jaw dropped. It seemed like he couldn't remember how to breathe. In an instant he remembered that what the senator said was true. He remembered almost as in a dream that he chose this task before he was born. Nothing like this had ever happened to him before. It was like super charged déjà vu.

"Hello, are you still there?" Senator Kinkaid asked. Scott gasped for breath.

"Are you Ok?"

"Yes I am fine, please continue Senator."

"There's a lot of help that has been sent to you, more than you could ever know. Remember this and always take heart and never give up. Your path is not an easy one, but it will be very, very rewarding." Senator Kincaid didn't remember the exact words from the dream but it seemed to flow so easily from his mouth.

"Are you ready to move forward with this task?"

"I am," Scott replied.

"Well then I have another message for you. I was told to tell you to fasten your safety belt and put your seat in the upright position because the next two weeks are going to be a wild ride. Good luck, and God speed." With that the senator hung up the phone.

Scott sat in stunned silence.

"Take whatever you're needing. Take whatever you can.
We are broken from within. Run to another land."

Toad the Wet Sprocket

Chapter 3—The Phoenix

Kate Seymore spent a long day in Florida, and she was growing tired of covering the same story. Her private investigator had paid off and gotten her a phone number of some man named Scott Stahl in Phoenix, Arizona. Someone she had never heard of before. Her cameraman and her hadn't heard any talk about the Centrust Party among their colleagues, so they held out hope for an exclusive. Throughout the day he shot her a couple of glances that meant, *this could be our big break.*

Kate called her editor and told her that she was onto something and that she would like to travel to Phoenix as soon as possible.

"I must have rocks in my head to even consider letting you leave Florida," her editor said.

"I was informed by a source of mine in Washington that something big was about to happen in the world of politics. I'll tell you what, I'll be back and forth in less than a day. From what we know about what's happening around here tomorrow I don't think I'm going to miss much," Kate said.

"Ok, one day but this had better be huge."

"Oh, it's big all right," Kate assured her. "We just have to make sure we can get the exclusive."

She held the phone number in her hand as she stood in the safety of a phone booth on a rainy November night in Florida. She was shaking with anticipation, because she believed this could be the biggest break of her career and if it wasn't her editor would be less than happy. She dialed the phone number and a woman on the other end answered.

Meanwhile, Scott sat in his office trying to figure out how he was going to explain all this to Elizabeth. He wondered if she would miss the $100.00 a month. He seemed to be locked in a trance. He was just too excited, too scared, and two humbled to even produce a thought. He decided to go downstairs and get it over with.

When he came into the kitchen Elizabeth was on the phone.

"Oh come on now. Who is this really? Annette is that you? Who's pulling my leg here?" Elizabeth asked.

"This is not a joke." Kate glanced at her watch. "If you turn on your television to CNN you'll see that in about two minutes I will be interviewing a former state of Florida election official named Bob Kuchansky."

"Yeah sure," Elizabeth replied and then hung up the phone.

"What's going on?" Scott asked.

"Oh nothing," Elizabeth replied. "Someone's playing a joke, trying to convince me that they were calling from CNN. Kate Seymore, as a matter of fact."

A lump formed in Scott's throat.

"Hold on a second," Elizabeth snapped. She made her way around the couch to retrieve the remote control from the coffee table. She sat down and tuned the television to CNN. Just then the news anchor explained they were going to go to an interview recorded earlier with Kate Seymore and Bob Kuchansky, the former state of Florida election official.

Elizabeth jumped up and screamed, "Oh my God!" The phone rang and she ran over to get it.

"Hello."

"Maybe we should try this again," Kate said. "My name is Kate Seymore and I am with CNN. I would like to speak to Scott Stahl about the Centrust Party."

Elizabeth stood there as white as a sheet. She handed the phone to Scott and said with a somewhat terrified look on her face, "It's Kate Seymore from CNN and she wants to talk to you about the Centrust Party."

Scott paused for a moment holding the phone in his hand and then the image of the tall slender correspondent with short blonde hair came to mind.

"Hello," Scott said.

"Hi Mr. Stahl my name is Kate Seymore and I am a reporter with CNN—

"How did you get my number?" Scott asked.

"I have my sources," Kate replied. "The reason for my call Mr. Stahl is that I'm planning to get on a plane this evening and fly to Phoenix. Tomorrow morning I would like to get an exclusive interview with you and see what you are up to with the Centrust Party."

"Could you hold on for a moment?" He asked.

"Sure," Kate replied.

Scott put the phone to his chest and let out a deep sigh. Elizabeth was standing there staring at him with a look on her face that was a combination of suspicion and awe. He really had no desire to meet with a reporter so quickly, and then he thought about the phone call from the senator in which he said, "Many will be sent to help you. He thought about Jeff Kline, about their meeting and how quickly that had happened. In an instant he knew that Kate Seymore was one of the people sent to help him.

He got back on the phone and said, "Sure Ms. Seymore come on out and we'll talk."

"Great! I will fly into Phoenix tonight, and call you first thing in the morning," Kate replied.

"I'll see you then, and thanks for calling," Scott said.

Scott explained the whole story to Elizabeth. He told her about the dreams that he had been having and about making the trial web site. He reviewed with her all the materials he had been investigating over the last few years about tax reform, industrial hemp, and campaign finance reform.

"I put all these issues into a format that made sense to me." He told her. "With my new software I created a Centrust Party web site. It was just for practice until last night when I got disgusted watching that political program. In my frustration, I put the web site out there."

Throughout the conversation Elizabeth kept looking from Scott to the materials and back again with a look of amazement on her face.

"When I checked my e-mail this morning it was full! I mean, Elizabeth there were 250 e-mails waiting for me." Elizabeth's eye's got even wider.

"Wait!" Scott said. "It gets even better. The server company called me this morning and told me they had 3000 more on their server."

Elizabeth jumped out of her seat and began to pace the kitchen floor.

"One of the first emails I read was from a man named Jeff Kline, he owns a web page design company," Scott said.

Elizabeth paced her way back to where Scott sat at the kitchen table and said, "over 3000 emails!"

"I know isn't it great? Anyway, Jeff Kline and the folks at

New World Web Design are going to turn it into a first class web site in less than 48 hours—

"Over 3000 emails," Elizabeth said.

"Yeah that's right over 3000." Scott thought Elizabeth sounded like an old record player that was stuck on a scratch. She seemed to be in a daze and Scott figured this was as good a time as any to let her in on the cost.

"Jeff got us a very good deal on another web service that can handle the volume of hits that we're getting. It's only going to cost $200.00 a month to start and Jeff said he would split the cost with me."

Elizabeth didn't even bat an eye about the cost. Scott figured she was probably just in shock. He had done some pretty crazy things in his life, and had been out on a limb before, but this took the cake. He saved the best for last when he told her about the phone call from the senator. Her mouth dropped wide open when Scott told her everything the senator said.

Elizabeth and Scott had lived a spiritual life throughout their marriage. They were accustomed to the coincidences and synchronicities of life. They had even gained spiritual insight into why certain people had come into their lives. Nothing, however, had prepared her for something of this magnitude. The dreams, a new political party, and calls from reporters and senators. It took Elizabeth a long time to get any words out.

"Boy, Scott from now on you had better stay busy at work. When you get sidetracked a lot can happen!" She quit pacing and sat down at the table.

"Sidetracked?" Didn't you just hear me when I said that the senator told me I was born to do this?" Scott said

"Yeah well, I just don't know what to say Scott. This whole thing is just completely unbelievable." She paused for a moment.

"After you do this interview tomorrow we will be in the national spotlight. Did you give that any thought? This is most likely going to turn our lives upside down. Did you even think about consulting me about this?"

Scott sat there with a blank look on his face.

"Consult you about this? Sweetheart, this all happened in less than a day." He stood up and leaned against the counter to remove himself from her penetrating stare.

"It's been less than twenty-four hours since I fired up the web site last night.

If I had known beforehand what was going to happen, I probably would have been too scared to do it. I had no idea that the response would be so overwhelming," Scott said.

"My mother always told me being married to you was going to be very, very interesting. I don't think she had any idea about how *interesting*." Elizabeth said. She began slowly shaking her head back and forth.

"It's a good thing I'm going to be done with my classes soon, because if you are starting another political party…I can't believe those words are coming out of my mouth, like starting a political party is some kind of normal thing."

"What are you going to do about work?" She asked.

"Hey, let's slow down here and take things one moment at a time. As far as work goes we're very slow right now. This will give me something to do until things pick up again."

"Huh, something to do you say? I think I know you a little bit better than that."

This was something she loved so much about Scott. He had an ability to jump into the water with both feet, and ask questions later. This made their lives exciting. She always loved him for it, even though sometimes she wanted to strangle him because of it.

Scott looked up at the clock; it was 7:45 pm already.

"What do you say we get something to eat? My stomach's been growling for the last half hour," he said. He walked from the kitchen table to the refrigerator.

This was her husband. Jumping in with both feet, moving at one hundred miles an hour, and still having time to think about his stomach.

He stood with his back to her with the refrigerator door open looking inside wondering what to say next when she walked over and put her arms around him giving him a hug from behind.

Father Morales had been waiting for two long days to receive the message on how to proceed. He passed the time this evening sitting on his balcony, first enjoying every moment of a beautiful sunset, and then the appearance of the stars one by one in the night sky. As he gazed into the sky he wondered when he would be delivering his important message.

He went back into his bedroom off the balcony and lay down on his bed to meditate when he fell fast asleep. In the middle of the night he began to dream. In his dream everything began to unfold once again. He looked into the night sky and saw the huge red ball of fire that was laid out in the prophecy he received. There were millions of people waiting for something. Then he saw the world being returned to balance once again. This scenario played over and over again in his dream.

After the world regained its balance the voice of all that is spoke to him and said. "Senor Morales." In his dream he smiled because he loved the way God addressed him. "Are you ready my friend?" The voice asked.

"I am," Father Morales replied.

"It is time for you to travel. Make a copy of the prophecy put it into an envelope and seal it." He was then told what name and address to put on the envelope. "Put the envelope into a FedEx package and send it to Patrick Kincaid in Washington DC. Mail the other copy of the prophecy to the Council of

Cardinals in Rome. Tomorrow you'll be leaving for Salt Lake City, Utah. Mail both envelopes from the airport. When your plane has landed you will be informed on what to do next."

Father Morales awoke immediately from his dream, and wrote down the name and address that would go on the envelope inside the FedEx letter. He also wrote down the senator's name and address in Washington DC.

He had fallen asleep completely clothed, and his shirt was soaked with sweat. A conversation with God can do that to a man, he thought.

He walked back out onto the balcony after stripping off his shirt. The cool evening breeze dried his chest and awakened his senses. He stood alone and at one with everything around him for quite some time as he stared up at the stars wondering what he would do in Utah.

He was careful not to think about this for very long, because thoughts are energy, and that energy can be tracked. There are legions that did not want to see these changes take place, and the world return to balance once again. Fear would run rampant. He became sad as his thoughts turned to how unaware humans are about their divinity and the possibilities that come with it.

He walked back into his bedroom, got undressed, and crawled back into bed. He lay with his hands folded on his belly and thanked God for entrusting him with such an important message. He fell asleep completely grateful even though tomorrow he would be saying goodbye to El Salvador.

Scott lay awake in bed the next morning staring at the ceiling. He took a minute check to see if the events of the last couple days were a dream or reality. He looked at Elizabeth lying next to him and realized it was not a dream.

He and Elizabeth stayed up late into the evening talking about how starting the Centrust Party was going to impact their lives. Realistically it was impossible for them to tell how far and how wide this impact would be. Elizabeth was somewhat fearful about it, but Scott, in his normal fashion seemed unaffected. For him the glass was always half full. Little did he know that in the next couple of years it would take everything he had, and the help from people he didn't even know yet to hang on to his eternal optimism.

Scott was the one who was always up cruising around in the stars. Elizabeth kept them grounded. She would always give Scott the permission to fly, and she always had permission from him to bring him back down to planet earth when necessary. This was one of the most beautiful aspects of their relationship. The couple allowed each other to continually redefine who they were in this world, without being threatened. They put a lot of effort into maintaining this delicate balance.

The remainder of their discussion involved dreaming about what kind of impact Scott's new party could have on this country and the world. They both knew that man had an astonishing amount of creative power, and could in fact create a world of incredible beauty. Together they dreamed of an America that cared more about its impact on the planet than spreading its consumerism around the world. They realized this would mean that Americans would have to face their fears.

Even after their long discussion both of them spent time lying awake in silence praying and listening for answers on what to do next.

Scott's answer came in a dream in which he heard the divine voice again. His dream detailed how to interact with Ms. Seymore this morning. It was only 7:00 am, and the couple hadn't even got out of bed yet when the telephone rang.

As he walked to the phone Scott knew it was the reporter.

"Hello," he said answering the phone on the fourth ring.

"Good morning Mr. Stahl this is Kate Seymore. I'm sorry to call you so early in the morning, but I feel we need to get on with this interview as soon as possible. The process will most likely take a few hours, and I want to roll some tape on the air as soon as we can."

"I agree with you there. It will probably take me a couple of hours to sort out everything that has happened in the last 24 to 48 hours," Scott said. He paused for a moment remembering his dream, and cleared his throat.

"Ms. Seymore you are the one who found me first, so I believe you should get the exclusive on interviewing me. There is something that I need from you however."

"Yes," she said.

"I want you to think long and hard about your answer, because it will determine the nature of our relationship." Scott knew that he was using the fact that she was already here in Phoenix, and anticipating an exclusive as leverage, but at the same time he was giving her choice. It was up to her.

Scott had seen her on television several times and he admired her presence. There was something about her that the television couldn't hide. Maybe it was more of a feeling of things to come.

"Well what is it that you want?" She asked.

"Right now this election is in the public eye, not only in this country but around the world. It is a very hot topic of discussion, and is the number one issue on most people's minds. Everywhere you go people are talking about it. People who say they don't care are not being honest with themselves. Now is the perfect time to launch another major political party, because of all the media attention."

Scott paused for a moment, took a deep breath and continued.

"The time is also perfect because this media attention can be used to focus the spotlight on some critical choices

Americans and the world will need to make very soon. The window of opportunity will not stay open for long, however. Soon we will have a president-elect. The Centrust Party will remain in the limelight for awhile, due to the unprecedented circumstances surrounding the election, but after that a long dry spell will come." Scott was merely repeating the things that had been revealed in his dream the night before.

"The commitment I want from you is that during this dry spell you'll continue to cover what the Centrust Party is doing, and do whatever is within your power, ethically, to keep us in the limelight. I see a future stretch of disillusionment, so to speak, and a period when people's passion for change will not burn so intensely. I will give you this exclusive interview today, and many more to come if you will do this for the Centrust Party."

There was a moment of silence and then.

"Wow!" Kate said. "It sounds like you've got this whole thing figured out." Kate's immediate reaction was to say yes to Scott's proposal, but for some reason she felt she needed to think about it.

At that moment Scott said, "I don't want you to answer immediately, but I need to know that you will do this. Otherwise, I believe someone else will."

"Ok," she said. "I'll call you back."

By this time Elizabeth had gotten up and started brewing a pot of coffee. Scott went back into the bedroom and threw on a pair of shorts and a T-shirt. He came back out into the kitchen and sat down with Elizabeth. Scott was a little on edge about whether Ms. Seymore would take his proposal or not. His mind began to race. Where would I find another reporter and one that I could trust to follow through?

Elizabeth touched him on the arm and gave him a warm smile.

Back at the motel room Kate Seymore sat on the edge of her bed contemplating Scott's proposal. She was already fully dressed for the interview. Her briefcase sat next to her on the floor packed and ready to go. Even though it was only 7:00 am she was fully prepared to do the interview right now.

She had not anticipated Scott's request though. How could she? She was unsure if she could make a promise like this without her editor's permission. She immediately tossed that thought out because there was no way she could ask that of her editor. This would have to be between Scott and her.

Suddenly she had a tingling sensation all over her body. She didn't know what it was so she stood up. She then experienced what felt like a column of energy coming down from above through the top of her head. Simultaneously a column of energy from the earth entered the base of her spine and joined the other column of energy around the area of her heart. The energy swirled around her heart center and then moved out from the middle of her chest to envelope her in a milky white substance. This was accompanied by a powerful sense of déjà vu. She felt like she already knew about the events to come this morning before they happened, but was only remembering them as they unfolded. After this energetic experience she sat back down on the edge of the bed where she went into a trance. She sat there for quite some time. In fact she lost track of time, which for her was something quite unusual.

At the kitchen table Elizabeth and Scott took their fifteen minutes together with little dialogue.

"Well honey, your political ambitions aren't going to put me through school, so I guess I better get dressed and ready to go," Elizabeth said.

On the way back to the bedroom she stopped and turned to Scott.

"I can't believe this whole thing is happening. It seems like a dream. The other thing that amazes me about it is how calm I am." She disappeared into the bedroom to get ready.

Scott sat there by the phone at the kitchen table for what seemed to be an eternity, but was actually only another fifteen minutes before the call came.

"Hello," Scott said.

"Hello Scott this is Kate Seymore."

"Boy, I thought you were never going to call back," Scott said.

"Yeah, I'm sorry about that, I guess I kind of lost track of time." Kate said not really buying her own explanation. "I've decided I will do what you've asked. However, I want you to understand that I will first and foremost always maintain my objectivity as a reporter."

"I wouldn't want it any other way," Scott said.

"I would like to share with you my opinion now before we begin our professional relationship. I don't know if I will ever have the opportunity to bring it up again." Kate told him.

"I have felt for some time that a good deal of change was needed in this country, especially in the way our government operated, but where would this change come from? There's almost no difference anymore between the Democratic and Republican Parties; they are both bought and paid for by special interests and big multinational corporations and neither is likely to promote change. Therefore the seeds of change will have to come from outside the status quo. It is because of my feelings on these matters that I am agreeing to your conditions. I will do what I can to keep the Centrust Party in the spotlight. I will stay in touch with what your new party is doing, and how it will hopefully continue to grow.

There is something else that I can help you with, and that is to help you find someone to deal with the press. I have a friend in mind, but I must contact her first and talk to her about it. After I talk with her, if she is willing, I will forward her contact info to you."

"Great!" Scott said. "That's more than I expected. Thank you."

"No. Thank you," Kate said.

"Where do you want to do the interview?" Scott asked.

"We will do it at one of our affiliates here in downtown Phoenix."

She gave Scott the address of the affiliate and asked him to please get there as soon as possible.

Father Morales awoke the next morning, showered, shaved, and got dressed like it was any other morning. He took his suitcase downstairs and stashed it away where no one could see it. He found Juan, one of the men who helped around the church, and arranged for him to give him a ride to San Salvador where he could catch a flight to the United States. He explained to Juan that he could not tell anyone where he was taking the priest. This, he explained, was for his own protection.

Father Morales wasn't asking Juan to lie. Later when Juan would be asked if he knew anything about the priest's disappearance, he would actually have no recollection of ever helping Father Morales escape to the airport.

As the two men drove away in the little automobile the priest turned and looked out the back window at the little church he loved so much. A tear made it's way down his face. It was a moment filled with sorrow and joy. Sorrow for what he was leaving behind, and joy for what had begun. They bumped and jostled their way along the road to San Salvador where he bid farewell to Juan.

He went to the FedEx location in the airport. He addressed the envelope that contained a copy of the prophecy to Patrick Kincaid. He sent the other copy to the Council of Cardinals in Rome. He would contact the council when he felt the time was right.

The priest had to book a flight into Los Angeles first, and from Los Angeles he would fly to Salt Lake City. He seemed unconcerned about leaving a paper trail. Later his name would mysteriously disappear from the manifests of both flights.

As he sat waiting patiently for his flight, he thought that to most people it would be absolutely terrifying to leave their homeland and travel to a place they had never been before, to meet people they didn't even know, with only the clothes on their backs and a small suitcase packed with belongings. He laughed at himself as he realized that to a mystic like him, it really didn't seem out of the ordinary. The prophecy he had just mailed however was anything but ordinary.

He had felt for some time that this prophecy was coming. He had gotten glimpses during his meditations and dreams, but never the whole thing at once. He believed for some time that either he or one of the other prophets that worked for the church would deliver a prophecy from the earth about the way mankind had treated her.

While he sat there alone in his street clothes waiting for his flight he prayed that those, in the western part of the United States who had been given that monumental task wouldn't fail. Every once in a while all the pieces of the puzzle come together, but it is up to man to fit them into place. When it came to this particular puzzle, time was of grave importance.

Before leaving the house, Scott gathered together everything he had collected over the last couple of years that contributed to the Centrust Party website. He grabbed a briefcase and tossed everything into it, hopped into his car and headed downtown.

He laughed hysterically as he drove off realizing that in a span of less than three days he would be going from a small business owner in Phoenix, Arizona to a national celebrity. His laughter ended with the realization that he was going to be interviewed for national television in less than an hour. This realization led to a slight feeling of nausea. It felt like there was a huge rock in the pit of his stomach.

Scott found the address Ms. Seymore had given him without any problems. He took a couple of deep breaths as he sat in his car in the parking lot.

He took his briefcase and the rock in his stomach and walked inside. He told the receptionist who he was, and whom he was there to see and they shuffled him off into a studio where Ms. Seymore was waiting for him.

She smiled warmly at him and said, "Hello Scott, it's a pleasure to meet you."

"The pleasure is all mine," Scott said. He extended his hand to shake hers.

She noticed his palms were sweaty. "A little nervous? Is this your first time on television?"

Scott took a deep breath. "Yes it's my first time on television Ms. Seymore, but hopefully it's not going to be my last, and I'm looking forward to getting on with it."

"Please call me Kate." She pulled a yellow legal pad and a pen out of her briefcase. "You have nothing to worry about. I'm sure you're going to do just fine."

"Why don't we take a seat over here." She motioned to a couple of high stools located in the middle of the set. A woman came in and spent a few moments applying makeup to Scott's face.

"I thought perhaps we could work through a couple of questions to get you warmed up a bit before we roll tape," Kate said.

"That sounds good to me," Scott said.

This worked well for Scott and he began to feel more and more relaxed. He shifted from being a nobody receiving his fifteen minutes of fame, to a person talking about his passion to someone who seemed like a friend.

Fifteen minutes into the conversation Kate realized that Scott was someone special. He had a keen wit and a clear sense of what people wanted from their public servants, and he had absolutely no problem articulating it.

"Scott could you excuse for a minute."

"Sure," Scott said.

Kate went into the engineering room and asked them to start rolling tape. She would start the interview right now while Scott was relaxed and doing so well.

After returning to her seat Kate asked him, "When did you first become interested in politics?"

"The Watergate scandal," Scott replied without hesitation.

"You must have been pretty young at that time."

"I was eleven years old," Scott said. "I watched the Nixon resignation with an extraordinary amount of interest for someone my age. After that I followed the problems that plagued the Ford and Carter administrations."

"Could you tell us how you got to the point just thirty-six hours ago when you launched the Centrust Party website."

"I would be glad to," Scott said. "I am a small business owner who loves politics, and like many Americans I'm appalled by the performance and behavior of some of our public servants lately. I believe what Americans really said on Election Day was that they didn't want either candidate. Half of us saw the democrat as someone who played upon people's fears, while the rest of us saw the republican as a figurehead for big business and the oil industry that would really be running the country. My frustration reached a boiling point so I started the Centrust Party."

"What do you consider to be the most important issue for Americans today, when it comes to politics?" Kate asked.

"The elimination of special influence by special interest groups," Scott replied. "This must be accomplished with complete campaign finance reform, accompanied by tax reform resulting in a progressive flat tax with no deductions. Americans also need to feel that they can be an integral part of their government. The majority of people feel that having a say in running this country is currently out of their reach.

The one power that every American has is his or her right to vote. In our highly advanced technological society, at a time when it mattered most, our government couldn't even correctly count the votes. This has left a lot of Americans completely discouraged. Campaign finance and tax reform will once again level the playing field. With this in mind the Centrust Party will only accept donations by individuals within the current campaign finance law, until campaign finance reform is complete."

"On the web site you state that you consider the Centrust Party, to be the true conservative party. Could you explain this?"

"Absolutely. Our top priority is to stop and reverse the environmental destruction of our planet. We consider this to be the ultimate conservative act. What could be more conservative than caring for the planet we rely on for our sustenance? We are calling for our government to come forward with all the facts concerning our environment and enlist the public's support in building an economy that can be sustained for many generations to come. An economy that focuses on renewable resources and alternative energy sources by supporting industries or corporations that makes this their top priority. We do not believe that the dream of building this type of economy can be accomplished without eliminating the influence of special interests. That is the reason why campaign finance and tax reform are essential. Our philosophical goal is to leave the earth in better shape than it came to us."

"Surely, you don't want to eliminate the deduction for charitable contributions?" She wondered how he could possibly counter this.

"If we allow a deduction for charitable organizations, then it would only be a matter of time before we allowed a deduction for something else. This is a self-perpetuating process that led us to the ridiculously complex tax code we have today." Scott paused for a moment and thought carefully.

"People do not give to charities just simply for the tax deduction. They give to charities because they want to help those who are less fortunate. Many people who give to charities know that to give is to receive. A progressive flat tax would give every American an overall tax savings. This would mean more money available for every individual to use, as they like, including giving to their favorite charity.

We need to remember that taking care of every American is the highest form of personal responsibility. This includes the use of our tax dollars for welfare and other social programs. Many people who experience the joy of giving in their own communities, or to various charities look at the welfare system with contempt. Perhaps this is because of abuse of the system. We urge the government to empower all workers at every level to stamp out abuse, and we urge all Americans to view all our government's social programs as another avenue for giving to those who are less fortunate.

I believe many of our problems in this area stem from viewing ourselves as separate from one another. This sense of separation is one of the biggest problems we face in this country, and on this planet today and governmental bureaucracy only perpetuates it. When we take the time to think about it, we remember that we are all in this together. If each American didn't view themselves as separate from every other American, then we would be more concerned about equality, respect, love, and the well-being of the majority rather than the few."

Scott continued to defend the progressive flat tax further by addressing the mortgage interest deduction.

"Americans don't own their own homes because of the tax implications. They own their own homes because of the pride of homeownership and the investment value. Most probably own their own homes because they prefer it to the alternatives."

"What is your position on the estate tax," Kate asked.

"After the turn of the last century Teddy Roosevelt became concerned about the concentration of wealth and power in the hands of a few families. Therefore he proposed the estate tax as a means of preventing this. This continues to be a concern for our society today. On the other hand a wealthy person pays taxes on their income all their lives and I believe it is fundamentally wrong for the government to take any portion of their estate after their passing. Perhaps a good compromise would be reforming this tax so that, regardless of their value, family businesses and farms do not have to be sold to pay estate taxes.

Our government, through waste, misplaced priorities and an impossible tax code, is taking too much money from the private sector. It is time for all of us to expect our government to operate at least at half the efficiency of one of our successful American companies. Eliminating unnecessary levels of governmental bureaucracy will reduce the burden it places on its constituents. Americans will then be much more willing to make the changes that are going to be required of them in order to provide a better life for their children."

"Could you speak a little about visibility?" Kate asked.

"Certainly," Scott replied. "Most Americans have no idea of the effects that our consumerism has on the environment, or the effects it has on other countries around the world that provide much of our resources and labor. I believe that if Americans had the facts in this regard the majority would change their lifestyles. A few minor changes in the way we do business could have an incredible impact on our environment. These changes will go a long way in letting the rest of the world know that we are onboard with environmental protection.

Visibility, that is, making the facts available to all Americans should be the responsibility of our elected officials. At the Centrust Party we will make it our responsibility. We will be able to do this because we are relying on individual contributions, instead of special interest financing.

As with any kind of change, fear is our biggest enemy. If Americans can overcome their fear of change, we will be able to realize our potential as a nation. Together we can build something sustainable, and our actions will encourage the rest of the world to do so as well."

"Where do you stand on social security reform?" Kate asked.

Scott smiled as he thought of his answer. "Social security should provide just that, social security. For many Americans all they will save for their retirement is through the social security system. For them, and for all Americans we need to provide a better rate of return."

He paused for a moment and added. "For the many Americans who rely on social security as their only form of retirement savings, it would be nice if they had the choice to leave this to their children when they don't use all their funds."

"This sounds a lot like the republican plan." Kate commented.

"Other people have good ideas also," Scott said. "I think we will make a lot more progress as a nation if we acknowledge when someone else has a good idea and build on it, rather than attack it because it came from a member of our political opposition. I realize that in a democracy the person or party that gets credit is important because this recognition leads to votes. But isn't it the responsibility of our elected officials to come up with the best possible solution to any problem, regardless of who gets the credit? Shouldn't outcome have a higher priority than getting re-elected?"

Amazing. Where did this man come from? Kate wondered.

"I would say in a perfect world yes to both questions…. Is there anything we didn't discuss that you would like to mention?" Kate said.

"As a matter of fact there is Kate. Teachers in our society should be among the highest paid and the most respected of our professionals. Currently we entrust the education of our youth, our very future, to people who we say we respect, yet our actions indicate otherwise."

"In closing I would like to bring your attention to the last item on your web site. You encouraged democrats and republicans that are fed up with their parties, along with independents to join you in helping to build the bridge you call the Centrust Party. Do you actually think this can happen?" Kate asked.

Scott sat there for a moment with his hands folded in front of him and then said.

"God help us all if it doesn't."

That was the end of the interview. Kate told Scott that she had been rolling tape the whole time. He told her he figured that was the case.

"Do you believe I got my point across?" He asked.

"I believe you did," Kate replied.

They reviewed the interview together, which Scott would find out later was uncommon. Scott thanked her for helping him to make a good first impression, and left the studio to return home wondering what would happen next.

After Scott had left the studio Kate sat alone for a few moments pondering what had just happened. She wondered why she had taken it so easy on him. Then she realized that in her heart of hearts she really wanted things to be different. She thought about the phone call from Patrick Kinkaid and how it completely slipped her mind to ask Scott about it.

Next time I speak with him I've got to remember to ask him if there is any connection between the Centrust Party and the senator.

"Never gonna break down the walls
and build a prison with the stone.
Cause you and I know what love is worth,
gonna build a heaven on earth.
Put it in the wheels of fortune turning water into wine.
Gonna make love the bottom line,
gonna find a peace in our time."

Eddie Money

Chapter 4 — The Flight

"Good morning sweetheart," Jack said. He sat down next to his wife Susan at the kitchen table with his first cup of coffee.

"Good morning honey," she replied. He leaned over and kissed her.

"There's something very interesting in the newspaper this morning." Susan said.

"What's that?"

"Today on page four of the Republic there's an article about a property purchase in Flagstaff. There is a thousand acre meadow that borders the highway and extends all the way to the foot of the mountains. The property had been vacant forever and was assumed to be state trust land. However, a private party owned it and was going to sell it.

"Now they're going to be a very wealthy private party. A thousand acres in Flagstaff is like owning your own gold mine," Jack said.

"It gets better Jack ,listen to this." Susan paraphrased from the article.

"The people in Flagstaff really didn't want another housing development especially one that would lead up to the foot of the mountains destroying the meadow. The city of Flagstaff didn't have near enough money to purchase the property so the sale went ahead as scheduled. An anonymous, wealthy individual bought the property and then announced that it would not be developed after all. Instead the property would be left in its natural condition. People would be able to use it for mountain access, to snowshoe, and cross-country ski in the winter as they had for years. The new owner asked only for people to respect and care for the property leaving it in its natural condition."

"That's pretty unusual," Jack said. He felt intuitively it was time to clue Susan in on some of the things that had been going on.

"Susan do you remember a few years back when I went up the mountain to do a vision quest?"

"Yes."

"I was on the mountain by myself with no food or water for 2 days crying out for a dream, and I started experiencing visions. Do you remember afterwards that I really couldn't reveal what the visions were about?" Jack said.

"Yes."

"This was for two reasons; one I had to honor the experience, and two I had to wait for things to develop more thoroughly so I could understand the visions myself."

"Uh-huh," Susan said. She nodded her head. Jack noted her facial expression. She seemed to be anticipating something big.

"My visions were about a time that would be coming soon, a time of great change. The consciousness of the planet is increasing and as a result millions of people will be waking up and no longer walking through life asleep—

"Well we've talked about this before, Jack."

She had a notable look of relief on her face.

"Well there is a little more to it than that." Jack said. The look of concern returned to Susan's face immediately.

"There is going to be a major shakeup politically, economically, and spiritually. In the end, I believe everything will work out to be much better than things are now. However the outcome of this change is not determined and it is not fixed in time. The future is always subject to our free will. Therefore, it is very important for the people who have raised their awareness to stay focused." He paused for a moment and then added. "I was also informed that many others know about this also."

Susan could tell that Jack was speaking purposefully. She believed he was asking Spirit what he should and should not tell her in this conversation.

"Before Ben and I went up to the rim to have ceremony, you and I went to the supermarket together. Do you remember that?"

"Yes I do," She said.

"We were trying to purchase cage-free organic eggs."

"Uh-huh," Susan said.

"Right then I heard the voice of Spirit say to me. 'Jack it's starting!' I didn't need to ask what was starting because I knew what it was. This shift was starting! A political and economic shift that is being brought about by God and the earth, because the earth can no longer endure our abuses." The excitement was growing in Jack's voice despite his attempt to control it.

"Susan, it was revealed to me during my vision quest, that I would play a major role in this shift." The other shoe had dropped and Susan realized that her husband's destiny was at hand.

Jack realized that he had been talking so intently that his eyes had been closed. When he opened them he saw the look on Susan's face and said, "Oh no sweetheart, there's nothing to fear.

This is a grand opportunity for me, for you, and for everyone else who calls this planet home."

"What do you say we get on the Internet and see what else is happening out there like this situation in Flagstaff?"

"Ok," she replied.

While the couple waited for their computer to boot, they discussed the seemingly limitless possibilities of what a shift of this magnitude could mean for the earth and everyone on it. As Jack explained to Susan that it was their chance to make an immeasurable contribution to the causes they held so dear, he could see the color start to return to her face and the sparkle return to her eyes. Susan sat on Jack's lap as the two surfed the Internet looking for other stories similar to the one they just read in the paper. She could feel the energy of their mutual love.

In other various news publications they were able to find some philanthropic land purchases, land that was purchased to be left as open space. After moving through a couple of other subjects they found a story about electric cars in India. The cars had not even been released yet, and they were sold out for two to three years of production. The manufacturer was skeptical about even being able to come close to keeping up with future demand. A major Japanese manufacturer was going to have their electric car ready five years ahead of their original schedule. The emission regulations were not going to go into effect until 2010, but these cars would be ready in 2005.

"Wouldn't it be great if people in this country got turned on about driving alternative fuel vehicles?" Susan said.

"That could make a huge difference," Jack replied.

Susan got up from his lap walked over to the window and looked out over the valley. She could remember days when she would look from this window and be able to see all the way past downtown Phoenix to the mountains on the other side. Today she couldn't even see the mountains this side of downtown let alone the buildings or the mountains on the other side of the city. There was a brown cloud hanging in the air obscuring the view, but not her memory.

"Now that the kids are on their own, maybe you and I could get one of those two-seater alternative fuel vehicles." Susan said.

"That's a great idea," Jack replied. Susan walked back over to the desk and sat down on Jack's lap again.

"You know Susan, it's of vital importance to focus our prayer and meditation for more and more people to come forward and demand products like these. We can also send energy to those who through faith are purchasing these products now."

The couple decided to sit down right then and meditate together. During their meditation the couple focused on their love for the earth and all the people who call it home. Susan visualized a massive wave of consumerism. This wave of consumerism however was friendly and healing to the earth. Jack used his power to send a message out to all those who had ears to hear. It was a message for everyone to step up and start using their buying power to bring about global change. Jack then moved an enormous amount of kausai energy to those companies that were working to save, restore and preserve the environment.

Susan knew something special was happening, because she became very warm. She began to cry softly. In college she majored in environmental studies and had never been able to turn a blind eye to the things that we're happening to the planet. She wasn't a shaman like Jack, but she loved the earth every bit as much as he did. When she opened her eyes she was amazed, yet not surprised that Jack's eyes were looking softly into hers.

"Everything is going to be just fine," Jack said.

It was nearly 11:00 pm Utah time, when Father Morales arrived in Salt Lake City. He was not surprised that there was no one waiting for him at the airport, because he arrived at such a late hour. He flagged down a taxi to take him to a motel close to the airport. For someone who had just left his country for what might be the last time he slept surprisingly well. When he awoke the next morning, however, he felt like a stranger in a strange land. He knew he was supposed to be there, but the day had taken on dream-like qualities.

After showering and shaving Father Morales began to get dressed. While he was dressing he got the urge to wear his black shirt and collar. When he had made the decision to bring these clothes with him he thought this was strange. Yet he couldn't seem to leave them behind. He had written this off as an attachment he had to the priesthood. As he finished dressing in his priest's clothing he felt even stronger that he was on the right track.

Father Morales locked the door to his motel room behind him and headed for the front office. The clerk informed him the food across the street was as good as any and so he decided to have breakfast.

After leaving the front office he stood on the sidewalk gazing across the street at the restaurant. Standing there he realized he would not have to spend another night at the motel. While crossing the street the sense he was headed in the right direction grew stronger and stronger. When he entered the restaurant there was a sign to his left that read, "Please seat yourself." So he took a seat in a booth where he could see the door.

A weary waitress made her way to his table. He made a conscious decision to be a light and brighten her day. As the waitress came closer to his table he could feel her spirits rise. He greeted her with a warm smile. She returned one with no effort.

"Would you like some coffee this morning, Father?" She asked.

"I sure would. Thank you," he replied. After the waitress left the table the bells on the front door jingled as someone entered the restaurant.

Father Morales looked up to see a rather tall Native American man wearing a cowboy hat and sunglasses. The man had shoulder length hair, and he was gazing around the restaurant as if he was looking for someone. As the man's eyes scanned the room, Father Morales realized he was there for him. The man took off his sunglasses to take a closer look at the restaurants occupants. This time when his gaze hit Father Morales his face lit up and he grinned widely. The dream-like quality returned as the man walked across the restaurant and sat down across the table from him.

"My name is Bob Talking Bird Walker," the man said after taking a seat.

"I am a Ute Indian from the Uintah Ouray Indian reservation in eastern Utah"

"Hello, it's nice to meet you," Father Morales said.

"Have you eaten yet?" Talking Bird asked him as he picked up a menu.

"No I have not."

"Well that is outstanding because I'm starved. At three o'clock this morning, I was awakened by the seer in our tribe who told me that I must leave immediately for this restaurant in Salt Lake City. I barely had time to get dressed. Hurry! Hurry! He said otherwise you'll miss him."

Talking Bird laughed and shook his head back and forth.

"I was almost off the Indian reservation when it dawned on me, why do I need to hurry? Did you see me there or not?"

Talking Bird gazed down at Father Morales's collar. "This seer, our medicine man, was told that a man of power was coming. We would know him because he would have a white band of power around his neck signifying that he spoke the truth. As I was leaving this morning he reminded me, 'Look for the white band of power. Look for the white band of power.' He repeated it over and over again and on the way driving over here I couldn't get it off my mind. I kept wondering what the white band of power would look like. Would I see a band of energy around someone's neck? I thought about and visualized several different things, but I have to be honest with you, I never thought of a priest. Now I have to laugh because it makes perfect sense."

"I can understand you wouldn't think of a priest. Very few people realize that there still are mystics involved with the church," Father Morales said. "Many members of the church don't know about the church's prophets and seers."

Bob Talking Bird Walker had very gentle eyes yet they were always on fire. Father Morales believed he was one of those personalities who was always going a mile a minute. The waitress returned and took their orders. While eating breakfast, Talking Bird held up most of the conversation. Father Morales was very hungry since he had not eaten after his meal on the plane. The office clerk at his motel was correct. The food was very good.

Talking Bird stopped eating and talking long enough to notice Father Morales's plate. "You don't eat meat?"

"No I don't," Father Morales said.

"Why is that?"

"I stick to a plant based diet because eating food that is alive brings more life force energy into my body. This helps my seeing."

"Hmmm that's interesting,…. Where are you from?"

"I'm from El Salvador"

After their breakfast Father Morales went back to his motel, gathered his things and checked out of his room to embark on the journey of a hundred lifetimes. He joined Talking Bird at his pickup truck in the motel parking lot, threw his things in the back and jumped into the cab.

He laughed as he turned to Talking Bird. "By the way, where are we going?"

Talking Bird smiled at the priest and said. "We're going to the rez. The medicine man, our tribe's seer, is waiting to meet you. He has known you were coming for over a year now. For the last week he has been so excited he's had trouble containing himself. He's hardly been able to sleep."

Father Morales noted that this was about the time he started to receive the prophecy. The two men headed east from Salt Lake City towards a little town on the Uintah-Ouray Indian reservation called Mountain Home.

"Our medicine man told us that in his vision he saw medicine men and women, holy people from of all walks of life coming to our reservation. Together these men and women would form a council whose collective power had not been known on earth for some time. The foundation of this council was that all its members were caretakers of the great Mother Earth. Despite their different ethnic and religious backgrounds their great love for the mother and all the people on her belly would form a bond of power that would vibrate throughout heaven and earth. This council will sit in ceremony together on our reservation, and actively participate in saving the planet," Talking Bird said.

"That's a tall order," Father Morales said.

"You got that right. It has always amazed me how you mystics hook up together. You receive a prophecy, take a plane to another country, then you sit in a restaurant and wait for someone to show up…. To know that someone else would be there …. I just don't know how you guys do it." Talking Bird had a look of amazement on his face.

"Well, I guess it's not for everyone." He looked at Talking Bird and smiled.

"I don't suppose so," Talking Bird said shaking his head slowly back and forth.

Talking Bird lived up to his Indian name, and Father Morales heard his whole life story before they were halfway to the Indian reservation. He also told the priest how the Ute Indians had a creation story, just like the Christian's did.

"The great Creator had gathered a bag of sticks that was completely full. He had left the bag of sticks in the care of Coyote. Coyote could wait no longer for the creator to let the sticks out of the bag. Coyote then opened the bag, and when he did all the sticks escaped. Coyote pleaded with the sticks to come back into the bag, for the Creator would be back soon. The sticks would not cooperate." Talking bird turned and smiled at Father Morales. "They were the people of the earth and they did not want to go back into the bag. When the Creator saw what Coyote had done, he admonished him for letting the sticks out of the bag, because they were not ready yet. The Creator explained that the people had not been scattered correctly across the earth, and therefore there would be many wars among the people. For this act Coyote was banished forever to live on the earth. This is why Coyote howls at the moon, because he wants to return home.

There were some people left in the bag and these people were the Ute Indians. The Creator then took the Ute Indians and placed them on the mountains, and proclaimed that they were the special people. The only people who were complete," Talking Bird said.

Father Morales thought about how the story Talking Bird had just told him was not unlike the creation stories of other traditions in that part of the story establishes its people as special in the eyes of God. He wondered how long it would be before all people realized that we are all connected to the creator in the same amazing fashion.

His thoughts were interrupted when Talking Bird said. "The medicine man from our tribe told me that the native peoples of America had fought bravely to keep their land and way of life when the white man swept across this country. He also explained that what happened before was a battle and what was coming was the war. This time however, it wouldn't be the white man against the Indians. This war would be fought on the spiritual front, and its participants would not be divided by race or creed. One side would not even consider the other side an enemy and this is precisely how it would be victorious. He told me that if one side had an enemy all its power would be lost"

"That's interesting," Father Morales said.

Talking Bird thought for a moment. "I've thought long and hard about this and I still haven't straightened it out in my mind yet."

"And the meek shall inherit the earth," Father Morales said.

Father Morales escaped again into his thoughts. He felt a deep sense of sorrow for all that had been done in the name of religion to indigenous people around the world. In South America, Mexico, the United States and Africa to name a few, the native people's way of life and commitment to the divine were trampled underfoot by those who would seek to force them into another way of life, all in the name of God.

"You've probably already figured out that I live up to my Indian name, and have a tendency to ramble on. You've been through much the past couple of days, and I will leave you to your thoughts while we continue our drive. Enjoy the scenery. If you wish to talk some more we can; however, I have told you all I know about the council and what lies ahead."

"Thank you," Father Morales said. The two men drove along in a comfortable silence, and Talking Bird left Father Morales alone to his thoughts.

Father Morales thought about how the church had tried to become more open in the last 20 years. However, it was an institution run by men. Man would always remain fallible, and problems came when he valued his own point of view above the best interests of his brethren. For some reason his mind drifted back to when he was a young man not even 20. He began to have dreams about things that had not happened yet. These dreams were soon joined by daydreams of the same nature. By the time he was eighteen he reasoned that somehow he was able to step outside of time. This was the only explanation his mind could come up with. He spoke to his parents of these things, but they didn't know what to think of their son's abilities and discouraged him from pursuing them for fear of divine retribution. Even as a young man he knew that God was not a vengeful, overbearing deity that cast people's souls into hell. He understood God to be the all-encompassing spirit of love that informed all life on this planet and the universe. He knew that this lifetime was just one of many in which men journeyed to find out who they really are. His parents however, were not quite ready to hear this.

He was quite surprised when he received the message to join the priesthood. At first he thought the message was something of his own mind, and not a divine calling. Over time there was no doubt that the message was indeed from God. He used to joke that God dragged him kicking and screaming into the priesthood. He felt that religions represented following rules rather than following one's own path into the divine. What concerned him the most was their use of fear to control people.

It was in the seminary that the church found out about Jose Morales's abilities. He enjoyed his special status among his peers. This helped him to forget about what he didn't like about the organization. He spent time in Rome and several places in Europe. His longing for home became too much, however, and he was able to convince the church to let him return to El Salvador by threatening to leave the priesthood.

Rome reluctantly decided that he could serve the church in El Salvador and send his messages to Rome from there. He was a very talented, clairvoyant mystic, and it was better to have him in the priesthood at a distance, rather than not having him at all. Over time he came to believe that his purpose was to help the people of El Salvador. He believed this was the reason he joined the priesthood. This was very rewarding to him, and he loved serving the people of his community. However for the last five years he had knowledge that something big was going to happen, and he would somehow be involved.

The two men began chatting again as they entered the Indian reservation. They drove until they reached the little town of Mountain Home.

"We will go straight to the medicine man's home," Talking Bird said.

Talking Bird and Father Morales stood at the front door knocking when Father Morales spotted someone moving around the side of the house from the corner of his eye. The person moved up on them very quickly, so quickly in fact that Father Morales was shocked when he turned to look at an elderly Indian man who had to be at least 80 years old.

"My name is Joseph Kindred," the old man said. He extended his hand to shake Father Morales's.

"My name is Jose Morales," the priest said as they shook hands.

"Pleased to meet you," both men said at exactly the same moment. The three men enjoyed a laugh as they entered Joseph's home.

"I told you he would have a white band of power around his neck," Joseph said.

"Yeah, but you didn't say he was going to be a priest," Talking Bird said.

"I didn't know he was a priest, I knew he had a white band of power around his neck."

"Please come and sit down," Joseph said to Father Morales. He turned on the television set. "We are about to witness something very special to all of us. Talking Bird, what channel is that CNN on? I always forget."

"Channel 42," Talking Bird said. He got up from the couch to get something cold to drink from the refrigerator.

It was about 1:00 pm Arizona time when the phone rang at Jack's house. The caller ID indicated it was Ben.

"Hey Ben, how are you doing?"

"Hurry up! Turn on CNN, right away," Ben said.

"What's going on?"

"Just turn on the television, hurry!"

"Susan, could you turn on CNN please?" Jack said. She set down her book reached for the remote, and turned on the television.

There was a young woman interviewing the man from Jack's vision. The phone slipped from his hands and hit the floor. When he picked up the phone the first thing he heard was Ben's laughter.

"Do you recognize him?" Ben said.

"Ben, I'll call you back after the interview," Jack said. He hung up and joined Susan on the couch.

Together they all watched; Jack and Susan, Ben and his wife Patricia, Joseph Kindred, Father Morales and Talking Bird, as a man in his early 40's talked of his disgust for American politics. Thanks to divine universal timing an apparent accident had thrust this man named Scott Stahl into the limelight.

This stranger to the American political scene spoke eloquently and intelligently about the current crisis in the election of the President. He talked about Americans tolerating a lack of results from their federal government.

"As Americans, nowhere else in our lives would we tolerate such pitiful performance," he said. "Neither political party has been able to step up and take care of the people's key interests in a timely fashion, because they are bought and paid for by the power brokers that fund their campaigns. No longer do these two parties represent the majority of Americans. Therefore it's time for politics in America to evolve just like everything else on this planet. For that reason we've started the Centrust Party."

When that statement was finished there was hooting and hollering on the Indian reservation. There were high 5's going on all over America. Jack and Susan sat in awe with their mouths wide open as they watched the interview. One man in spite of himself, and almost by accident, had started something that millions and millions of people wanted to happen.

After the interview was done airing on CNN, Scott got up from the couch and headed upstairs to his office.

"Where are you going, sweetheart?" Elizabeth said.

"I am going to try and weed through the rest of the emails I've received so far," Scott said. "Today is a workday, and all my customers and clients are at work. Tonight most of them will most likely see this on the news, and tomorrow my phone will ring off the hook."

Scott stood on the stairs for a moment. "Would you like to help me?"

"I was just waiting for you to ask," she replied. Elizabeth went over to their home phone and shut it off. Scott looked puzzled.

"Not everyone we know is at work right now," she said.

Scott copied half the emails over to Elizabeth's computer and the couple started the long task of sifting through them. More and more emails continued to arrive, and it became obvious that two people could never keep up if each email was read. They were simply unprepared for such an incredible response. The two decided to let their intuition guide them to which emails they would read.

One email that caught Scott's attention was entitled. "You're going to need a lot of help." When he opened the email he found its author's name was Sam Jameson who lived in Minnesota. He was actually one of the people who were instrumental in starting the Reform Party. Sam said he was very proud of Scott, and offered his services. He had the experience of what it took to start a new political party. Sam had also left his phone number.

That afternoon Scott and Elizabeth poured through as many emails as possible. Scott phoned the Internet service supervisor he had spoken to the day before. He retrieved more of the emails that had come in and now the count was up to 7850. This was in spite of the web page being down several times. Scott thanked the supervisor for his time and told him that Jeff Kline from New World Web Design would be contacting him.

At one point that afternoon as the couple poured through the emails, Elizabeth said to Scott, "This feels very strange. It's as if we are living someone else's lives."

"Our lives sure have taken a quick turn, and there's this dreamlike quality to the whole experience," Scott said.

Scott wondered if this turn in their lives just might write history.

"If there ever was a time we needed to stay completely present in the moment this has got to be it," Elizabeth said.

Scott called Sam Jameson and it was better than he could have hoped for. Not only was Sam in between jobs, but money was not an issue for him.

"If you'd like I could fly to Phoenix as soon as possible and help you get things started out on the right foot," Sam said.

"That would be greatly appreciated," Scott said.

"Scott, do you have any idea about how huge this is? You've opened the door to a path that many people have been wanting to walk for some time."

"Well, I really can't take any credit. It all kind of happened by accident."

"I guess so…I mean…. That is if you believe in accidents," Sam said.

"Ok. Well, give me a call when you get into town and I'll give you directions to my house," Scott said.

Sam began laughing.

"What's so funny?"

"I'm watching a reporter out in front of your house doing a live shot right now. I don't think I'll have any trouble finding your place," Sam said.

"Ohhhhh No," Scott said.

After the conversation with Sam, Scott thought it was interesting that he had trusted so easily someone he had never met. Scott would find out that this was only the beginning of many coincidental meetings and circumstances that would change his life forever.

"What's going on?" Elizabeth said.

Scott turned on the television and said, "Look!"

"Oh brother," Elizabeth said. They were watching a reporter standing on the sidewalk in front of their home.

"Lets go take a peek," Elizabeth said.

They left the office and went to a bedroom in the front of the house where they could see the street. They peeked out the window and sure enough there were two television station trucks parked in front of their house. They giggled like a couple of kids and were careful not to be spotted spying on the scene below.

While the two were checking out the reporters in front of their house Scott's business phone rang. He let the answering machine pick up the call, but when he heard Kate Seymore's voice he ran into his office and picked up the phone. Kate gave Scott the name and phone number of her friend in LA, Helen Shultz, who was interested in handling their growing press coverage.

Shortly after her conversation with Scott Kate realized she
had forgotten to ask him if there was any connection between
Senator Kinkaid and the Centrust Party. For the first time in her
career she had the thought that if this slipped her mind, perhaps
she wasn't supposed to know about it. This thought surprised
her, but nonetheless she made the decision to drop the matter all
together.

After hanging up with Kate, Scott dialed Helen's number
immediately.

"Hello."

"Hi, this is Scott Stahl may I speak with Helen Shultz
please?"

"This is Helen."

"I was referred to you by Kate Seymore. She said that you
might be interested in helping me handle the press."

"Well, I really can't think of a better reason to get involved
again…. I saw your interview with Kate today. You did a great
job," Helen said.

"Well thank you. Kate made the whole thing pretty easy.
She really is such a sweet person," Scott said.

"Yes she is, for a reporter that is. I'm just kidding, I love
Kate we've been friends forever. I'm not kidding about reporters
though, anything you say in public, or even to people you might
consider your friends could wind up on national television.
You've got to be prepared for it every time you talk to the press
from this point forward."

"Can you help me?" Scott hoped his voice didn't sound like
he was pleading.

"I believe in what you are doing and at the very least I think
it could all be good fun. If you would like I could drive over this
evening and we could meet sometime tomorrow morning,"
Helen said

"Are you kidding me? That would be awesome. Thank
you," Scott said.

"I want to thank you Scott for what you've started. There is one condition."

"What's that?"

"Don't talk to the press until after I get there," Helen said.

"No problem," Scott said.

Scott gave Helen his address and telephone numbers and told her he looked forward to meeting her in the morning. After the conversation he was once again amazed at the way everything was fitting into place.

Jack and Ben spent the afternoon on the phone chatting while watching the various news channels. They were thrilled because what they had seen in their vision was now starting to take place. Jack and Ben understood that the ending or the beginning, depending on one's perception, was not yet established. The difference between them and those who haven't awakened their vision is that these two men would consciously take part in these events.

The two men found some humor in what different people had to say about the formation of the Centrust Party. A reporter remarked that its formation was an indication, just like the election, that America no longer identified with either political party. A well-known politician, however, passed it off as, "some Internet thing."

"When the election process is complete in Florida, and America has a new president, the Centrust Party will fade into obscurity," one elder statesman remarked.

Jack laughed. "Some of these folks have no clue what's really going on here. Do they Ben?"

"Well I guess they don't realize that the Centrust Party is just part of a force that is growing in America and around the world," Ben said.

"Just wait until this force reaches critical mass. Then global consciousness will shift and no one will be able to stand in its way," Jack said.

"Can you imagine what the world will be like when the majority realizes what doesn't suit them with honesty and without fear?" Ben asked.

"Yup, and what doesn't suit us will be cast off. Then everyone will realize they have the power to dream the world into being," Jack said.

"Hey, what do you say we stick around awhile and help this one along?"

"Sounds like a plan to me. I'll talk to you later Ben."

After their phone conversation Jack continued to daydream about a world awakened that no longer lived in the prison of fear. He visualized this coming about in a peaceful way rather than the alternative that he and Ben had witnessed during their ceremony the other night.

"Oh people look around you, the signs are everywhere.
You've left it for somebody other than you to be the one to care...
Rock me on the water, maybe I'll remember,
maybe I'll remember now."

Jackson Browne

Chapter 5—The Prophecy

During the next couple of days Scott and Elizabeth did
their best to enjoy the events taking place. The day after the
story broke, Scott's business line rang off the hook. Customers,
clients, friends and associates were calling him asking quite
frankly what the hell he was up to. Many of them were republicans and they were not appreciative of a lot of the things Scott
had said. Some remained skeptical and told Scott that he was
proposing pie in the sky changes that could never take place.
However, as Scott went through the agenda with them, others
began to respect what he had done and came to see the things
that needed attention.

Scott listened to everyone's fears and suggestions with an
open heart. He made a commitment to himself always to do
so. When the day was done, however, he could not help but
have a feeling of nervous anticipation about stepping into the
public eye and what affect it would have on his business and
his livelihood. He also wondered if his relationship with any of
the people that called would ever be the same again.

Scott set up a meeting with Jeff Kline, Sam Jameson, and Helen Schultz. The meeting would take place at the offices of New World Web Design.

After the meeting got started they laid out their agenda for the next couple of weeks and each person had specific goals to accomplish. They elected Scott Stahl as the party's first chairman. Sam Jameson would be in charge of all business operations for the party. He would be responsible for setting up the party as a legal entity, its tax status and everything else that was involved with running the business end of a political party. Helen Schultz would be the press secretary, and would be in charge of disseminating public information and handling all press releases. She would also individually instruct the party members in interacting with the press as necessary. The new web site was now up and running, and the founding members reviewed it with great pleasure.

Scott and Elizabeth would continue to answer emails that came in from the web site. Now, however, they would be organized thanks to the work of Jeff Kline and his company. Scott couldn't thank him enough for this.

"You have no idea what it's like to sift through thousands of uncategorized emails a day," Scott said.

They also agreed that whenever possible Helen Shultz would be contacted before speaking to the press.

The party's founders decided to treat no one like an enemy, even groups that used their money and political power to take advantage of the system. This would be a different approach, and given America's disdain for the current political situation it would be hard for the other parties to attack them when they were not treated as enemies. The Centrust Party would merely point out that the fears of a few were dictating legislation for many, and they didn't believe these were the principles this country was founded on. The meeting was a smashing success and they all agreed for the time being to conference call once a day.

Scott and Sam had really hit it off, and after discussing it with Elizabeth they opened up their guest room to Sam. This would make it easier for them to work together to get things established. Helen decided to return to Los Angeles for a couple of reasons. Los Angeles was a major press hub and giving the press releases there would deflect some attention from Phoenix allowing Scott and Sam time to get more work done.

On the way home Scott, Elizabeth, and Sam drove along in a comfortable silence for quite some time.

"I can't get over how all these personalities and talents have fit together so well. It just seems like there has been one coincidence after another that has changed this improbable task into something that I am starting to believe is achievable," Elizabeth said.

Scott's eyes met with Sam's in the car's rearview mirror and he said,

"That's because there are no coincidences, right Sam?"

"You've got that right," Sam replied. There was a moment of silence, and then Sam put into words what was apparent in the look on Elizabeth's face.

"What we are dealing with here is so powerful and important we couldn't have planned it. Yet I can't help but have this feeling that we all agreed to our part beforehand."

The three spent the rest of the ride home in an appreciative silence.

Father Morales spent the next few days getting to know Joseph. Joseph and Father Morales compared notes about what each one of them had seen as their roles to be in the upcoming events. It was amazing how much each man's vision complimented the others. The two comrades would work together in spirit and in truth to do their part in bringing about the shift in America's consciousness.

Neither man felt threatened by the other's different spiritual background, because together they shared a mystical bond that transcended race, religion or creed. Father Morales was most interested in learning everything he could from Joseph. Joseph was inspired to know that so much love could exist in one person, as it did in Father Morales. Father Morales asked Joseph to teach him the medicine way.

"Your power is great, and the depth of your love is special, I felt you coming from thousands of miles away. Your decision to work through the medicine wheel will strengthen our energetic tie. It will increase our power together immeasurably. Together we will then be of the same lineage," Joseph said.

The next morning, Joseph entered Father Morales's room.

"Good morning compadre."

"Good morning Joseph. How are you this morning?"

"I am good. Listen, I thought tonight could be our first fire ceremony together. What do you think?"

"That sounds great to me. Today is an important day and ceremony would be a good way to end it." Father Morales said.

Since he awoke this morning he had been in constant prayer and meditation, because today he would call Rome and speak with Cardinal Delmar. The letter that contained the prophecy arrived in Rome yesterday and today he would make the all-important phone call.

After leaving the priest's room Joseph poked his head back in and said, "you can use my phone whenever you are ready." Father Morales nodded and smiled.

To a seer, a man of true power, thoughts that contain a lot of energy are easy to read. Thoughts that contain a lot of emotion are right on the surface, and easy for a seer to pick up on. The priest had been aware of this ability for years. It was strange for him however, to be in the company of someone else who had the same gift.

As was customary Cardinal Delmar made seven copies of the prophecy received from the Central American priest. Cardinal Delmar was Father Morales's contact in Rome. His job was to coordinate information received from the church's seers and present this information to a council of cardinals for review. Usually the cardinals that sat on the council would review the information at their convenience, and then a meeting would be scheduled for them to review it. The magnitude of this prophecy, however, would dictate that a meeting be called immediately. Cardinal Delmar's mind was preoccupied with the contents of the prophecy. He believed that the council would probably call the priest a heretic.

The meeting had just gotten under way and Cardinal Delmar could already see he wouldn't be surprised by its outcome. Cardinal Talbott was in charge of the council, and he was fuming.

"I cannot believe you have called an emergency meeting of the cardinals."

He glared at Cardinal Delmar. "This prophecy is obviously not authentic. It cannot be from God!" A couple of the cardinals shook their heads in agreement. A few sat as if they were stone figures, unable to speak, perhaps knowing in their hearts the prophecy was true.

"Since when does a Catholic priest call the earth his mother? This among many other things contained in this blasphemous document make me doubt its authenticity. Have you heard from this priest Cardinal Delmar?" Cardinal Talbott asked.

"No, I have not," Cardinal Delmar replied with an insolent tone.

The two cardinals glared at one another across the table.

Cardinal Talbott broke the uncomfortable silence.

"Cardinal Delmar you have been the contact for this priest. We've all met him on one occasion or another, but you know him the best. What do you think of this prophecy?" He sat back in his chair with his arms crossed waiting for a reply.

Cardinal Delmar thought for a moment. "It is disturbing to say the least. Father Morales has been without a doubt our most accurate prophet. It is for this reason that I am so disturbed. He has been receiving bits and pieces of this prophecy over the last year. He has had time to approach God again and again regarding its content. He would not have come forward if he didn't believe the prophecy he received was authentic."

By authentic the cardinals meant that a particular prophecy was received from the Holy Spirit and not the thoughts or desires of the prophet's mind. Prophets have been around for thousands of years. Some are better than others. Father Morales is a very gifted seer, yet he is still a human being. Could this prophecy be in error? Could it be the creation of the priest's mind? These were the questions that the cardinals faced.

One of the cardinals who had been shaking his head in agreement with Cardinal Talbott spoke,

"The church has always been a caretaker of the earth. We have never condoned the malicious destruction of the earth and its resources. We may not believe that the earth is a living conscious being, but nonetheless we have treated it with respect, and have encouraged our members to do likewise."

Another cardinal asked. "Has Father Morales ever delivered a prophecy that came from the Mother Earth before?" Everyone looked around at each other and then all eyes turned to Cardinal Delmar.

"None that I can remember," Cardinal Delmar replied.

"You see, this alone indicates there is a problem with this so-called prophecy." Cardinal Talbott said. He looked around nodding his head and encouraging the others to nod their heads in agreement also.

He continued, "There are some things within this so-called prophecy which the holy Church of Rome will never consecrate. Who is this man anyway, to bring these requirements upon the church?" He waited and there was no reply.

Two of the cardinals began to look nervous, and Cardinal Delmar hoped he was not looking nervous also. Two were shaking their heads in agreement with Cardinal Talbott and now a third seemed to be leaning in that direction. Cardinal Delmar could see which way the vote would go. Although he never thought it was in question before he entered the room. In other words, he knew they would decide to discredit Morales.

"If the Church were required to change some of its policies, do you not think that the Pope would have been informed? Would God not have gone to the head of the church and told its leader of the need for change?" Cardinal Talbott asked. He glared again into the eyes of Cardinal Delmar.

Cardinal Belmont thought, but dared not speak it. *Perhaps the Pope was too busy to listen.* This prophecy not only made sense to him, it spoke to his heart also. He could tell that it spoke to a couple of the other cardinals, but they were afraid to voice their feelings.

Cardinal Talbott broke his stare with Cardinal Delmar and summoned one of his assistants over to him. After whispering something in the assistant's ear, the assistant left the room. Cardinal Delmar believed that this could not be good.

The cardinals finished discussing the various points of the prophecy and then put it to a vote. In the end there was only one vote that proposed sending the prophecy onto the Pope, the vote of Cardinal Delmar. Four cardinals voted to shelve the prophecy two abstained. Cardinal Delmar had sensed that the other two cardinals wanted to vote to forward the prophecy, but they were afraid to go completely against Cardinal Talbott, because he was such a powerful political figure.

After the meeting was adjourned, Cardinal Talbott stopped Cardinal Delmar in the hallway.

"I have summoned Father Morales to Rome because we need to look into this matter further. All of us need to discuss this prophecy with the one who received it."

Cardinal Delmar's heart sank. "Are you interested in talking with the priest or do you want him here so you can keep an eye on him," he asked.

"Come on, face it! You know as well as I do, that if this prophecy somehow became public knowledge the results could be disastrous—

"Or people might actually decide that change was appropriate. But, that would involve granting them the power of choice, wouldn't it?" Cardinal Delmar said.

He turned and walked away leaving Cardinal Talbott standing in the hallway.

Cardinal Delmar had trouble sleeping that evening. He had tried to contact Father Morales during the day and had been unsuccessful. As he drifted off to sleep he wondered what would become of his old friend and what would become of this world if the prophecy were indeed accurate.

The next morning Cardinal Delmar spent in prayer seeking God's guidance and asking for enlightenment on the prophecy. After a couple of hours of prayer and meditation he sat down to read it again one more time.

It read…

A Prophecy From the Earth

As received and transcribed by the hand of Father J. Morales during the year of our Lord AD 1999

The earth is facing a time of great change for the people who live on her belly. It is up to the people

who rely on her for life to decide whether this will be
a peaceful loving transition or a time when mankind's
population will be needlessly and drastically reduced.
This choice is up to mankind. Mankind has always
had free will to evolve to Christ consciousness anyway
it chooses. "Armageddon" as man chooses to call it, is
not necessary. The future has always been made of
potter's clay that takes a long, long time to harden.
This clay is molded and shaped by the hands of man
collectively. As time has passed mankind's decisions
have hardened the clay and made it less and less
pliable. The Mother Earth has been watching and
waiting for her children to wake up and remember
several things. Indeed many of her children have been
waking up, and practicing conscious living. The pace
of this awakening has accelerated in recent years.
This is very pleasing to God. The universe has asked
the earth to delay her decision a little longer, and she
has agreed.

  The Mother Earth wants mankind to awaken
from its slumber and remember its true destiny, which
is to become enlightened, and realize its divine nature
as apart of God. This is what all the masters have
experienced, and is the destiny of all. How mankind
realizes this destiny and what experiences it creates is
entirely up to it.

  These are the requirements of the Mother so she
can maintain her place as mankind's caretaker:

  1) Love your neighbor as you love yourself. If you
   don't know what love is, or how to love, find out
   quickly and make it a priority in your life.

  2) Live consciously and make a pact with me: to
   love and care for me on every level and in every

aspect of your existence. Everything you have including your body comes from me. Be mindful of this and no longer waste my resources. This can be accomplished very simply by paying attention to what and how much you buy, how you eat and taking care in conserving the resources I provide you.

3) Remember you are a part of nature, and not apart from it. Mankind as a whole has done it's best to forget this fact. Many of you have been trying to live outside the laws of nature, the laws that every other species lives by. Regulate your population. This is the natural order of things. I cannot sustain a population that is growing so fast. I cannot and will not let the destruction continue. This destruction has no purpose and certainly doesn't serve who you truly are.

The next part of the prophecy was entitled:

The Role of the Church

1) Apologize for all past wrongs against any of mankind. The inquisition, participation in the extermination and mistreatment of indigenous peoples etc.

2) Abandon your stance on birth control and encourage it. Population control is the natural order for all species. Mankind is no different on this account.

3) Declare that women are equal to men in all things. Allow them and encourage them to have any post they desire, within and outside the church. Women because of their ability to bring forth life, and their natural tendency to love

unconditionally, tend to be closer to the divine than men.

3) Fear and intimidation must no longer be used to control people. This includes using the threat of eternal damnation that doesn't exist. This is not helping people to achieve enlightenment, which was one of the messages of Christ. We understand that this will be a leap of faith for the whole Christian church, and all of my children. Yet these changes are necessary. They are in fact, requirements.

The next part of the prophecy was entitled:

The Choice

Two years ago I conspired with the universe to create a condition that would ensure my survival. I am a living conscious being, and most of mankind has forgotten this. I have used my consciousness to draw an asteroid to myself. This asteroid will wreak enough havoc to reduce the human population by 80%. I will then go about healing myself with the help of the universe as I have done before.

Astronomers will become aware of this fact one year after the inauguration of the new American President. The truth about the asteroid will not become public knowledge at first. Astronomers will correctly calculate a time of impact at seven years, seven months and seven days from the day of its discovery. If mankind turns from it's present course, and realizes it's true role as my caretaker; if it proceeds with respect for me, with the intent to heal me, and at least honors the requests made in this prophecy, then mankind's love for its Mother will deflect or make the asteroid disappear altogether.

This was the end of the prophecy received by Father Morales. Reading it for a second time left the cardinal feeling even more helpless then he did when he first read it. The cardinal sat in silence staring at the letter in his hand when an assistant walked in and informed him he had a telephone call.

The cardinal picked up the phone; it was Father Morales. "Where are you, Jose?"

When the cardinal asked this Father Morales saw in his mind's eye two big black cars pull up to his church in El Salvador. He saw people exiting the vehicles and frantically searching for him. He knew now that this was another reason he had to leave El Salvador.

"If I told you where I am then the Church would know where to send its people to retrieve me," the priest replied.

"It wasn't me Jose, who sent those people. It was Cardinal Talbott."

"I know that you wouldn't do something like that; you and I go way back even before I lived in Rome." Father Morales said.

"I could never forget, those were good times," the cardinal replied.

Cardinal Delmar knew intuitively that this would be the last time he would speak with Jose Morales.

"The prophecy has been discredited, has it not?" Father Morales asked.

"It has been shelved for now. The others wish to know who else knows about it and its contents."

"What did you think of the prophecy?" Father Morales asked.

"It is most disturbing to say the least."

"Well don't worry Patrick. The Church's position on the prophecy will ensure that more energy will be directed at bringing forth this information from another source." Father Morales said.

It increased the cardinal's faith to know that somehow the

truth would be told. On the other hand he believed a truth of this magnitude would undoubtedly rock the foundation of our modern culture.

"It will most likely come from several sources, our church was just the first political structure to receive it in written form. Mystics of many cultures from every corner of the globe have been hearing this same message from the earth. The words of this prophecy are in the songs of every bird, they are in the whispers of the trees as they talk to one another while their leaves rustle in the wind," Father Morales said.

Cardinal Delmar let out a sigh.

A million and one thoughts were swimming through his mind and he was experiencing emotions from all of them at once, ranging from pure unadulterated fear to eternal hope for the possibility that mankind might join together to straighten out what is wrong in this world with a new conscious intent.

"I must get off the phone now Patrick. I'm resigning my position with the Church and I'm sure you've figured out that I won't be coming to Rome," the priest said.

"I'm going to miss you Jose."

"Likewise, well, hopefully we will see each other again in this lifetime," Father Morales replied. He let out a soft uncomfortable laugh.

A cold chill went down the cardinal's spine. What a weight for a person to carry he thought.

"Goodbye old friend."

"God bless you Patrick."

Cardinal Delmar left to tell the other cardinals that he had heard from Father Morales.

"We scheme about the future, and we dream about the past,
when just a simple reaching out might build a bridge that lasts."

John Hiatt

Chapter 6 — The Meeting

Over the next few days, under Helen's guidance Scott interviewed with each one of the local television stations. He and Elizabeth worked feverishly to reply to as many emails as possible. Scott, Jeff, Sam, Helen and Elizabeth were moving forward with something that now had almost completely taken over their lives and become a passion for everyone involved. It was Friday afternoon and the world was waiting for a ruling from the Florida Supreme Court. Scott felt that the heat was off for the moment and wanted to leave the house and get some fresh air and run some errands.

Elizabeth gave Scott a list of things to pick up from the organic food store and the name of a book she wanted. Scott opened the front door prepared to break his way through the barrage of reporters who were always waiting for a comment on the latest events in Florida.

As he drove through the few miles of Sonoran desert that still remained between his house and the rest of Phoenix he could not help but replay the events of the past few days over in his mind. It was late November and he rolled down the windows to let the cool desert air blow across his weary face. He allowed the unique aroma of the freshly rained-on-desert to remove the recent events of his life from his mind. From time to time when he became troubled about one thing or another he would recall the smell of the freshly rain soaked desert. This had such a calming effect that he found it hard to worry or stress in that state of mind.

His first stop was the bookstore. At Elizabeth's insistence he had brought a baseball cap and sunglasses to help hide his identity. Wearing them made him smile at himself. He found the book Elizabeth wanted and purchased it. He was relieved when no one recognized who he was. After purchasing the book Scott got back in his car and drove to the food store.

Jack was standing at the gas pump filling up his car when he realized he had been staring at the organic food store across the street. He didn't think too much of it, and nothing seemed familiar to him. He spent the last few days waiting patiently for Spirit to let him know how to proceed. He paid for the gas and got into his car to drive away.

As he started to drive away from the gas station he couldn't take his eyes off the organic food store. In that instant he realized his preoccupation with the store's sign was not an accident. After pulling into the street the urge to go to the food store became overwhelming. Finally surrendering to this urge he pulled into the parking lot, parked his car, and headed inside. While walking into the store Jack made a conscious effort to connect energetically to everyone he saw. His mentor referred to this as being a light, and this was one of the tools Jack used in practicing conscious living. Today, because of this incredible urge to enter the store, he would raise that consciousness up a notch. He shifted his perception to that of the cat, the jaguar who is ever vigilant, aware of every moment, of everyone, and everything around him.

He grabbed one of those little shopping baskets, so at least he looked like a jaguar with a reason to be there. As he walked through the store he made eye contact with every one he passed and in an instant knew each one of them. One by one he eliminated each person as the reason for his being there. Jack looked up at the aisle signs, and the sign with the number three on it was luminous. It wouldn't take flashing lights and ringing bells to let him know he was in the right place; a luminous aisle sign would do. After entering the aisle he stopped for a moment, turned towards the shelves, pulled out one of his business cards from his wallet and headed down the aisle to a man wearing a baseball cap and sunglasses.

Jack recognized the man at the end of the aisle as Scott Stahl. After seeing his face several times on the television for the last couple of days there was no mistaking him. As he walked the last few yards to approach Scott he didn't have the feeling that he was meeting a stranger. It felt more like a reunion.

He approached Scott and said, "Excuse me."

Scott turned cautiously to face Jack and very slowly took off his sunglasses.

"Yes, can I help you with something?"

"You don't know me yet—

"Listen, if you're a reporter I've told everybody—

"No, no," Jack said. He smiled and shook his head. "I'm not a reporter, I'm a shaman."

"A shaman? Well, I'm not sure I even know what that is," Scott said.

The events of the past few days had worn Scott thin. He could feel the impatience welling up inside him, and he could tell that his eyebrows were furrowed.

Then something told him, *Relax Scott this is important.* He could feel the tension leaving his face.

"Most people don't know what shaman is, and that is quite all right. You don't really need to know what one is right now. The point of the matter is that I have been sent to help you," Jack said. He paused for a moment, looked deep into Scott's eyes, and Scott had the feeling that this man could somehow command his attention. He was unable to look away.

"The first time I became aware of our eventual meeting was three years ago at a ceremony. I've been sent to be your helper, to offer a different kind of help than you've had until now. Over the past year I began to have more and more visions of you starting a movement of some kind, and the importance of your mission."

Scott's head was reeling with a million questions. His knees felt like they might buckle; yet he could not look away from this man's powerful eyes. They seemed to be holding him up, and keeping him from collapsing into a pile of flesh on the market floor.

Jack continued in a calm but forceful tone. "The Centrust Party is a very large part of something bigger that is happening for the whole planet."

"Wait a minute, hold on a second here," Scott said. He suddenly got a hold of his senses.

"This all sounds like just a little bit too much for me," Scott said,

I knew I was going to run into some weirdoes, I just didn't think it would happen the first time I got out of the house.

Fear began to grip him, and he started to long for his old life back, when he realized he had never looked away from Jack's gaze.

At that moment Jack smiled and a feeling of peace enveloped Scott and began to dissipate the fear. The rest of the market seemed to melt away, and it felt to Scott like the two men were standing alone face to face in a place where time did not exist.

"I understand the reason for your suspicion, but there is no need to fear," Jack said. He smiled kind of matter-of-factly. "The senator told you that several people would be sent to help you. Did he not?"

Scott's jaw fell open.

He had only told one person in the world about the senator calling him and that was his wife Elizabeth. For some reason Scott felt he would never tell anyone else about the phone call from the senator. Yet, standing in front him was some stranger named Jack who seemed to know about it. His mind raced through a series of questions including whether the senator or his wife Elizabeth had told others, but he quickly came to the conclusion that this was highly unlikely.

Suddenly Jack spoke again, snapping Scott back to the present moment.

"What you are involved with has been coming into being for longer than your mind is capable of imagining at this point. Changes of this magnitude, happenings of this kind of beauty take time and energy for the universe to create. The senator who you respect so deeply told you that helpers would be sent to you, and I am one of them."

"Here is my card." He slipped a business card into Scott's palm while shaking his hand. "I have put my home phone number on the back. Don't lose this card, because it's going to be very hard for me to get a hold of you. You can call me anytime day or night." Scott nodded his head.

"The shaman is a servant. Remember this when you hesitate to rely on me. The shaman is also a person of power, and I have been sent to help you stay on this very important path of yours. Right now people all over the planet are helping you and your new friends. They are sending prayers and energetic power. Your resources are beyond your comprehension.

I am here for whatever you need me for, Scott. If you need someone to unload on, or perhaps just someone to talk with, I am here. If your load becomes too heavy, I can help you lighten it. As things come up that require extra energy, call on me. Perhaps it will help you to think of me as the first person in an incredibly large prayer chain. These prayers contain a creative power that will be invaluable to you and your new companions.

I have to get going now but before I do I would like to say, you and I both know that regardless of the media's desire for this current election to continue indefinitely, it will come to an end soon. When it does, the media coverage for your new party will slow down to a trickle. This will be the time when you will be tested. You will need strength, courage, and faith to continue with your purpose and that is another one of the reasons I've been sent to you. This power that I've spoken of will be like the wind at your back."

Scott was amazed that Jack not only knew about the phone call from the senator, but he knew about Scott's dream of the coming slow time.

"Thank you," Scott said.

Jack put his right hand on Scott's left shoulder. "Take care, and stay the course." Scott could feel an intense wave of excitement pass through his body from Jack's hand, unlike anything he had ever experienced before. Scott put his sunglasses back on, and Jack turned and left walking at a quick and effortless pace.

Upon his return Scott burst into his house passing his daughter.

"Where is your mother?"

"Well it's nice to see you too, Dad," she replied.

Scott flashed her a smile and repeated his request. "Where is your mother? I really need to speak to her right away."

"She's in your room."

Scott swept into the bedroom like a blustery March day. "Elizabeth, when I was in the food market I was approached by a guy…hey, have you ever heard of a shaman?"

"I think a shaman is an Indian, or a medicine man," Elizabeth said. She had a quizzical look on her face.

"Well this fellow was no Indian, I'll tell you that much! His name was Jack, and he said he knew about me and what I'm doing with the Centrust Party three years ago." Scott paused to take a breath. "Can you believe that? Well I couldn't believe it either." He was so excited he was walking in circles waving his arms as he talked.

Elizabeth had to grab him by the shoulders. "Scott slow down take a deep breath, and tell me what happened."

"Yeah, you're right," He said. He took another deep breath and sat down on the edge of a chair. "My mind has been racing a mile a minute since I left the store, and I'm probably not making much sense." Scott looked up at Elizabeth from the chair.

"Elizabeth, he knew about the phone call from the senator."

"What? Wait a minute here, start from the beginning," Elizabeth said.

Scott took a couple of moments to calm down and then told Elizabeth the whole story. He repeated how this man named Jack had approached him in the market. He told her that he said he had known of Scott and the Centrust Party for about three years, and that many other people from all different walks of life had been waiting for this to happen. Scott explained that at first he thought Jack was just some crazy that had come out of the woodwork as a result of all the recent television coverage.

Elizabeth nodded in agreement, but then Scott repeated, "Honey, he knew about the phone call from the senator. The only person I told about that phone call was you. Since I know you didn't tell him, and it is highly unlikely the senator told him, the only way he could have known would have been through some supernatural means. Besides, he not only knew about the senator calling me, he knew about the senator telling me that many others would be sent to help me." This erased the growing look of skepticism on Elizabeth's face, and she sat down on their bed across from the chair where Jack was sitting.

"Oh my God," she muttered. Scott could see her mind trying to come to grips with what he had just told her.

"Well, maybe the senator did tell someone," she said.

"Remember Elizabeth, the senator asked me not to divulge the conversation to anyone and I haven't except for you. For crying out loud, a United States senator called me and told me he had been instructed in a series of dreams to contact me. I don't believe for a second he would risk telling anyone about it" Scott paused to catch his breath.

"Do you think it could be? I mean, do you think that thousands of people could some how be involved behind the scenes with what is going on right now with you, me, and the Centrust Party?"

Elizabeth didn't answer she just sat there staring at Scott like a deer caught in a car's headlights.

"When I was talking to this man my initial skepticism was replaced by an overwhelming feeling of peace and purpose. The experience was electric, energetic, and mystical all at once. The night before I put up the web site, I had a dream and I heard a voice speak to me in the kitchen, but I thought it was my own mind playing tricks on me. So I haven't mentioned it until now."

Silence fell over the room for a few moments.

"I've often wondered about those who were involved in events of great importance throughout history," Scott said. "Were these men and women conscious of the magnitude of their contributions to the world? Where they aware or did they even have a sense of the impact their actions would have on human history? Compared to just being hopeful?"

After Scott's flurry of rhetorical questions, Elizabeth got up and began to pace the bedroom. "A new political party?... Our faces on the evening news…. A shaman, senator, reporters. This is blowing my mind!"

She stopped pacing and looked directly at Scott.

"We really need to stay focused in the moment if we are to make the right choices. Otherwise this whole damn thing could overwhelm us."

Looking up Scott and Elizabeth noticed their daughter was standing in the doorway of their bedroom. There was no need to ask her how much she had heard of their conversation, because the look on her face gave it away. They invited Michelle into their room and Scott went through the whole story again.

This was how their family dynamic worked. People didn't keep secrets from one another, and things were discussed openly. Maybe sometimes a little too passionately, but things were always discussed openly.

Michelle was thrilled with her father starting a new political party. She had enjoyed the attention from the reporters who had been at the house, and also at her school. She found the mystical twist of this afternoon's events especially intriguing.

"Cool," was the word she used. Scott and Elizabeth believed that she understood the importance of keeping today's events to herself.

Father Morales found the fire ceremony that evening to be an incredible experience. He had read many different things about Native American ceremony, but this was the first one he had attended. He was excited throughout the entire evening. There were many rituals involved with the ceremony, just like in the mass, and these were performed with impeccable intent. There was an all-encompassing presence of unity and power. He found himself becoming absorbed by it, and whatever apprehension he might have had beforehand melted away in the presence of this power. Everyone participated in some way, either by chanting, singing, dancing, drumming, or rattling.

Some, including Father Morales, were so swept up in the moment that they managed several of these things at the same time. This focused group consciousness created a feeling of power and grace that was tangible. It was electric! The ceremony succeeded in transporting everyone into a mystical realm.

At one point during the peak of the ceremony Father Morales had a vision. He saw people of many different faiths praying for the seed that had been planted in the western part of the United States, called the Centrust Party. Recent events had caused a window of opportunity to open up and a few souls have stepped forward to care for the seed, but mankind's collective will was responsible for the seed bearing fruit.

Could America live up to its guiding principles, and take its place in helping to lead the world out of the mouth of environmental destruction? Father Morales prayed that it could, and visualized a world where America stepped forward to become a caretaker of the earth, instead of its largest consumer. There was a new generation of Americans being born, and being born again into a complete awareness of its role in life. This generation was no longer consumed by greed, and no longer willing to sacrifice the future of its nation or the world for short-term gain.

While the priest walked back to the Joseph's house, he wondered if the people who started the Centrust Party had any idea about the forces that had gathered to support them.

That evening Elizabeth had a very vivid dream. She had had dreams before that she felt were important. Some of her dreams even had great significance in her life, but none affected her as powerfully as did this dream.

The dream began with her seeing groups of people in different parts of the world simultaneously. She saw a light in the middle of every person's body. This light was located around the area of their solar plexus. From this light, a luminous strand stretched out in an arc to some distant point. Elizabeth thought this energy looked like a smoothly curved lightning bolt. There were millions and millions of arcing strands of energy coming from all over the world converging at one location simultaneously. In an instant she realized that one location was Phoenix, Arizona.

Her initial surprise was replaced by a sense of, warmth and joy, as she realized that these strands were emanating from more people than could be seen or counted, and they were here to support the growing consciousness that she and her husband had become an integral part of. This was certain to provide the momentum that was needed to fulfill their mission.

Up until this point Elizabeth had been referring to recent events in their lives as, "the Centrust Party ordeal." It had been her way of dealing with the drastic changes that had occurred over the past week. To call it an ordeal meant that one assumed it would end. In this dream she had the clear notion that she should refrain from calling it the Centrust Party ordeal.

Elizabeth never recalled being directly informed in a dream before. Upon awakening she remembered the entire dream. Every last detail was clear in memory including being told to remind her husband to stay in touch with Jack Anderson.

Scott woke up Saturday morning when he heard the front door gently close as Elizabeth returned from her walk in the desert. He lay in bed relaxed and rested after the first good night's sleep he had in a couple of weeks. Scott lay there just staring at the ceiling, really feeling good all over, when he remembered what had taken place over the last five days. On Monday a Florida Circuit Court judge rejected Andrew Knight's contest of Florida's election results, but yesterday his appeal to the Florida Supreme Court was successful, and the court ordered a statewide recount of every under-vote. The under-votes were ballots that, when run through the vote counting machines, failed to register for either candidate. Florida law did not account for a statewide recounting standard and today they would start counting by hand or machine every under-vote throughout the entire state.

As soon as he remembered this he leapt out of bed. Threw on a pair of shorts, and a T-shirt, and dashed upstairs to the office, where Sam Jameson was seated at Elizabeth's desk on the phone. Scott had just gotten up, and it seemed that Sam was already doing five things at once. The television was on, tuned to ABC; he was on the phone; he had the Centrust party web site up on his computer, and some governmental site loaded on Scott's computer. Scott enjoyed having Sam stay in the guest bedroom the past week, because the two had developed a deep camaraderie in an amazingly short time. He couldn't help but wonder however, what his next phone bill would look like.

Sam had what Scott thought to be an unequaled ability to work at a feverish pace for incredibly long periods of time. Scott had tried to keep up with him the first couple of days, but was unable to do so.

Sam had told him not to worry about trying to keep up. "I have worked this way all my life, and have never met anyone who could keep up with me," Sam told him.

Sam quite regularly preferred to handle four or five tasks at a time, all the while being on the phone. Scott sat there in amazement for a few minutes watching Sam talk on the phone, work on the Internet and watch television without ever missing an important detail from all three information sources.

Sam also had a way of making Scott feel at ease, which was not an easy task considering their present set of circumstances. Sam had been through this before in helping to start the Reform Party, and this time he felt a burning desire to get it right.

This morning Scott's duties involved sifting through emails from the party web site. He was also drafting the party's political agenda. With all the press coverage the party had been receiving, the emails were multiplying rapidly.

Over the last week, Scott had received several phone calls from various congressman and senators. Some from the republican side were not very happy at all. The democrats seemed to be trying to feel them out. He also received many calls from different political action groups. Many of these groups had something to do with the environment and Scott had noticed that many of the people whom he talked with had a discouraged tone in their voices. Sometimes he could even feel the hatred they had for their political opposition.

Scott had spoken with Elizabeth about this hatred for one's opposition, because it was obvious to him that hating one's opponent was detrimental to the progress that these groups were so desperately trying to make. He knew that hatred and opposition was not the same thing and being able to separate emotion from the issues was critical to constructive dialogue. Elizabeth reminded him that these people had been arguing their causes for a long time, and had perhaps become entrenched in that kind of dynamic. A clear vision like that being created by the Centrust Party could provide the energy these groups needed to revitalize their commitment to their individual causes.

Scott was only halfway through his first cup of coffee when he was jolted out of his daydreaming by Sam saying, "Yeah, yeah, I'll turn it on right now. I've got to go I'll talk to you later."

Sam flipped the television station from ABC to CNN where the state- wide recount of under-votes was getting under way. A reporter was interviewing a political analyst who had been closely following the events in Florida from the beginning and the analyst was beside himself.

There were counties calling in from upstate Florida wondering which votes needed to be recounted, and how to go about it. The analyst, a former Florida election official, explained that there was such confusion that some of the counties had even called him asking for direction, even though he no longer worked for the state.

"Oh brother this is really bad," Sam said. He took the phone off the hook, the scene before him now had his undivided attention.

The analyst's face was flushed, and his eyes spoke of big trouble coming. Florida was crawling with attorneys from both sides arguing one thing or another in county after county. The scene resembled mayhem. Some election officials were running some of the under-votes back through the machines. The additional chads produced as a result could only create more reasons for argument among the myriads of attorneys. The cameras panned from one county seat to another. Some were hand counting, some were running the votes back through the machine, some were waiting for instruction on how to count, and some were listening to attorneys argue.

It was obvious to anyone who was watching that any recount undertaken without a statewide standard would be called into question. Up to this point most Americans had not realized how flawed our vote counting process was. What was going on that Saturday morning in Florida was utter chaos, and any result that came from this process would be doubted, con-tested and only serve to deepen the bad feelings one side had for the other. What the two men saw that morning saddened Scott deeply, and for once in his life left Sam at a loss for words. Even the media was in a state of confusion. There were too many stories going on at one time to cover any of them effectively.

This whole mess started on election night with every net-work calling the state of Florida for Andrew Knight before the polls had even closed in the state's panhandle. Later that evening they would have to retract and in the early morning hours of the next day they declared Robert Kelton the winner. However, this would have to be retracted before sunrise that morning because the Kelton's lead had dwindled to within the margin of error.

What has taken place since then has been one bizarre turn of events after another that culminated on this Saturday morning where even the media didn't know which way to turn. It was a morning created by lawyers, politicians, and the media, and it was a disaster for America, one that her people would not soon forget.

The republicans had ceaselessly interrupted and stalled the hand counting. Knight had proposed recounting the whole state of Florida, long before this Saturday, but after it was allowable by Florida law, knowing full well that this would portray Kelton as someone who didn't want all votes to count. Texas had specific vote counting procedures that Kelton had signed into law while he was Governor and now he was opposing applying these same standards in Florida. Knight had only wanted to recount highly populated counties that would obviously favor his candidacy. He figured by recounting these counties he could find the thousand votes he needed to put him over the top. The Democratic Party had done their best to deny as many military votes as possible, believing they would highly favor the republican.

The whole situation had long since been a mess, but on that Saturday morning it took an ugly turn for the worse. There was no way that what was unfolding before them would convince America that an accurate count of votes would come out of Florida.

It was clear to Scott and Sam that the mayhem in Florida needed to be stopped immediately.

"You think the market was in bad shape yesterday," Sam said, "just wait until Monday if they let this fiasco continue."

They watched in horror as CNN switched from one county seat to another, and the confusion increased. Even Sam couldn't take it any longer. He walked over to the TV turned down the volume, shook his head in disgust, and returned to his seat at his desk to continue working. In a minute he was back on the phone again.

Scott couldn't contain his sadness any longer. He put his head down into his arms on his desk, and began to weep. At first they were just tears, but his sadness was too great, and tears gave way to uncontrollable sobbing.

"Hey, I'm going to have to call you back later," Sam said. He hung up the phone and walked over to where Scott was sitting at his desk and placed his right hand on Scott's left shoulder. He turned and walked silently downstairs to leave Scott alone with his tears.

Scott cried because the ordinary American was so far removed from the political process that all they could do was watch these events unfold on television. He wept because of the great blanket of apathy that smothered America. This blanket was so heavy that it kept Americans from speaking the truth, even to themselves.

This growing apathy continued to lower standards by which Americans measured their public servants. He thought, *Who am I, to think I can do anything about this anyway?* He wept because of the stressful changes starting this party had already placed on his life and his family. He doubted whether laying everything on the line, family, business, and his personal life would in the end make any difference.

His sadness went the deepest as he thought about his children's children. What would he tell them? That we were 10 to 30 years away, depending on whose estimate one used, from permanent irreparable environmental disaster, and rather than take immediate action we argued about what to do. Some of us were afraid of losing our jobs, or changing our lifestyle. Rather than having faith in our ability to adapt, we chose to live in fear and continued our destructive trend.

Could he look his middle-aged grandson in the eye and tell him that we were the richest, most powerful country in the world, and rather than lead the world into an age of environmental care taking, we chose to perpetuate unsustainable consumerism, and only woke up after it was too late?

Would his grandson ask: *You mean to tell me grandpa that you were too afraid of hurting your economy? You mean that all that would've been required was for people to switch from one job to another? Now you left us this, just because people were afraid of change?* Scott didn't think he could live with this.

He looked through his tears and imagined the look of bewilderment in his grandson's eyes. He now felt that what had started, as tears of cleansing, had become tears of self-pity. He wouldn't stand in front of his future grandson and tell him that he did nothing while the destruction continued. Scott would tell his grandson how he and his friends led the charge to do things differently. That as a result of his efforts, millions like him led the battle to increase people's awareness and live consciously.

He wanted to be able to tell his grandson that alternative sources of energy were developed long before fossil fuels ran out, or the earth's atmosphere could no longer accommodate their pollution. He wanted to tell his grandson that people took responsibility for how they ate and what effect their eating had on the planet, as a result this saved the remaining rain forest. He wanted to tell his grandson Americans were willing to put up with very minor inconveniences in order to leave future generations an earth as beautiful as the one he was born to. He wanted ed to tell his grandson that men began demanding that women be treated with respect, reverence and as equals. What became the most admirable trait of a human being was the quality of their character, not the size of their bank account—this would be what Scott would like to tell his grandson.

After his own heart called him back to duty through the vision of his unborn grandson, Scott could weep no more. He sat up, dried his eyes, took a few deep breaths, walked into the bathroom, and blew his nose. He splashed some water on his face, toweled it off, and walked out of the office to look down and see Sam and Elizabeth sitting at the kitchen table. They both looked up at him for a moment and Elizabeth broke the silence.

"Are you ok, hon?"

"I'm ok now," Scott said. He looked at Sam. "Are you ready to get back to work my friend?"

"That I am," Sam replied. Sam jumped up from his seat at the kitchen table, poured himself another cup of coffee, and motored up the stairs.

Scott had already taken his seat in front of his computer by the time Sam made his way into the office. Sam walked over to Scott and once again put his hand on Scott's shoulder. "They sure have made a mess of things, if you didn't start to cry I would have."

Ten seconds later Sam was back at his desk, and on the phone again. Scott couldn't help but let out a sigh. He couldn't remember ever weeping so much.

With that Scott sat down to write an essay for the Centrust Party web site. What he wrote about had its birth in the tears he just shed. He opened his word processing program and this is what he wrote:

> America is once again at a crossroads. The rest of the world anxiously awaits our decision on how we will move forward from this point. Our collective attitude and spirit will be the foundation for the changes that are needed and they will shape our experiences from this point forward. Will we choose a foundation of fear, selfishness, anxiety, stress and hatred, or will we choose a spirit of love, brotherhood, forgiveness and community?
>
> Our economic prosperity over the last eight to nine years has been unprecedented. Yet there is a pervasive underlying unease among the people of our nation. Many married couples are working ten to twelve hour days when you include their commute.

Some are doing this to preserve their standard of living, some so that they can buy and accumulate more things, and some are working these hours just so they can survive. The effects of so much work and stress, and not enough time for love, family and community are also evident in the statistics that relate to our children. Crime and violence, dropout rates, drug addiction, teen pregnancy and suicide rates are still to high. Apathy has caused us to develop a hard skin around our hearts.

Respect and reverence for women has deteriorated. This can be seen in the startling rise of crime and violence against women. It is not coincidental, in our viewpoint, that the rising violence against women coincides with the accelerated pace at which we are consuming the earth's resources, and destroying her ecosystems. Women bring life into this world and nurture it. These attributes are in direct opposition to our rampant consumption of natural resources.

People know intuitively something very wrong is happening. It needs to be stopped and a new course of action needs to be adopted without hesitation. This underlying urgency to embark on a new path is fueling the furnace of change once again in America. We all know that these steps are necessary and that our politicians don't seem to have the courage or desire to take up the challenge.

The energy of this confusing time has spawned the creation of the Centrust Party. Of all the sweeping changes that were proposed on our original web page, and those that are being formed by the new members of our young party, the following have emerged as the cornerstones of our party platform:

1) The elimination of exclusive influence on our

political system by special interest groups. This is only possible because of the huge sums of money that are needed to run a political campaign and stay in office. The Centrust Party asks for your input and inspiration on how to set up campaign finance reform that is not only constitutional, but also assures that every person in America will have equal access to his or her senator and representatives as does the leader of a special interest group. In other words we've elected some very bright and talented people to public office. Let us trust them to do the job they were elected to do, and let them decide which issues are important to their constituency, the country, and the world. Any person who has an exceptional idea should have the same power to affect positive change that a special interest does to further its political agenda. Until meaningful and deep campaign finance reform is enacted this won't become a reality.

2) The influence of power enjoyed by special interests cannot be eliminated without abolishing the IRS as we know it, and establishing a progressive flat tax with no deductions. There must be no deductions, without exception. Otherwise special interests will once again be able to position themselves and increase their influence within our political system. The progressive flat tax must be implemented in a way to encourage people to increase their income, and to leave those with higher incomes not feeling like they've been penalized for making more money. The current tax code is an unacceptable waste of time, money, and energy, not to mention paper.

This time, money, and energy could be used to get in touch once again with our families, communities, and politicians.

The majority of individuals support the kinds of sweeping changes that we are proposing, because they make sense for all of us. However, when you arrange the same individuals into a special interest group, and motivate them using fear, they no longer care to promote change that will benefit millions. They are instead more interested in protecting themselves from their own fear at the expense of everyone else, and our planet. It is as if they forget the value of what happens every time they have helped another human being. They can no longer remember that there is a ten-fold return of joy and energy as a result of their consideration. This must be the focus of our efforts if we are to overcome our collective fear, and enact the kinds of changes that we all know in our hearts must occur.

The elimination of preferential consideration and access to our public officials by the special interest groups will not be easy. When we say special interest groups we mean all of them including domestic industries, multi-national corporations and labor unions, among many others. We are not saying that their access would be eliminated it would just be given equal consideration along with anyone else. Access to our public servants should be determined by the importance of the issue to the public servants constituency, and the nation as a whole. We realize at the Centrust Party that some groups will strike out against us in fear. Their attacks may become vicious, and personal. We don't believe this is necessary, and we stand ready to discuss our agenda with anyone.

The Centrust Party encourages any individual or group of individuals to join us, and become a member of our party. There are only two requirements and we insist that any prospective member consider them as long as necessary before joining us:

1) Forgive your enemies or opposition, and let go of the past. This will change the energy dynamic of your individual cause moving forward.

2) Commit to helping us mold the Centrust Party from the heart with love as our sponsoring motivation. That is a love for all people, and the earth as well. Debate among ourselves, and with our colleagues in the opposing parties must be held with respect and love as the fundamental principle. This doesn't mean one has to agree with the opponent's viewpoint, but one must acknowledge the spirit of his opponent and always hold that in higher regard than his own opinion.

We encourage people of all races, religions, and political affiliation to come forward and join us. Help us to create something new in American politics, something that will be an expression of our great potential. Thank you all for your time and consideration, and may God bless America.

Scott finished editing what he wrote and signed the bottom of the page. He had the document in the fax machine when he remembered his agreement with Helen Shultz. They agreed that she would review all documents that were to be made public. She was the expert when it came to public relations and he had no problem running the document past her. He was just glad he remembered to do so.

He called Helen and indicated to her he would be sending a fax that contained something he wanted to add to the Centrust Party web site.

"Can you believe what is going on in Florida this morning?" Helen said. Her voice had the tone of someone who had lost their footing and didn't know if they would find it again.

"If I didn't see it myself I wouldn't have believed it. As a matter of fact that is the inspiration for what I am faxing you," Scott said.

He faxed the document while the two chatted briefly on the phone. Helen glanced at it and told Scott she would read it and call him back.

Scott had given the document to Sam to read before he called Helen and somehow he managed to read the document while still keeping an eye on the television.

"Hey look!" Sam shouted. "The Supreme Court has stepped in and is stopping the vote counting in Florida."

"Boy, that was close," Scott, said under his breath.

"This is good stuff Scott," Sam said referring to what Scott had written for the web site.

"Thank you," Scott said.

"I liked what you wrote about molding the party from our hearts. If we can persuade enough people to get out of their heads and start living from the heart our new party might stand a chance."

"Let's hope so," Scott said.

Scott thought that Helen would have called him right back, but when she didn't; Scott and Sam broke away from work to have a late lunch.

In Los Angeles Helen Shultz must have read the essay at least ten times. Scott had written about things that they all wanted to accomplish, of that there was no doubt. But to come right and put it on the table like this…. She couldn't help but wonder if politically, this was the right thing to do. Helen thought that she would wear through the carpet in her family room as she paced back and forth contemplating the implications of making Scott's essay public.

Finally out of the blue it occurred to her. Truth is truth; maybe we should play politics with the truth. "Lets use the truth," she said to herself. As she accepted this idea a feeling of warmth overcame her.

This is indeed what we are trying to do, she thought. We want to create something new. If we operate from the heart center and speak the truth as we see it, we'll enter into debate with love, just as Scott put it. Then we can always speak the truth as we see it, and have no fear about tackling such important issues. Issues that in the past, because of their potential to become political bombshells had been avoided until reaching a crisis point.

Helen then came up with an idea to help with the campaign to start the Centrust Party. The first political buttons for their party would read.

"Help us create something new. The Centrust Party. "

Scott began to wonder if Helen was ever going to call him back. It was driving him crazy. Sam thought Scott was ready to jump out of his skin, as he waited anxiously for Helen's call. When Helen did finally call she said that she thought the whole message should be left intact.

Scott let out a big sigh of relief. "I will fax it to Jeff Kline right away."

Helen then shared her idea about the campaign buttons with Scott. Scott told her he thought it was brilliant. After finishing her conversation with Scott, she spoke with Sam to arrange having the buttons made, and to go over a couple of other details.

Scott spent the rest of the weekend relaxing and trying to recover from that emotional Saturday. Sam finished the rest of the work that he felt he needed to do immediately, and on Monday he left to return to Minnesota. Scott hugged his new friend at the airport when they said goodbye. Sam was leaving rather regrettably; he had been talking the past couple of days about possibly moving to the Phoenix area. Scott hoped this would come to pass. Sam complained bitterly about returning to Minnesota just in time for the long winter.

On Tuesday Robert Kelton was selected by the Supreme Court to be the next president of the United States of America. That evening Andrew Knight bitterly conceded. In his concession speech he used the word fight, Scott remarked to Elizabeth that this was one of the problems he saw with the way things were being done now. The word fight naturally invokes aggression in the human spirit. Time however can blur the lines between what a man believes is right or wrong, and later Scott would be tempted to attack.

The initial work of starting the party was over. Elizabeth would be done with school in about another week, and would put off becoming a teacher to work on a full-time basis for the party under Helen's direction. Scott needed to return to his business and concern himself with making a living.

The campaign buttons were bright yellow with blue letters that said: "Help us create something new: The Centrust Party". They were being manufactured on a rush basis because Helen wanted them for an upcoming media event she was planning.

This media event would take place in Phoenix, at the same office complex where Jeff Kline's company was located. The Centrust Party headquarters would also be located there. Helen and Sam were arranging it so that the headquarters would open the day after the presidential inauguration. There would be a news conference out in front of the new headquarters to let people know they were now open for business. After the ribbon was cut to signify the opening Scott and Elizabeth, Jeff Kline and his wife, Helen Shultz along with Sam Jameson would be the first people to officially register as Centrust Party members.

When Helen spoke of the upcoming events she would become so excited she could not talk about them and sit down at the same time. She would get up and pace around the room as she was talking. What set Helen apart and made her so attractive was her strength this was in contrast to her fine features and tall slender build. She had an aura of power about her. When she spoke about stealing the limelight on the president's first full day of office everyone in the room could feel that power surge through them.

When the republicans got wind of the young party's plans to hold a press conference on their candidate's first day in office they were livid. They didn't hesitate to let the founders know exactly how they felt about it. They insulted them privately and publicly. Nevertheless, Helen sent a press release a couple of days later to announce the opening of the Centrust Party Headquarters with a public invitation to register. A high-ranking republican was a guest on one of the political talk shows. He went on at length about how the timing of this event was yet another example of the spirit of divisiveness that was so prevalent in this country.

The program's host found the whole thing kind of amusing. "You have to admit they're squeezing the most publicity they can out of the events at hand."

"That's the problem, this should be a time of healing for America and for all of us to come together behind our new president. Not a time for seeking publicity on the president's first full day in office," the republican said.

"Well I haven't seen anything from the Centrust Party yet, that indicates they wont be supporting our new president," the host said.

In response to this comment the republican skillfully changed the subject.

The founders of the Centrust Party watched from their various locations, satisfied with the free publicity. They felt the republican official's attacks demonstrated yet another reason why so many people were supporting the Centrust Party.

The republicans felt quite confident that if the Centrust party even survived long enough to make it to an election, they would pull the majority of their votes from the democrats.

However, the republicans made clear their intentions to damage the Centrusts politically. They would do this not out of fear of losing votes, but because they didn't want the new party to keep the public focused on the reasons that the election ended in a tie.

"Someone told me long ago there's a calm before the storm.
I know, it's been coming for sometime"

Creedence Clearwater Revival

Chapter 7—The Fundamentals of Transformation

One day about a week before the inauguration Scott was having a particularly bad day. He could have handled a bad day at work, and the pressures of taking care of party business, but when a steep market decline was added he began getting scared. Fear made him begin to question everything he was doing. Elizabeth sensed her husband's confidence was waning and she was going to suggest that he call Jack Anderson. When she approached his office the door was ajar and she could overhear Scott who was on the phone. She listened briefly as she stood at the door, and she was amazed to discover that her husband was already on the phone with Jack.

"I don't know why I called you today," Scott said.

"Are you having a rough day, Scott?"

"Too many things going wrong in one day. Business has been terrible lately and I believe that's because we're entering a recession. If things don't pickup pretty soon we're going to have to make some serious cutbacks around here," Scott said.

"Uh huh," Jack said.

"The Centrust Party is taking a up so much of my time and sometimes I wonder if it's even going to make a difference anyway."

"Well that sure qualifies as a bad day in my book," Jack said. "Whenever I let fear get a foothold, I start questioning my purpose too."

"Yeah I know, it's just that all this responsibility gets to be overwhelming sometimes," Scott said.

"You're tired Scott, and your energy is very low. You need to refuel, try being kind to yourself. Take a break and do something that helps you to relax. It's not every day that someone starts a political party. Remember what the senator told you, there are many who will be sent to help you." Jack paused a moment for effect and then said slowly.

"Many. Think about that for a moment Scott and let it sink in."

"Yeah you're right, I need to remember that."

"Don't forget that to one whom much has been given, much shall be required. You have answered a calling my friend. Give yourself credit for that. Many people don't answer that call in a hundred life times. I am here to help you whenever you need me, and I am not alone. Many others are helping you even though you are not aware of it. If you pause and become still even for a moment, you can feel that power and love all around you."

"Thanks a lot for listening Jack," Scott said.

"It's been my pleasure." Jack's tone told Scott that he meant it.

"I promised I would stay in touch, and I wish we could've talked more since we met in the market," Scott said.

"I have a feeling we're going to have plenty of time to talk," Jack said.

"Since our meeting that day, my life has been one big crazy miracle after another. Meeting you and hearing from the senator, were a little different though. These events involved the presence of Spirit. There is really no other way to explain them," Scott said.

"You're right, there is no other way to explain them."

"Well, thanks Jack and I'll talk to you soon."

"I'll talk to you later. Be good to yourself," Jack said.

Scott felt a deep sense of serenity after hanging up with Jack. Following this short conversation Scott's business problems, the Centrust Party, and the market slide seemed like a distant memory, even though these matters had him consumed with fear only minutes earlier. He was relieved to have many of the things that were bothering him off his chest. This is something that had helped him in the past. He felt sorry for people who didn't know how to do this, or had no one to listen. There was something very special about Jack's presence though. Scott couldn't quite put his finger on it, but this man, who he had only met once, spoke straight to his heart.

The next few days leading up to the presidential inauguration confirmed to Scott that something needed to be done about the political status quo in America. The outgoing president refused to leave quietly. Many presidents have pardoned people of questionable character, but a few of this president's pardons really angered the public. Once again it didn't seem to matter what the spirit of the law was that grants the president the authority to pardon, what was more important was how he could use that power for personal gain.

"We will never be able to pass enough laws to insure that any man listens to the voice of his conscience," Scott remarked to Sam on the phone one day in reference to these events.

The inauguration came on Saturday and Scott watched it paying particular attention to the president's speech. He thought it was a very well written speech, and it was delivered aptly. Robert Kelton's history had been one of bringing both democrats and republicans together, and this was a major element in all his speeches. Scott appreciated this about him regardless of his stance on other issues.

That evening Elizabeth and Scott had a hard time falling asleep, because the next day was the press conference, and the opening of Centrust Party headquarters. Sam and Helen were both in town, and Elizabeth commented that neither one of them would probably get much sleep that night either.

Scott finally fell asleep sometime around 1:30 am, only to awaken about an hour later. He glanced over at the clock it read 2:35 am. His mind began to wander. He wondered if it could really be the time when Spirit guides our country's leaders once again? Could this be the beginning of a time when public servants serve from the heart and do what is right for the majority of their constituents, and this country, rather than playing on the fears of people to remain in power? Could these same public servants have the courage to speak the truth, rather than worry about what is politically advantageous?

If this was the beginning of a shift in American politics, a shift that corresponds to the larger shift in global consciousness, could it all have begun with a random web site created in his home? Is that possible, he wondered? This whole ordeal had almost been too much for him to grasp. Every time he thought he had his arms around it, the magnitude of it would hit him like a locomotive. This would send his heart racing, but not tonight, tonight he felt an incredible sense of peace and gratitude.

He wondered about Jack Anderson. He seemed to know a lot about what was going on without being directly involved. Jack also alluded to knowing about what was to come. Scott couldn't help but wonder about these things that Jack knew, wonder if he should know about them also. Scott grinned as he lay there in bed acknowledging to himself that, if he had known in advance about the events that had taken place over the last four to five weeks, he would have been too afraid to participate in them.

Scott went back in his mind to the phone call he received from the senator. Obviously there was a greater force at work here than the motives of one man who was disturbed about the current state of affairs in his country. Could it be that God or whatever name people use to try and name the unnameable, could that living force be behind the Centrust Party?

There was really no other explanation for how all these occurrences could come together at the same time. Scott thought about all the amazing coinciding events that had occurred to form the Centrust Party and believed there had to be something greater at work here. This thought made him a little nervous, and immediately he longed for the peace he felt only minutes ago. Would he measure up? Could he continue to carry the ball? He felt an overwhelming sense of responsibility, and then he remembered that the power of intent, the same universal force that got him this far would carry him forward.

"All I have to do is stay present in each moment." He told himself. This statement brought back the comfortable feeling of peace again. Sleep soon found him and he drifted off repeating, "Stay present Scott, stay present."

The following day Scott, Elizabeth, Jeff Kline and his wife Judy, Sam and Helen rode in Jeff Kline's van to the new party headquarters. They arrived thirty minutes before the press conference was scheduled to begin. Jack and Susan, Ben and Patricia drove down to the party's new headquarters to be among the first people to register.

The press had gathered there long before the six of them arrived. It seemed only a couple of minutes had passed before it became time for Helen to give her speech. They all filed outside, took their place behind Helen as she walked slowly up to the podium which they had placed in front of the entrance. She took a deep breath and began,

"I want to thank each and everyone of you for being here to commemorate the opening of the

Centrust Party headquarters. Today is also the first day that people will be able to register as members of the party. Our slogan is, "Help us create something new". This is what we are asking each and everyone of you to do. Judging from the response to our web site and the buzz from every one's lips lately, I would venture to say our party is the manifestation of what has been in the hearts and minds of many people for some time.

Making a successful run at breaking into and influencing American politics will not be easy. It will not be easy because we are taking a truthful common sense approach to government. However truth can be like the shining of a light. To all of you out there who know and feel in your hearts that it is time for a new approach, we ask you to pick up this light and shine it, without fear or blame, on every aspect of our government and political system that needs to be changed. In recent decades we've come to expect more and more from ourselves while at the same time we accept increasing waste and apathy from our government. We ask one another what can we do? Fear grips our hearts when we try to answer this question, and sometimes we even believe that we are powerless.

Special interest groups, and those who believe falsely that they need to maintain the status quo, will not want us to succeed. The Centrust Party believes that the time for change is now and time is of the essence.

We believe that most Americans have love in their hearts for the principals that this country is based on, and enough Americans care too much to let our government waste billions of dollars while important programs like social security go bankrupt. We believe there are enough people who care too much to watch our government waste billions of dollars while there are children in this country who go to bed hungry every night.

There are too many other issues to try to cover in my opening comments. These issues will come to light as the party gains the support of concerned Americans. Let me close by saying we believe that Centrust Party has the answer to the age-old question we have all asked ourselves at one time or another. That question is: "What can I do and how can I make a difference?" The answer is to become a part of this new force for change that has, as its focal point, the founding principles of the Centrust party. The five founding members of our party will now register each other and then who ever wishes to, may also step forward to register. Thank you all again for your love and support, and God bless America. I will now take a few questions."

"Yes Ms. Seymore from CNN."

"Ms. Shultz what will be the next move for the Centrust Party?"

"The Centrust Party will continue to develop and clarify our party platform. We will be doing this in two ways; first, by incorporating the comments we receive in emails on our web site. Second, from the mail that we receive at our party headquarters."

"Do you really think that you'll be able to get enough of a coalition to change Washington into a three party town?" another reporter asked.

Helen took a long moment to formulate her response. "230 years ago the British predicted that they would unhinge the principles of our founding fathers and crush this upstart nation. We defeated them against all odds. The British were defeated first and foremost because the great experiment called the United States of America was destined to be. The second reason our founding fathers succeeded in defeating the British was because they believed they could, and the British were too arrogant to see the power of that intent. The third reason for our victory over the British was that men and women are meant to be free. America is the greatest country in the world and our freedoms surpass those of all other nations. However, if we are honest with ourselves and truly look around at what we see, can we say that this is the best we can do?

Those are enough questions for now," Helen said. "We will now register the founding members, and then the rest of you can come in and register if you would like."

Ben and Patricia, Jack and Susan filed inside with the others and were among the first to be registered. Jack was really excited about the number of people that were there. He could see from the look in Scott's eyes that he was also excited.

Ben and Jack stepped outside together. There were still a couple of reporters wandering around out front interviewing people.

One of the reporters approached Ben.

"Excuse me sir, how do you feel about being one of the first registered Centrust Party members?

"It feels great," Ben said. "It's about time someone in the political arena stepped forward, and just told the truth. I believe Americans really want the truth and are ready to hear it."

Ben turned to see if Jack would make a comment also, but he was no longer standing next to him.

Interesting, Ben thought.

Scott, Elizabeth and the others continued registering people. Jeff Kline remarked with a smile that it was much easier to let people do this at their web site. They were all elated to be there and were overwhelmed by the turnout and the positive response. Over two thousand people registered not including those that registered over the web.

The next couple of months seemed to fly by. No one knew how she did it, but Helen Schultz managed to get Scott booked on the Larry Stein show on the president's 100th day in office. Scott wondered if it was Helen's magic or if Larry just thought it would be good fun to needle the current administration. Scott stood back stage with a feeling of nervous anticipation in his stomach. He was led to the stage where Larry Stein waited for him.

They reviewed some of the things they would discuss, and Larry did his best to make Scott feel at ease in front of the camera.

Larry started the program by introducing Scott as the founder of the Centrust Party. After having Scott summarize his incredible journey over the past several months Larry asked, "Why do you believe it is time for another political party?"

"The republicans have what they claim is a conservative approach to government. Their vision includes less government, lower taxes, and less governmental intrusion on our lives. We share this opinion.

The democrats have traditionally focused more on addressing the social challenges that face this country. We believe this is very important also.

We hold the opinion that taking care of this country's social challenges can and should be accomplished with less government, lower taxes, and less intrusion on our lives."

"That sounds very simple, but how do you expect to accomplish this?" Larry asked.

"One problem we all face is our government's close association with the businesses and industries they regulate. This association has prevented the American people from receiving the facts regarding many issues of great importance to them. In some cases it has caused half-truths, or even outright false information to be held out as the truth. I think it is unrealistic for any of us to expect our elected officials to always act completely in our best interests, as long as they have to rely on business and wealthy individuals with an agenda to fund their campaigns. At the Centrust Party we believe our goal of a well-informed public can only be accomplished through visibility. We believe visibility can only come about after complete campaign finance reform is enacted."

"Could you speak more about visibility when we come back from this break?"

"I would be glad to," Scott said.

As they went to the break the phone lines began lighting up with a flood of incoming questions and comments.

Father Morales and Joseph sat watching the show in a mobile home in Mountain Home, Utah. Jack and Susan had Ben and Patricia over for dinner. Afterwards they were glued to the television, sending love and energy to Scott and hanging on his every word. An outsider watching would have thought that Scott was their long-lost brother. On one level he was their brother, as he shared with them a common set of values and a commitment to see them affect change. The day was coming when the Centrust Party would realize how many people from their world were already behind them, and sometimes out in front of them.

A high-ranking politician in the Democratic Party phoned the Democratic Party chairman.

"Are you watching CNN?" the politician said.

"No; why, what's going on?" the chairman replied.

"Well you had better turn it on. What we thought was going to be a blessing and steal the limelight from the president, could prove to be a big problem for us. Scott Stahl doesn't seem to be going away very easily, and he's fairly sharp also."

"I'll turn it on right away," the chairman said.

After returning from the commercial break Scott continued to speak about visibility.

"Visibility is at the core of the Centrust Party's agenda. Knowing what our elected officials are doing with our tax money, how are government is affecting our freedoms and our environment is a top priority.

People need direct access to all kinds of information, in fact any information they choose, as long as it does not endanger our national security. At the Centrust Party we hold the conviction that it is our elected officials responsibility to present the American people with the facts regarding a myriad of issues, instead of the information that the corporations or special interest groups want presented. We believe this information can be provided through the Internet and with more public television coverage of what our government is up to on a daily basis."

"That's a tough row to hoe," Larry said.

"You're right, Larry. It is a tough row to hoe, but don't the changes visibility could bring about fill your heart with excitement?... It does. I can see it in your eyes," Scott said.

He smiled widely at Larry from across the table and then he wondered where that statement came from.

Fear began to creep into his mind as Larry pulled away from the desk slightly with a somewhat cynical look on his face. But suddenly Larry nodded and said, "I suppose it does...yes it does."

Scott seized the chance to continue. "Visibility needs to be created by the people, for the people, with a spirit of common cause. There are many changes needed and many things that our government is doing right now that are not in our best interest. To create effective change past mistakes (even those that happened yesterday) must be made visible to the public. The public in turn must be willing to provide constructive feedback to guide our elected officials toward appropriate action. We see forgiveness as being the key to unlocking the doors of change. This is not to say that we don't expect our politicians to be accountable, but we do wish to foster a spirit of working together with common cause. In this spirit, we hope to minimize judgment in an effort to create responsible change."

Scott paused for a moment, Larry was looking directly into his eyes.

"We are promoting a sort of paradigm shift here, Larry; one that requires us to think in terms of the greater good and the long term benefits to the public welfare and the environment. You might call this "right thought". And from right thought comes "right action". Hey, that's kind of catchy, Larry, Right Thought – Right Action! We may be able to use this as a new campaign slogan to communicate our vision. And you can say that it started on your show!

Thank you Larry!"

Larry chuckled and smiled. "You're welcome, Scott."

"In short visibility leads to trust. Trust leads to a proactive government, instead of the reactive finger pointing situation we find ourselves in now," Scott said.

"You've been critical or should I say one of the issues you have a big problem with is the role of the USDA," Larry said.

"The United States Department of Agriculture is responsible for educating Americans about healthy eating while at the same time promoting and regulating agricultural business. This is a classic case of the fox guarding the hen house. From 1988 to 1998 the congress received over $41,000,000 in campaign contributions from the food industry. More than 1/3 of this money went to the house and senate agricultural committees.

How can the same agency that is responsible for promoting agriculture concerns effectively provide the American public with information regarding their food choices?"

Scott paused as Larry shrugged in response to his rhetorical question.

"If the American people knew what the USDA knows about our food they would be appalled. I encourage Americans to find out more about the food they eat, what affects it has on their health and our environment. I personally believe if they did, Americans would demand that this agency be split up. This information is out there it just has not been presented in a clear and concise fashion because of the influence the meat, poultry and dairy industries have on our legislators." Scott could almost feel Helen squirming backstage.

"One of your concerns is the cozy relationship between the FDA and the drug companies. Could you elaborate on this?" Larry asked.

Scott took a deep breath and thought for an uncomfortable moment about what he was going to say next. He could hear Helen Schultz's voice in his head saying, remember Scott you can't walk on water, not yet anyway.

"The FDA unfortunately has a history of persecuting alternative health practitioners and doctors who come up with new forms of treatment. Alternatives to current drug therapies whether they come from a medical doctor or any kind of alternative practice, are in direct competition with the drug companies. This competition throughout the last 70 years of our history has led to many treatments being shelved that could greatly benefit people. There are many well-documented cases of this happening. Again the information is out there, I encourage people to find out for themselves by researching the Internet or alternative health magazines or books."

"It's very sad isn't it," Larry said.

"Yes it is, in fact one might accurately say that the FDA is one side, and the pharmaceutical companies are the other side of the same coin."

Backstage, Helen was up out of her chair and pacing the floor. "You're moving too far off center Scott," she said under her breath

Scott paused, thought for a moment and said. "Larry, I want to say at this point that the Centrust Party is not anti business. To the contrary we are pro-business. We are also not anti government. We would simply like to see a clear separation of government and business, so that the government can do what it is supposed to do, which is serve and govern the people. We are for social programs that work, that are run, and are managed, by people who are empowered at every level to get the job done. The Centrust Party is going to move this country towards a government that does much more for its people while taking much less from its people."

Helen stopped dead in her tracks let out an audible "thank you", and when Larry went to another commercial break she thought she might fall to her knees and praise God right there on the spot. She rushed to the stage (only having to knock one person to the side) and found a spot where she could make eye contact with Scott, and gave him a hand signal to bring the conversation back a little closer to center. Scott nodded in agreement.

Back in Washington DC, a phone call went out from the Republican Party chairman to the White House Chief of Staff. Unable to talk to the chief of staff personally he left a voice mail indicating he was recording the Larry Stein show. He urged the chief of staff to clear some time in his schedule in the near future.

"I've been watching this kid who started Centrust Party and we've got a big problem on our hands."

Back in Mountain Home, Utah Joseph turned to his friend and said, "Compadre, did you feel that?"

"It would have been hard to miss," Father Morales said.

A chill went up his spine.

"We need to have a ceremony for this mans protection, tonight!" Joseph said.

The two men got up and prepared to leave for their sacred location where they had been doing their fires.

In Phoenix Elizabeth, Michele and their son Jonathan who was home from college on break sat on the edge of their seats waiting for Scott to reappear on the television set. Elizabeth felt so proud of her husband. He had stepped beyond his fear and stood up for what he believed in. The pride she felt turned to a feeling of love, at which point Elizabeth remembered from her dream all the points of light sending energy to Phoenix, Arizona. Then something very different happened. In her mind's eye she had a flash, an instant, where she remembered that she had agreed to be a part of this at a time before she was born.

At the CNN studios backstage there was a commotion going on. It appears that the first person to speak from the phone lines this evening would be the governor of Minnesota. When Scott got wind of this he felt his heart leap in his chest. This was just what their party needed to cap off what he thought was a very successful evening. The governor took up a long portion of the show that was set aside for phone calls. He congratulated Scott and thanked him even, for stepping up to the plate to play a game that anyone else would have told him that he was unqualified to play. The governor also said what

Scott and the Centrust Party we're talking about is a common sense approach to government and politics. He let Scott and the rest of the country know that they had his wholehearted support. Before he hung up the Governor said he would be contacting Scott in the near future. Backstage Helen didn't know if she should jump for joy or run and hide.

Among the many other phone calls, one worth noting came from a person who asked why Scott had not brought up more environmental issues on the program this evening.

"Our policies regarding the environment are well documented both on our web site, and in the literature, which may be obtained from our party headquarters in Phoenix. I would like to thank the caller for raising this question. Tonight has been very exciting for all of us at the Centrust Party. The absence of truth and the wholesale destruction of our planet were the main two reasons that I started down this path four and a half months ago. We do not see economic growth and the destruction of our planet and its ecosystems as a take one and leave the other proposition. We will be having an environmental conference sometime in August in Las Vegas, Nevada."

"Las Vegas in August, ouch!" Larry said.

Scott smiled and replied. "It's cost effective Larry. Dates and times of specific meetings will be posted both on our web site and in future press releases. We ask all concerned individuals and the various environmental groups to come with an open heart, and an open mind. Help us to shape a policy that will reverse our present course, and lead us to becoming responsible caretakers of this planet. We want to encourage every person who cares deeply for this issue to join us in Nevada. Together, let us create a proactive environmental plan, rather than continuing to react to the growing number of environmental disasters."

After Scott answered this question Larry sat for a long moment and then asked, "Scott, if the Centrust Party accomplishes, but one thing, what would it be?"

"That's a tough question Larry."

"That's what they pay me for."

"That would be for an awakening on a massive scale to take place in which all people get in touch with the spirit of the earth and become caretakers of this planet. When this happens everything else will fall into place."

That was all the time that was available. Larry thanked Scott for being on the program. The light on the camera went off, and Scott let out a deep sigh of relief.

In New Orleans, Tom LeClaire the senator from Louisiana got up to turn off the television and wondered if his mentor the judge had seen the program. He laid back down in bed and thought. *This kid has really put all the pieces together.*

Joseph and Father Morales sat bouncing in Joseph's pickup truck as they headed out to their sacred place to begin their fire ceremony for Scott's protection and that of his household. Father Morales's mind was preoccupied with the church, knowing that they were trying desperately to find him. He could feel their presence and he knew they were closing in.

He was lost in those thoughts when Joseph broke in and said, "The world in which we live has been turned completely upside down. Humanity though not at the peak of it's suffering, is at a turning point. People who were previously unconscious are beginning to intuit that something is very wrong in their lives. Their pursuit of separation has led them to unhappiness. They are searching for a cure on a global scale. More and more people are waking up to the fact that the separation between you and me is at the material level only. In fact it is an illusion."

Joseph paused in thought for a moment. Father Morales was looking right at him as he drove the pickup truck.

"On the next step of your journey through the medicine wheel you will begin to practice the art of invisibility. Invisibility is achieved by allowing yourself to be completely seen and by having nothing to defend. You will learn to pull your energy in, and you will be amazed how people fail to notice your presence."

They pulled off to the side of the dirt road to park, and take the short walk to their fire site.

"I know you have been concerned about those that are looking for you. You feel their presence closing in. I have felt this also. As you learn to master the art of invisibility they will get no further in tracking you," Joseph said.

Father Morales let out an audible sigh of relief.

"Surely you didn't think that they would actually be able to find you?"

"No I didn't, but you know how that is, It's always nice when you receive a confirmation from someone else's lips," Father Morales said.

The fire was very friendly to both men that evening. They received a lot of energy to move forward with their mission. Joseph and Father Morales believed they were successful in sending Scott Stahl and his family a great amount of love and energy for protection. They visualized an energetic shield around the whole Stahl household. In the fire each man saw other groups forming around the world for the same purpose. Joseph chanted and sang while Father Morales had a vision. His vision was about a bridge between those that followed Christ and those who practiced the old ways. Father Morales joined Joseph in his chanting and the two men settled into the same rhythm. Both men experienced peace beyond measure during which they saw groups of people scattered all over the world sending energy to Phoenix, Arizona.

In another vision they saw the giant red ball of fire and the sorrow of the Mother Earth. It brought pain upon her to do what was necessary to ensure her own survival. She loved all the people who lived on her belly, and did not want to harm them. She sent a wave of love and gratitude over each man reminding them that the giant red ball of fire was not necessary.

After the fire ceremony the two men packed up their belongings and started the drive back to Joseph's mobile home. As he watched his friend drive the old pickup truck along the bumpy dirt road Father Morales felt a sense of companionship he had never felt before.

Here was a man whose ancestors had all but been wiped off the face the earth and then were forced to live on reservations. Yet when he was in this man's presence he knew that all Joseph cared about was that people would awaken from their limiting dream. All he wanted was for everyone to make the journey within and find the joy he knew in his life.

Joseph broke the long silence, "My friend, to continue with the conversation we started on the road up here, people are trying to achieve a sense of security and peace through separation from one another. You and I know love and peace comes from realizing there is no separation, or should I say that separation is an illusion. One man would not hurt another man, or even have bad feelings towards another, if he realized that all men were one. As you and I know, our mission is to help to create this common vision. How do we get so many people and luminous warriors on the same page, dreaming the same world into existence? Now that is a tough one. The events that have unfolded so far lead me to believe that the answer will be revealed to us."

"Seek and you shall find," Father Morales said.

"Indeed, compadre, indeed," Joseph said. It made Father Morales feel at home when his friend called him compadre.

Later that night Father Morales had another one of his dreams. In his dream God told him how they would join all the groups together. "I have given man a great and powerful gift, a gift to make his life easier, so he could work less and spend more time with his family and friends. The computer has provided yet another chance for man to free himself up and spend more time renewing his connection to spirit. Instead man has used this great gift to work even more hours in a day, and further the separation, one from another that has led to his unhappiness. Many people no longer even talk face to face; they do this over the Internet. You, Jose Morales, will use this Internet to spread a message of hope among thousands of prayer groups, meditation circles, and people who still practice the beauty way. It will be entitled the Ten Fundamentals for Global Transformation. Jose, get up and write them down now."

Father Morales awoke instantly went to the little desk in his room, pulled out a sheet of paper, and then in a mystic trance wrote down the following:

Ten Fundamentals for Global Transformation.

1) Love all people as you love yourself. This can be easily achieved when one remembers and embodies the secret that we keep from ourselves.

2) Create an awakening in young people. Let them know we are sorry for not waking up and accepting responsibility sooner. Encourage them to forgive.

3) Create a wave of forgiveness that flows like a cool breeze through all people. To propel humanity to move forward unshackled by the past.

4) Visualize the love of the earth coming up from it's core into all people. Show them they can step beyond fear and violence.

5) Send love and energy to all world leaders so their ears will no longer be closed to the message the earth has been sending.

6) Commit to striking out against the opposition (real or imagined) with love and light. To battle darkness with darkness is to become the darkness.

7) Become stewards of your thoughts for they affect your collective progress. Create an awakening for others to become stewards of their thoughts also.

8) Commit little acts of mercy for the Mother Earth, daily if possible. These are most powerful if done alone with no one to witness.

9) Commit little acts of mercy for other human beings, daily if possible. These are most powerful, and will affect the greatest amount of change if no one knows of them but you.

10) Consciously make your personal part of the light brighter for all others to see. No one will need to be told of this; they will be attracted to it. However do not let others feed on it.

Pass this map on to others who meditate and pray. Consciously create the world that you want to live in.

The next morning Father Morales told Joseph about the dream and the list that he was told to write down. He informed Joseph that they were to put this on the Internet, send it out to prayer and meditation groups, and those who still practiced the beauty way.

Over the next several months and into the New Year Father Morales finished working his way through the medicine wheel. As they continued their fire ceremonies, they became aware that others were being drawn to Mountain Home to take an active role in creating the critical mass that would be required for the collective consciousness to shift. Then the world would be returned to balance again. Joseph borrowed another mobile home from a friend, and set it up on his property and furnished it for those who would be joining he and Father Morales soon.

Because he knew that those looking for Father Morales might be able to trace the email back to the reservation, Talking Bird came up with a plan to visit Internet cafes all over the West to release the list of ten fundamentals for global transformation.

Father Morales traveled with Talking Bird while Joseph stayed behind to prepare for their visitors. The priest greatly appreciated the opportunity to see this beautiful country. It helped him to deepen his connection to the Mother Earth, the Mother who provides such a deep sense of security to man. He continued to practice the art of invisibility and the seers who worked for the church lost sight of him somewhere in the western United States.

The spotlight on the Stahl household slowly faded in the two months that followed Scott's interview on the Larry Stein show. Scott had been very busy running his business and working with the others establishing the party. It was mid-June and Scott was preoccupied with the upcoming environmental conference. A large banquet hall had been booked in Vegas, and the response so far had been less than encouraging even though Kate Seymore had done her best to keep the party in the public eye. Elizabeth continued to contribute by retrieving important e-mails from the party web site and bringing them to the appropriate person's attention.

In her spare time, which she had more of since she would not be returning to school until the fall, Elizabeth had been keeping track of a transformation of another sort. She began to notice that when the party first formed there seemed to be a shift in consumer habits. Everyone else associated with the party, Sam, Helen, and to some extent Scott included, had been too busy to notice this. Elizabeth kept a kind of scrapbook of different events that she felt were representative of the change in consumer behavior.

Shortly after the Larry Stein interview Elizabeth had a dream. In this dream Christ came to her, which she thought was unusual, because she was not particularly religious. He told her that he was very pleased with her for noticing and keeping track of the shifting consumerism. Christ showed her a vision of the major corporations of the world, and she felt their unharnessed power. He then showed her a group of people who loved and cared for the earth and all the people on it. As Christ showed her this group of people she could see and feel their numbers increasing. This brought great joy to her heart. Christ directed her attention to the way those people felt about the major corporations. She could actually feel their love turning to resentment as they shifted their focus to the corporations. He then told her that one of the reasons he instructed people to love their enemies was because in doing so they would no longer perpetuate opposition.

He then directed her attention once again to the corporations. She could see a visible energy being emitted from the growing group of people, and the corporations began to follow it and feed on it. Christ was pleased with Elizabeth as she realized that the corporations were simply reacting to what the people wanted. She realized that if the group would forgive the corporations then they could harness their power and accelerate the shift in consciousness that could save the planet.

In the weeks following her dream, Elizabeth intensified her focus on the shift in consumerism. If there was something that applied to this topic, be it on television or some other news medium, it would leap out at her, and she continued to catalog it. Car dealers across the nation were unable to keep alternative fuel vehicles in stock. All the auto manufacturers were in a race to develop these vehicles, even ahead of the government-mandated targets. People whom Elizabeth had never heard talk of their love for the earth we're now talking about buying alternative fuel vehicles. None of these events escaped Elizabeth's attention.

Organic food sales were growing twice as fast as food sales in general. This was happening despite the higher cost of organic food. Vegetarianism was spreading like wildfire. She had statistics to back all of this up. She also noticed that more and more manufactures were claiming to use recycled materials. She wondered if there was a particular company or organization that verified whether corporations were actually using recycled materials or not.

It was mid-June when she received the chain email entitled ten fundamentals for global transformation. Scott was also working in the office that day and the two began to talk about it.

"What a transformation that would bring if people of all different faiths were praying and meditating on the same ten fundamentals," Scott said.

"I think this has great significance for us and the Centrust Party," Elizabeth said.

"Let's hope so," Scott said.

At this point Elizabeth felt that it was a good time to mention the things she'd been keeping track of. She also shared with Scott the dream she had.

"How come you haven't told me about these things?"

"You've been so busy," She said. "Besides with the other work I have been doing for the party, and with everything else that's going on, it has taken me sometime to gather the information and statistics."

"Well I guess I have been too busy because this is really important stuff," Scott said.

"What I'd like to do is write an article about this consumer trend for a magazine. With our current notoriety I believe we can attract an audience and bring this message of hope to everyone's attention," Elizabeth said. Her face was filled with excitement.

"I will call Helen first thing in the morning and speak to her about this. Would you mind submitting the article to her to before you publish it?"

"Sure I don't see why not," Elizabeth said.

"Great, because it's the best idea I've heard for quite some time, besides it could help us drum up some support for the environmental conference. Lord knows we could use it, " Scott said.

Later that day when Elizabeth picked up the mail, she noticed there was a letter from the Internal Revenue Service. Her heart sank, and fear reached out to take her in its grasp. When Scott opened the letter he confirmed what she already knew. They were being audited for the last three years. Although it could probably not be proven, they suspected their opposition had waited for public scrutiny to die down, and now they would start playing hardball.

Scott immediately initiated a conference call with Sam, Helen, and Jeff Kline. The topic of conversation was the likelihood that the rest of them might come under attack.

Before everyone said goodbye and hung up. Helen asked Scott to stay on the line.

"You know me Scott, I'm not good at beating around the bush, so I will get right to it. As this situation with your audit evolves you need to make sure that I am the first person in the loop, ahead of every one else. I can be your knight in shining armor if you need one, but you have to keep me informed," Helen said.

"Ok, You've got it. I don't want to go through this without you."

"Good, good. We are agreed then. I will see you soon," Helen said.

When Scott came downstairs and sat at the kitchen table, he noticed his wife was intentionally making herself busy. He wasn't fooled and he could see the fear in her face. As she tried to make her way past him he stood up in front of her and gave her a great big hug.

"They wouldn't come after us if they didn't think we could make a difference," Scott said.

"I know. It's just that the IRS really scares me."

"Mother Earth will feed our hunger. Father Sky will love her well.
Make me worthy of this vision
that no human tongue could ever tell.
Give me strength to learn the lesson. Make me wise to understand,
what it takes to walk in beauty
as I learn to walk this sacred land."

Red Thunder

Chapter 8—The Initiation

The four weeks preceding Elizabeth's birthday on July 20th, were stressful to say the least. Thankfully, Frank the family accountant who was now a registered member of the Centrust Party donated his time to work on Scott and Elizabeth's audit.

"I must have marbles in my head for continuing to work for you. You're going to put me out of business," Frank said to Scott on the phone one day.

"Well—

"You know I'm just kidding you Scott, if a substantial tax cut can be achieved by simplifying the tax code, then I'm all for it."

After their conversation Scott thought that what we needed were more people like Frank, people who were willing to look beyond their fear and short-term gain and invest their energy in something that could benefit so many other people.

Helen and Sam happened to be in town on the weekend of Elizabeth's birthday, and Scott asked Elizabeth if she would like to have them all over to celebrate.

"Thank you that would be nice," Elizabeth said.

"Great, that's what we'll do then."

"I would also like to invite Jack, his friend Ben and their wives," Elizabeth said.

"Well I guess that'd be Ok. We just won't be able to talk about party business in great detail," Scott said.

She smiled at him. "I know, won't that be great?"

Scott returned her smile and laughed at himself.

I have been in contact with Jack, more and more lately and it would be nice to see him again, Scott thought.

"I'll call them today and invite them over, and I'm sorry for not being more considerate. Centrust Party politics have taken over our lives, and we shouldn't let them take over your birthday," Scott said.

On Friday night Helen and Sam arrived together. Jeff Kline and his wife arrived shortly thereafter. Jack told Scott that they wouldn't be able to make it until a little later. This week brought another tax audit. Sam Jameson was the target this time, and he didn't try to hide that he was upset about it. Jeff Kline was undergoing the most grueling audit of all. Not only was he being audited personally for the last three years, but the IRS and the State of Arizona were also auditing his company. He had an unusual look of weariness about him and the air at the Stahl house was thick with tension. It was such a shame that everyone was so down on Elizabeth's birthday. They all tried to remain upbeat, but without much success. Then Jack and Susan Anderson arrived with Ben and Patricia Winston.

Scott answered the door and led the two couples into the family room where everyone else was seated. Elizabeth noticed immediately the energy of the whole room changed. The first thing she noticed is that these four people were smiling.

Ben couldn't help himself. "Is this a funeral or a birthday party?"

Helen let out a laugh, and was the first one to come over and introduce herself. After the two couples settled in the atmosphere of the whole party changed for the better.

Elizabeth noticed that if a particular conversation turned negative Jack or Ben would guide the conversation back to all the positive things the Centrust Party founders were doing. Almost magically the conversation would then turn to something that had nothing to do with politics. Scott shot Elizabeth a glance from across the room, because the effect that these four people had on the energy and atmosphere of the room didn't escape his attention. Interestingly enough everyone in the room remembered Ben from the day the Centrust Party office was opened. No one seemed to remember Jack however, and Elizabeth thought this was a bit odd. She passed off this observation with the thought that maybe it had something to do with Ben's height and quick sense of humor.

The remainder of the evening was very pleasant, and Elizabeth enjoyed her birthday dinner immensely. It made her happy to get together with all these people that she had grown so close to. The attraction that everyone seemed to have for Jack and Ben was peculiar; it was hard for her to put her finger on. It was obvious to her that everyone in the room felt it. Sam was the last one to come out of his bad mood. Even he couldn't resist the presence that accompanied these two men. Helen couldn't help but wonder if there was something in particular that Sam was worried about with his upcoming tax audit.

After dinner there were cake and presents, Helen and Sam were the first to leave, and Jeff Kline and his wife left shortly thereafter. Jack and Susan, Ben and Patricia stayed on after everyone else had left. Elizabeth believed they did this intentionally.

The conversation between the three couples easily drifted from one subject to another. When it was discovered that both

Jack and Scott loved to hike, Ben steered the conversation towards hiking in the sacred canyon.

"Have you ever hiked the sacred canyon?" Ben said.

"No I haven't. Where's it located?"

"It's in the central part of the state, about an hour and a half from here." Ben turned to Jack. "You were going to go hiking there tomorrow weren't you Jack?"

"Yes I was," Jack said.

Elizabeth moved up onto the edge of her seat

Jack turned to Scott. "Would you like to join me?"

Before Scott could even answer Elizabeth chimed in. "I think that'd be a great idea honey. Why don't you take the time and go."

"I don't know…we've got a lot things going on right now," Scott said.

"Whatever you decide. I'll be leaving at about 7:30 in the morning," Jack said. There was a look of obvious disappointment on Elizabeth's face. Ben and Jack seemed not to notice.

The couples talked for another ten to fifteen minutes before Jack, Susan, Ben and Patricia got up from the table to get ready to leave. As Elizabeth and Scott were showing the two couples to the door, Scott seemed to be contemplating.

"On second thought I think I'll join you tomorrow for that hike, Jack, if the offer is still open?

"Of course it is," Jack said. "I'll swing by and pick you up at 7:30."

Elizabeth let out a notable sigh of relief.

The couples said their goodbyes and as they drove away Scott and Elizabeth waved goodbye from their front porch.

The next morning Jack swung by Scott's house and picked him up for the hike. At first conversation didn't come easy, so Jack took the initiative, and as he talked, Scott could feel himself beginning to relax, then he felt comfortable enough to let Jack in on what was bothering him.

"The party has committed to a large convention hall in Vegas for the upcoming environmental conference and so far the response has been less than encouraging." Scott said, feeling a sense of burden starting to drain his energy.

"Sometimes don't you just wish you could go back and take the blue pill, instead of the red one," Jack said. This brought a smile to Scott's face.

"I really love that movie."

After Jack's reference to the movie *The Matrix*, the atmosphere lightened considerably. Jack had an uncanny ability for finding common ground between people, and using that to make them feel at ease. Scott thought for a moment that perhaps Jack should be the politician, and he could just go back to running an engineering company.

"I have to hand it to you Scott. I don't think I could be a politician." When Jack said this Scott had what seemed to be an insane thought.

Could Jack be reading my mind?

"I don't know if I want to be a politician either," Scott said. "Perhaps my job is to get this thing rolling, and let other people take it from there." Jack smiled when Scott said this, and not long after they rolled into the parking lot for the sacred canyon trailhead.

The two men got out of Jack's jeep and strapped on their daypacks. They walked from the parking lot towards the trailhead. At the trailhead Jack turned to Scott.

"This canyon is a sacred place. Do your best to stay conscious, and walk with beauty and grace while we're in it. If you have any questions or any problems you're confronting, you can bring them to these canyon walls. This area is ancient and sacred.

It was here long before us, and God willing it will be here long after us. If you can let go and let the energy of this place infuse you, the answers you seek will come."

"This sounds like just the place I need to be today," Scott said.

Jack led as they made their way up the trail. They dodged boulders and soaked in the beautiful scenery.

"There are two places of incredible power in this canyon. One is that spire right there," Jack pointed to a huge rock spire with a large rock on the top. "The natives call it Kachina woman. We'll stop there on the way back."

"That sounds great," Scott said.

"The other place of power is at the head of the canyon," Jack said.

As they walked along the trail the two men established a rhythm so they could continue to walk and chat at the same time. Scott noticed something peculiar about Jack, he didn't seem to be laboring at all. His movement seemed effortless and he appeared to glide along the trail. As he walked Jack seemed to be absorbing everything around him. Then Scott remembered what Jack had said about letting the energy of this place enter. He made a conscious effort to try this, and as he did a feeling of peace began to overwhelm him. The canyon walls seemed to embrace him, and assure him that everything was all right. Scott couldn't remember the last time he felt this way.

Amazingly Jack stopped walking and turned to Scott. "Doesn't this place bring you back to your center? Don't you feel at this moment that everything is Ok?"

"That is incredible, how do you do that?"

"Do what?" Jack said.

"I was just starting to feel at peace, and not worry about everything that is going on in my life. At that exact moment you turned to me to talk about the very feeling I was having," Scott said.

"I told you there is an energy to this place. Before you started to feel at peace your energy was contrary to the energy of everything around you. When you started to feel at peace and let the energy of everything here run through you, I could feel the difference, and that is when I spoke," Jack said.

Scott felt this seemed as good a time as any to ask, "Jack what is a shaman anyway?"

Jack stood there silent for what seemed like a long time. He gazed around at the trees, the bushes, and the canyon walls around them. Scott light heartedly wondered if Jack expected the canyon to answer the question. He stopped gazing around and looked up into Scott's eyes.

"A shaman, is first and foremost a servant, a servant to the earth and all the creatures on her belly. Shamans don't consider themselves separate from anyone or any living thing. He or she dedicates their life to the path of service and communion with spirit. The Great Spirit, the spirits of the animals, the plants, the people, and of course the earth. The shaman lives his life with one foot in this world, and one in the world of spirit. He can step into the other world sure footedly, and navigate."

Scott stood there with his mouth open, and a look of amazement on his face.

"It is impossible to answer that question completely right now, because we simply don't have enough time. Yet I hope this gives you a better idea," Jack said.

Scott was wondering whether Jack was someone Scott should be seen spending time with, considering the possible political implications.

"We've been waiting a long time for something like the Centrust Party to come into being. When I say we, I mean shamans, and everyone else who has heard the message the earth has been telling us for some time now. The message is that the earth can no longer sustain man's current rate of reproduction and consumption. You have heard this message also. It is evidenced in your writing."

Jack paused for a moment to think.

"The biggest problem we face is that of separation. This is

evidenced in the way our western culture perceives the environment. We talk about it as if it is something that is separate from ourselves. On the other hand, the shaman and people from some other cultures consider the environment as a part of themselves. When the majority of us realize that separation is an illusion we won't even consider doing many of things that today are excepted practice," Jack said.

He shrugged his shoulders and smiled. "Enough of all this serious talk, let's get back to our hike."

Jack and Scott began once again to walk up the trail towards the head of the canyon. Scott's head was swimming. Could all this be true? He wondered if Helen might have a fit if she knew he was spending time with some mystical shamanic practitioner.

The two men must have walked a half a mile in silence when Scott finally got back into the rhythm of everything around him.

Ah Ha, Jack thought, *much better Scott, much better.*

Up ahead on the trail was an anthill. Scott stopped to look; there were thousands of red ants everywhere. Jack acknowledged them and continued to walk right through the parade of ants, as if he didn't have a care in the world. When Jack was several steps up the trail Scott realized that Jack hadn't stepped on a single ant. Jack sensed that Scott was no longer behind him. He turned around and grinned widely. "Well, come on what are you waiting for?"

"Oh nothing," Scott said.

The trail started to get steeper. It moved into the forest and Scott noticed he was breathing heavier. Jack continued to glide up the trail in front of him with little effort. There were tree roots everywhere on the trail. Scott was grateful for the natural steps they provided as they continued their ascent. Then he noticed that Jack was not stepping on the tree roots. Scott remembered what Jack had told him about the shaman not seeing himself as separate from the world around him. Could it be that this man was not stepping on the tree roots because he felt the life that was in them? Scott was just going to ask him that very question when they reached the end of the trail. They were now at the head of the canyon.

Jack stepped to the side and motioned for Scott to pass him. Scott moved past Jack and into a clearing where he saw the most beautiful view he had seen in some time. The canyon was now only 200 yards wide. Its walls were red and white sandstone, the giant trees they had been walking through were below them now, and they stood like sentinels guarding the canyon floor. Scott stood there like a groom on his wedding day absorbing the beauty before him.

"C'mon Scott, let's go to a vantage point where we can see the whole picture." They climbed upwards on an angle toward a ledge that seemed to disappear around a corner.

When they got up to the ledge Scott could see that they would not be going around a corner. Instead there was a gradual elevation change of about 20 ft. where the ledge led out to a point. They moved out onto the point and sat down. From here they could see the whole canyon. Scott thought the view might take his breath away. Both men sensed that words would only interrupt the way they felt at this moment. Jack could see and feel the energy around them, and Scott could not help but think that all his problems seemed pretty small right now. He was reminded that one of the reasons he stepped forward, and took up the challenge of the Centrust Party, was so that places like this would always stay pristine and special, the way they are now.

After sitting in silence for about fifteen minutes Scott started to wonder when they would talk again. Moments after having this thought Jack turned to Scott and said,

"This place has great power. The veil between us, and all that is, is very thin at this location. Let's take some time and meditate about everything that is going on in our lives at this time. Perhaps we can see how our paths fit into the destiny we both desire."

"Sounds good to me," Scott said.

"Turn and face me and sit close enough so our knees are almost touching." Scott scooted around to face Jack.

"Good, now I believe you already know how to meditate, correct?"

"That's correct," Scott said.

"Ok. When you reach a very quiet state of mind, let me know," Jack said.

They closed their eyes, and let the energy of this beautiful place run through them.

Jack had been here to meditate many times, and he loved the way this sacred canyon made him feel. He thought about the many people who come here who don't realize the power of this place. He held a vision in his heart, where masses of people realized how much the earth loves them and they returned that love by becoming caretakers. Jack bathed in the beauty of his dream and he smiled as he remembered what happens when one dreams.

"Ok I'm ready," Scott said. Jack took a moment to confirm that Scott was ready.

"May I have permission to show you something?" Jack said.

"Of course."

Jack took a hold of Scott's hands. Immediately Scott could feel a cool tingling sensation move up his arms to his head, it seemed to pool around his head and then moved down his spine into the earth. He became a little unnerved.

"Don't be afraid," Jack said.

Scott relaxed again, and waited. Just as he was beginning to think that perhaps he wasn't going to see anything he started to see groups of people heading somewhere. Where are they going he thought? Then he could see they were going to Las Vegas. He saw that there were thousands of people converging on Las

Vegas and this made him feel very happy. He was so overjoyed that he forgot to hang on to Jack's hands and then Jack squeezed his hands to remind him to stay with the process. At this point his vision changed from the thousands of people to a stage with a podium. No one was standing behind the podium, but there was a red tailed hawk circling overhead. Scott felt a sense of panic.

Oh no, he thought, *there is no one at the podium.* Just then a voice came and told him. "Remember there is never a reason to panic. Look again."

Scott looked again at the podium and he was relieved to notice that someone was standing behind it. The hawk was sitting on top of a boulder looking down at the man. This brought him a great sense of relief. For some reason he couldn't tell who the man was, but he knew it wasn't him.

Jack let the sense of relief fill every part of Scott's being and after a couple of minutes he removed his hands from Scotts, and Scott slowly found his way back to the present. When he opened his eyes Jack was looking straight into them.

"I'm glad that you were relieved by this vision. I received it some time ago, and I didn't know how it would sit with you. You're the one, Scott, who stepped forward and started something that you agreed to do before you were born. I sensed that you were uncomfortable when you were on the Larry Stein show so I began to meditate about what your uneasiness meant. It was then revealed to me that the man I saw at the podium was not you—

"How do you know all these things, and what else do you know?.... It's a little unnerving to know that someone who I had never met before that day in the market knows so much about me, and my destiny," Scott said.

The two men were standing now, and Jack put his hand on Scott's shoulder.

"Do you think that God would give you such a monumentally important task, and not send you all the help you need?"

"I guess not," Scott said.

Scott noted that the calming effect was immediate the second Jack put his hand on his shoulder. He was amazed by the love and the power that came from this man.

"What do you say we take a couple minutes and enjoy this view, then head back down to Kachina Woman?" Jack said.

"Sounds like a plan to me," Scott said.

After standing there for couple of minutes and soaking in the beauty they headed back down into the forest that covered the canyon floor. Scott's head was swimming and it took a few minutes of hiking before he was able to come back to the present and focus on the hike. He engaged his senses as they walked. He let the smell of Ponderosa pine fill his nose and lungs. He felt the warmth radiate off the canyon walls. He took time to participate in the joy of the birds as they sang and chirped around them. Scott then noticed that the birds were no longer flying away as the two men walked by. On the way to the head of the canyon he had noticed that the birds remained in their perch when Jack walked by, but when he came up from behind the birds flew away. After walking for over an hour they reached the point where the trail went off to the left and up to the base of Kachina Woman.

Scott had a sense of great anticipation as the two men made their way up the steep incline to the base of the rock spire. When they both caught their breath from the steep climb they sat down face to face as they had done a little over an hour ago. Jack guided Scott in another meditation that involved becoming aware of the ladder.

"Scott, without opening your eyes look up and you will see a tunnel which I call the ladder. Do you see it?"

"I see it," Scott said.

"Do you want to travel up the ladder?"

"I do," Scott said.

"Allow yourself to leave your body and travel up the ladder.

Good, good. Now continue traveling until you reach a door and let me know when you reach it," Jack said.

After a minute Scott said, "Ok Jack I've reached the door."

"Look down, can you see the top of your head Scott?"

"Wow! I can actually see the top of my head."

"Do you want to open the door and go in?" Jack said.

Scott was overwhelmed with the sense that once he stepped beyond this door, things would never be the same. He started to become self-conscious about taking to much time to make his decision.

"Take your time Scott, take your time," Jack said.

Scott contemplated his decision for a few more moments.

"Ok, I want to go beyond the door."

"Well, then ask for the door to be opened," Jack said.

Scott asked for the door to open and when he moved through Jack was waiting for him on the other side. What Scott felt next was beyond anything he had experienced before in any meditation, dream, or in his imagination. He saw, felt, and experienced himself at one with everything.

Scott saw himself sitting in his office working on party business. He then floated up and began viewing this picture of himself from further and further away. At first he saw the top of his house, and then he saw his neighborhood. After this he was above the Phoenix metropolitan area. Next he floated higher and higher until he could view the whole world. He then saw thousands of bands of light coming from all over the world, and converging on Phoenix. He was immediately filled with a sense of complete gratitude.

A voice spoke that seemed to come from all around him.

"You see Scott, you have more help and support than you ever could of imagined. In the coming months and years look back upon this scene whenever you need to remember. Jack has been sent to you as your personal helper and he knows many ways to guide you that others do not.

The universe and the earth have conspired to bring together all these things at one time. Saving mankind from destroying itself is going to require help from every possible source. Jack is a great navigator of spirit. Do not forsake him and keep him close to you. Remember your apparent separation from everything else on your planet is only on the material plane. Come back as often as you like to keep this knowledge fixed in your memory. You are doing so well Scott, do not fret, just believe in your dreams."

After lingering for a while Scott found his way back to the door and the ladder. All he had to do was think of the door and he was there. He looked down from the door and saw the top of his head below. He moved back down the ladder until he was right above his body, and hovering there for a second he made the decision to go back into his body. He felt his hands, and he noticed his feet were numb. He opened his eyes to see Jack sitting on a ledge about 15 ft. away watching the breeze blow through the trees below them. He pulled out his wallet and took out the deposit envelope he had written his dreams on that first day after meeting with Jeff Kline and took a few minutes to read it and be with his dreams.

"Welcome back Scott. How was your journey?"

Scott got up stretched out his stiff body and walked over to sit down by Jack's side.

"You were there in the beginning," Scott said. "Where did you go?"

"I helped you get there, but once we were there I was told to come back and wait for you."

Scott explained everything he experienced during his journey. Jack smiled as Scott told him about the thousands of bands of light and how the voice of Spirit spoke to him. After this they stood up dusted off their pants, and made their way back down to the main trail.

After walking for a short period Scott turned to Jack. "Jack,

I want to thank you for listening to Spirit and showing up in my life."

"It has been my pleasure," Jack said. "I made an agreement a long time ago that when Spirit called I would show up."

"Well I'm sure glad that you did." Scott gave Jack a big hug and neither man could know at that moment how important this day was to each of them, or to the cause they felt so deeply about.

During the ride back to Phoenix the two men dared to dream together out loud. Scott felt a sense of bliss and amazement at how natural this seemed. Two adult men talking about making their dreams come true, and feeling the great difference this was going to make for everyone. At one point during a lag in the conversation Scott drifted off to sleep. Jack smiled remembering how tired he became after the first time he journeyed. Scott woke up as Jack's car pulled up to his house.

He opened the car door and peered back in at Jack. "Thanks again Jack, it was a great day that I'll never forget."

"Your welcome Scott. It was really my pleasure I'm just thrilled to be involved I'll see you real soon."

"Ok, I'll talk to you later." Scott walked up to the house where he knew Elizabeth was waiting, eager to hear about his day.

Jack drove back to his house filled with a sense of relief. He knew for some time that he was to be Scott's helper, but he had begun to wonder, even worry he had to admit, that maybe he was just going to help from a distance. He smiled as he realized that he had become attached to the outcome. He has seen time and time again how Spirit would work things out and this would be no exception. It made no difference to God that the matters at hand were so astronomical by his standards.

"Treat the earth well: it was not given to you by your parents, it was loaned to you by your children. We do not inherit the earth from our Ancestors, we borrow it from our Children."

Ancient Indian Proverb

Chapter 9—The Conference

Scott spent Sunday relaxing with Elizabeth and his daughter and there was no discussion whatsoever of party business. Elizabeth could tell that the time spent with Jack in the sacred canyon had a profound effect on her husband. It was nice for Scott and his family to spend the day, just being together and enjoying one another's company.

It didn't take long for things to start happening with the environmental conference in Las Vegas. Early Monday afternoon Scott received a telephone call from the founder of Planet Save. Robert West founded the popular organization shortly after writing a couple of books on vegetarianism. These books not only dealt with the health benefits of becoming a vegetarian, but they also laid out a plan for how a plant based diet could help to save the earth.

"The reason for my call is that I wanted to let you know that I plan on attending the conference," Robert said.

"That's great."

"I also wanted to ask your permission to put a notice on our web site about the conference and encourage our members to come," Robert said.

"Are you kidding me? We would be honored and thrilled to have your support."

"Well it's settled then, I've been watching the growth of your party and it's platform, and have been meaning to get in touch with you, but time has gotten the better of me," Robert said.

"I know how that is. Speaking of time, I was wondering if we could meet before the conference gets started, so we can get to know each other," Scott said.

"That sounds like a good idea. In the meantime if there is anything I can do to help with the conference, just pick up the phone."

"Thank you Robert, I really appreciate it."

"Thank you Scott, I'll talk with you soon."

This was one of those moments where Scott felt like he could really see the power of what he and the others were doing. Robert West was a famous author and he had just called Scott as if they were old friends and pledged his support. This was amazing!

Feeling very much like he was on a roll at this point. Scott called a dear friend of his Austin Wright. Austin is a professional speaker and founder of the Wright Impact Group. Scott had been trying to persuade Austin to MC the conference for some time, but Austin resisted because he was not an environmental specialist. Today Austin finally relented and Scott was overjoyed.

Over the next couple of weeks things continued to come together for the upcoming conference and Elizabeth continued working on her article about the shift in consumerism. Elizabeth's goal was to have her article finished before the conference got under way. Writing the article filled her with a great sense of excitement as she thought about the limitless possibilities consumers have to effect change.

Elizabeth's article not only brought what was happening in consumer behavior into the public eye but, it also explained concisely and simply the effect consumers have on the world we live in. She discussed in detail how some car manufacturers were moving faster than regulations had forced them, to develop alternative fuel vehicles and that this was done in response to the growing consumer demand. Elizabeth shared a dream of hers, in which consumers harnessed the power and money of the automobile manufacturers and affected the greatest change in our environment since the automobile was invented.

Elizabeth pointed out that organic food sales are on the rise, and many food companies are scrambling to purchase or make inroads into this fast growing market. People are eating less meat and according to a vegetarian resource group, the Zogby Poll, the percentage of the total population in America that is vegetarian has risen to 2.5%. Perhaps the most encouraging news is that this percentage jumped to 6% for the eighteen to twenty-nine age group. This evidence suggests there is a quiet revolution going on in this country as more and more people are changing to a plant based diet.

Elizabeth pointed out that if this shift in American's eating habits continues the possible implications for our environment are enormous, because livestock production is second only to automobiles as a source of pollution.

Elizabeth called on all Americans to live and shop consciously. She pointed out that despite the fact that computer technology had been touted as a way to save paper by switching to electronic information filing systems, the computer age has brought with it massive waste in the form of unused draft documents. She promoted printing on both sides of the computer paper, whenever possible and practicing simple quality control principals to avoid mistakes that result in discarded paper. She discussed how much of our forests could be saved, and how much reforestation could take place if Americans insisted on the legalization of industrial hemp for papermaking. She wrote that it is absurd that other countries are using this economic resource for clothing, rugs, and paper while we continue to consume our own forests and the forests of other countries instead. She asked all Americans to recognize that every purchase they make does make a difference.

The article concluded with a discussion of intent. She wrote: "Intent is what powers the vehicle of change. When one's intent is clear the vehicle runs smoothly and on all cylinders. The greatest battle we face is with ourselves. When we ask what difference does it make what I buy? I am only one person. What affect will my actions really have on the big picture? Our intent then wavers and the engine sputters and slows with indecision, sometimes never taking us to our intended destination. All great teachers including Jesus have taught that the little acts of mercy that are done in secret are the most powerful. They have a greater effect on the mass consciousness of this planet than any great act that is done by someone in public. The reason for this is because of the purity of intent. As human beings when we bring forth some little act of mercy for the earth or for another human being without anyone knowing, our intent is not confused or diluted by the desire for acknowledgement and self-promotion. Anything that is done with pure intent has the greatest power to effect change. This is how consciousness works."

Elizabeth closed the article by asking the reader to acknowledge the current changes in consumer behavior as an act of conscious intent. She also encouraged everyone to recognize the power that capitalism affords them to affect constructive change in our society.

Elizabeth's included the ten fundamentals for global transformation she found on the Internet in her article. She enthusiastically shared with her readers how powerful this could be if people all over this country, and indeed the world were praying and meditating on the same ten ideals. Helen Schultz and the other members of the Centrust Party quickly approved her article. It was printed first in the magazine Kindred Spirit, and later picked up by a magazine called Light of Consciousness.

The first week in August brought new hope to the founders of the Centrust Party. It was becoming obvious that many people were headed for Las Vegas to attend the environmental conference. Hotel rooms received a flood of reservations for the week of the conference, and interest spread among people who would normally not be interested in politics or environmental issues. Scott's vision of an exodus to Vegas for the upcoming conference was becoming a reality.

Things were slow in the news business at this time, and Kate Seymore was able to talk her editor into doing a story about the upcoming environmental conference. She interviewed ordinary people who were planning to go as well as celebrities like Robert West who had been outspoken about his plans to attend. The Planet Save organization's web site had been particularly helpful in promoting the conference. However, it was clear that making the conference a success would involve more than just getting people to come to the desert at this time of year. Achieving a consensus on an environmental action plan would not be easy when opinion and emotion often tended to the extremes.

Scott was confident that they could get the job done. The very fact that so many people were showing up for the conference was an indication people felt empowered and believed they could make a difference. Jack and Ben would be in Vegas to support Scott and the other founding members of the Centrust Party.

They joked with each other in the midst of the growing waves of energy focusing on Las Vegas. "I can't resist the temptation to see one of the worlds biggest arguments. Up close and personal," Ben said.

The turn out at the environmental conference was nothing less than amazing. People had come from all across the country and every major environmental group was represented. Even more important was that thousands of Americans who were not even affiliated with any these groups also attended. Many of these people planed their summer vacations around the event. This humbled Scott and the other founders of the party.

Jack and Ben spent their time mingling with the mass of citizens that had showed up for the conference. They would find out that many of these people had come just to show their support for the idea of creating a new way of doing things in America. Many citizens felt that last fall's bungled election actually created an opportunity for great political change.

Jack commented to Ben about the apparent pull of consciousness on everyone's psyche, "it really is happening isn't it Ben?"

"That it is my friend, and it's picking up steam," Ben said. They were overjoyed with the awakening that seemed to be happening right before their eyes.

Austin Wright opened the conference with an eloquent speech about the possibilities that lay before them all. He suggested that everyone hold a vision of success, not only for the conference but for the Centrust Party as well. He talked about the power we all have in creating our future as individuals, as Americans, and as a species. "If we all hold this vision this conference will be the first step towards saving this planet, and everyone and everything that calls it home."

Prior to the start of the conference it was decided that each of the environmental groups, along with a couple of citizen groups that wished to participate, would each elect one official to represent them on a board. Establishing the board took place on the first day of the conference. The board would then hear testimony on specific issues from representatives of the various groups. After hearing from the citizen and environmental groups, they would then draft an environmental policy for the Centrust Party.

On the second day of the conference Robert West was elected as temporary chairman of the board. Robert was faced with a tough decision, which the board asked him to make as soon as possible. The board had decided and Robert had agreed that serving as chairman of the board, could be viewed as a conflict of interest if he remained president of Planet Save. Robert was torn; he loved Planet Save, which he had founded and helped to grow. Working with the Centrust Party on the other hand could be a chance to affect the kind of global environmental change that he had been dreaming about. In the end he chose to leave Planet Save and become the party's environmental chairman.

The board spent the next three days hearing a variety of spirited debate. On day two emotions reached a peak when a cattle rancher took the floor. After indicating his support for the Centrust Party he was met with boo's and jeers when he expressed his opposition to the party's attacks on the livestock industry. There were other cattle ranchers in the audience and they came to the rescue of their friend who had the nerve take the floor and speak from the podium. A small scuffle ensued. The air in the conference hall was thick with tension, and progress had seemed to come to a halt when Scott decided to take the floor.

Scott spoke about his life during the first month of the Centrust Party's existence. He remarked how he had felt like he was living someone else's life, or he was stuck in a dream that he couldn't wake up from. Scott spoke about his life being turned upside down, because he was tired of the status quo. He mentioned that about three months after the presidential election, he realized that if he wanted to continue with the party he would have to lay everything he had on the line.

"This was not an easy decision to make, but I had to ask myself, how can I expect anyone else to find another line of work, or to change their lifestyle if I don't lay it on the line for this party and its future."

He addressed the cattle ranchers. "We are not trying to destroy the livestock industry in this country. Lord knows that I didn't want to give up eating meat." This statement was met with muted laughter. "However the facts are clear that the resources that are used to feed cattle could go much further towards feeding our all too rapidly growing population. Currently one half the earth's land mass is used to graze cattle. The Centrust Party wants only for Americans to have the facts on this issue and all the other issues that affect so many others, and our course as a species going forward. Right now Americans are not getting the facts because our government is intermingled with business. If Americans cut their meat consumption by 50% the environmental benefits alone would be significant. The savings in grain needed now to feed cattle would go a long way towards feeding the hungry people in this country and the rest the world.

Eating beef is as much a part of American way of life as apple pie or baseball. I don't believe that if Americans cut their meat consumption by 50% it would result in the death of cattle ranching in this country. It would however result in less importation of beef from other countries that can't even afford to feed their own people. The land in these countries, which is currently being used for cattle grazing, could be used to grow food to feed their own populations. The most important point in this whole debate is not whether or not any of the cattle ranchers of this country choose to support the Centrust Party. Rather it is whether or not we are willing to change our lives and our lifestyles to save this planet. If the majority of us here today say yes, I am willing to take a chance and make that change despite my fears. Then we not only have something special here, but something that is bigger than we are."

Scott took a long look around, walked away from the podium, and anyone could have heard a pin drop in the auditorium. As Scott walked down the aisle that parted the audience the cattle rancher who was previously at the podium stood up and started to clap slowly. Others stood up and began clapping, and before long the whole auditorium was standing in ovation.

Austin Wright seized the opportunity as the crowd quieted down and took the podium with a big smile on his face.

"What do you all say we get on with changing the world?"

There was a roar from the audience and the conference continued. Interestingly enough the news media carried the story about the scuffle, but Kate Seymore was the only reporter to cover the whole story including Scott's speech.

After more debate the conference ended with the Centrust Party drafting a document to be released to the press and posted on the web site. This document would establish the Centrust Party's environmental policy moving forward. Both the founding members of the party and the environmental board that were formed at the conference felt a great sense of accomplishment. To bring so many people with such a diversity of lifestyles together to form a consensus in such a short time was a miracle.

"This had to have been the hand of divine intervention," Robert West said.

"It was Robert, it most certainly was," Scott replied.

The foundation of the Centrust Party's environmental policies were released as follows:

1) Campaign finance reform is the first priority for the Centrust Party's environmental coalition. The party feels it is unrealistic for any of us to expect credible reform under the current system of political fund raising. The much-needed reform

to secure our future will be painfully slow under current campaign finance laws. Time is of the essence. According to most scientists we have a window of 10 to 30 years before irreparable damage is done and we will no longer be able to sustain our existence on this planet. Our elected officials must be free from the burden of having to raise so much money to run for office.

2) Developing alternative fuel resources especially for automobiles and trucks is our second priority. Not only are automobile and truck emissions the number one cause of air pollution, but our current rate of fossil fuel consumption cannot be sustained. According to some estimates the world's oil production will peak in the year 2010. If our current growth in oil consumption continues some predict we will run out of oil in the next 40 to 60 years. We need to use this limited resource in the manufacture and development of alternative fuel vehicles. Manufacturing alternative fuel vehicles needs to be prioritized immediately.

3) Reducing the bureaucracy within the EPA and establishing a spirit of cooperation between government, business and industry is the Centrust Party's third priority. Again time is of the essence in formalizing this cooperative effort. Many businesses are afraid to come forward with their environmental problems or concerns due to fear of substantial penalties and fines imposed by the EPA. What has happened in the past is in the past. We need to save this planet from environmental destruction by supporting as many people as possible in becoming caretakers of this planet.

4) Starting a new, mandatory education program between the government and business for the conservation of all of our resources is another priority. Employees of this country's corporations, local, state and Federal governmental agencies would be educated on energy and resource conservation at the workplace. The focus of this education would be on how our individual acts really do make a difference. When the majority of Americans recycle, conserve energy, and reduce their use of paper our collective impact on the environment can be dramatically reduced.

5) Increase incentives for businesses to use recycled materials in manufacturing. Encourage consumers to purchase recycled products even if in the beginning they cost slightly more. As consumers increase their demand for products made from recycled materials, more and more companies will scramble to provide them.

6) Legalize industrial hemp in this country. There is absolutely no reason not to. To suggest otherwise is absurd. Hemp has many uses including the manufacture of paper. The government should provide incentives to the paper industry and encourage consumers to support their transition to using hemp in the manufacture of paper. The DEA has opposed this move in the past, even though smoking industrial hemp will only lead to a headache, not a high. The environmental impact of using hemp for paper, and the economic impact for farmers would far outweigh the potential for abuse by drug users.

7) In many European countries, environmental groups are considered to be among the many "Non-Governmental Organizations" or NGOs that play an important role in approving, modifying, or completely scrapping plans for new industrial plants or plant modifications. By law, their involvement is required during the environmental impact assessment phase of any new project. American Industry needs to adopt a similar philosophy of working in cooperation with environmental groups. Similarly environmental groups need to adopt a responsible view of contributing to the broader public interest rather than taking a purely adversarial stance.

8) We would like the public to view environmentalists as being conservative rather than radical extremists. The most conservative course for our nation and this world is for us all to become environmentalists. Therefore the Centrust Party will not accept support or affiliation with any group that participates in the destruction of private property done under the pretense of protecting the environment.

Scott wrote a closing statement that said:

The Centrust Party does not wish for the American people to perceive our message as a message of doom. To the contrary, we feel our message on the environment, the changes needed in our government and its policies, and the power we all have as individuals, are messages of hope. America is the largest consumer of the earth's resources, and we are also the leaders of the free world. Other countries not only look to us for help and guidance, many of them also wish to emulate our lifestyles. Therefore, a few small changes in our lifestyles, which might not amount to more than minor inconveniences, have the capability to reverse our present course of environmental destruction.

If asked if they would make these changes, most Americans would answer yes. The problem arises when we get discouraged, and fail to value the importance of our decisions and their impact in the bigger picture. I know about this discouragement, because I have felt it myself. The quality of our intent is what makes miracles possible, and even probable. As each one of us makes these small yet crucial changes in our lifestyles with the intent of saving this planet, we collectively create the shift in consciousness that is needed to reverse our current course.

We believe it is time for America to be a leader in the shift in consciousness that must take place in how mankind views itself in relationship to its natural environment. When the majority of Americans become caretakers of this beautiful planet, we call home; the rest of the world will surely follow our lead.

"The world is headed for mutiny when all we want is unity.
We may rise and fall, but in the end we'll meet our fate together."

Creed

Chapter 10 — The Red Ball of Fire

In the weeks following the environmental conference the Centrust Party was running on all eight cylinders. Scott hoped there would be no stopping them now. The governor from Minnesota contacted him, and in a media fanfare declared that he would register with the Centrust Party.

A republican senator from Vermont left his party to become an independent. Scott, Helen, and Sam were very impressed and thought that it took a lot of conviction, because in leaving his party, he effectively gave the democrats the majority in the Senate.

This senator contacted Helen through an old friend, and obtained Scott's phone number from her. The senator and Scott had a long conversation regarding politics and reform. Without naming names the senator indicated that there were many other politicians that were unhappy with the current political system. They felt unable to perform the service they were elected to do and desired a significant change. When Scott told an eager Helen about his phone conversation with the senator from Vermont she lit up like a Christmas tree. Scott had never seen her so happy.

The party's founding members made it through their grueling tax audits. The audits were the kind of thing that would wake Helen Schultz's out of a sound sleep in the middle of the night.

In Mountain Home, Utah Joseph and Father Morales were very pleased with the progress of the Centrust Party, and the wave of waking consciousness spreading across the country. Despite everything appearing to be going very well they both experienced a subtle sadness and a drain in energy for a period of about a week. They discussed what the possible cause of these feelings could be. "I imagine we will know what it is soon," remarked Joseph.

Then it happened. On September 11th terrorists used commercial airliners as bombs and flew one into each tower of the World Trade Center, another was crashed into the Pentagon. There had been terrorist attacks before, but none were of this magnitude. The terrorists woke the sleeping giant and it dusted off the war machine. Of course the media wanted the Centrust Party's take on the events, and of course the new party stood firmly behind the President along with the rest of America. Reform was replaced by revenge in the minds of many Americans, however a spirit of unity began to emerge in the midst of it all. "It's a shame that it takes something like this for us to wake up and realize we are all in this together," Scott remarked to Helen one day in regards to the attacks.

The party's founding members wondered if the war on terrorism would greatly slow down or halt the shift in consciousness that had been happening they didn't even dare to speak about it, but it was on their minds. The Centrust Party had been a key part of this shift, and participating in it had propelled them into notoriety. The news was dominated with details and stories about the attack. Over the next couple of months, the Centrust Party faded into obscurity.

Scott began writing major speeches for the governor of Minnesota. He also went back to running his business full time and spent more of his time getting to know Jack better. The two men developed a deep friendship, and when Scott would get to feeling down Jack would always find something inspiring to say.

On one occasion he said, "C'mon Scott keep your chin up, the election is still three years away. We're still in the ballgame. Remember your vision of the man at the podium. Hang on to that vision, and hold it in your mind."

Father Morales and Joseph spent their time in prayer and meditation. The two men developed a bond based on the knowledge of who we really are, rather than what we think we are. They spent their time telling stories of their different spiritual experiences and cultures, discussing the mysteries of God, and their faith. They waited for the events that they knew were yet to happen. They also talked at length about how man over the millennia had developed religions that obscured or entirely missed the central point. Father Morales thought, that Joseph had a beautiful way of putting it. "It is the secret we all keep from ourselves."

Thursday, January the 17th. Patrick Kincaid went to bed early after a long hard day presenting a bill on the Senate floor. Shortly after falling asleep the voice came to him again in a dream, and told him it was time to send out the Fed Ex envelope to a judge in Louisiana.

"Make sure you do it tomorrow morning Patrick," the voice said, "send the package priority overnight. It must arrive on Saturday." The senator woke up and glanced at the clock to realize he had only been asleep for half an hour. He thought he might get up and make a note as a reminder, when he smiled at himself, because there was no way he could ever forget one of these dreams as long as he lived.

On Saturday morning the judge had been awake since 5:00 am, he suspected this day would be like everyday had been lately, filled with the pain and the occasional self-pity of a dying old man. It was about 10:00 am when the judge dozed off while watching the television. He found himself in a dream surrounded by white light. He was immediately overcome with a feeling that there was something left undone.

Then a voice spoke to him. "You're right Judge, that which you agreed to do so long ago, is not yet done."

"Who are you?" The judge asked. "What can I do? I'm old and I'm dying!"

"You're dying, because you're choosing to," the voice said. When the voice proclaimed this to the judge, he remembered that all he had to do was choose differently.

Before he had a chance to enjoy this feeling the voice spoke again. "After you wake you will receive an envelope. It is one of only two copies of a prophecy, and it is the truth. It has been entrusted to you, because of your protégé Tom LeClaire, and his future. Read the prophecy and come back to it and read it again when you need to. For now you are to show it to no one. You are also not to speak of it to anyone. Your protégé is about to embark on a path few men would dare to take, and he needs your help and support."

When the judge awoke he blinked his eyes a few times, and then sat up slowly on the couch. He immediately noticed his pain was diminishing. The doorbell rang and his wife answered it. She came walking in the room with a Fed Ex envelope and put it in the judge's hands, which immediately began to shake.

"Are you all right Judge?"

"I'm fine sweetheart," he said.

His wife walked back into the kitchen, and the judge realized he had been asleep for couple of hours and it already was lunchtime. He decided to read the letter at a time when his wife was not around. Walking into the kitchen the judge felt the pain start to return. He chose not to have it, and the pain vanished immediately.

Michael Fisher, an astronomy student from Boston University, could hardly wait for this day to start. This evening he would take his first shift at the Loneos telescope at Lowell observatory outside of Flagstaff, Arizona. He would be manning the computer station looking for ECAs and ECCs, which is short for earth crossing asteroids and earth crossing comets. He tried to sleep some during the day because he knew he would be awake all evening, but his excitement got the better of him. His work began shortly after sunset.

It was almost 2 am on Sunday January the 20th one year after the inauguration of the American president, when Michael first spotted an ECA. The first thing he marveled at was its size, but when he saw the calculation made by the computer tracking program his heart nearly stopped. Michael couldn't believe his eyes, so the first thing he did was run the ECA profile through the database of existing near earth objects to see if it had already been discovered. To his surprise it wasn't listed in the database. He continued tracking the asteroid as he waited for the computer to calculate an approximate impact day. Seven years, seven months, and seven days from today was the projected impact. Now it was definitely time to wake up the boss.

Michael picked up the phone and called Dr. Arthur the principal scientist at the Lowell observatory.

"Dr. Arthur I think you'd better come down here right away," Michael said as soon as the doctor answered the phone.

The doctor sat up in bed trying to clear his head. "Who is this?"

"Oh, I'm sorry Dr. Arthur this is Michael at the Loneos. Can you believe it? On my first night I found a new ECA, and its huge."

"I'll be down as soon as I get dressed, in the meantime double check your data immediately."

"Ok Doctor."

After hanging up the phone Michael's enthusiasm turned into terror as he double-checked his data. He had been so excited to make his first discovery that he forgot to contemplate the implications of it.

Dr. Arthur arrived and confirmed his data. "Michael you know the protocol here." While Dr. Arthur went into his office to make a phone call Michael thought about the responsibility that had been laid upon his shoulders. They were to tell no one of this discovery. Not even other staff who worked at the observatory. That was standard procedure.

Before the sun came up on January the 20th there were four Federal agents at Lowell observatory. Two of them secured the Loneos telescope, and Dr. Arthur and Michael Fisher briefed the other two. Michael never did learn the names of the two men who interviewed him and the doctor. The feds were very concerned about Michael being able to keep the secret. Although they didn't directly threaten him they made it clear that mentioning this discovery to anyone else outside of this room would be a big mistake on his part.

"We don't know if anyone else has seen it this morning. Besides someone else might also see it in the Far East later today," Michael said.

"You let us worry about that." The fed took a long hard look at Michael.

"Well I just don't want to get blamed for someone else opening their mouth. I know the protocol, I was cleared to work here," Michael said.

The Doctor reached over and touched Michael on the arm. "Calm down son, calm down."

Before the sun set that day, anyone who needed to know, knew about the ECA. It was a very short list of people. The rest of the world's governments that had observatories that could make this kind of discovery were notified also. Every possible action was taken to keep this under wraps. On Monday January the 21st the President of the United States was told that the asteroids projected course was to hit the surface of the earth at Latitude 41° 40′, Longitude 83° 35′. It was not a leak from one of the observatories that the world's leaders would have to concern themselves about, instead it was the fact that prophets from several different faiths knew about the asteroid well before any observatory could have spotted it.

The senator from Louisiana, Tom LeClaire, had not seen his mentor, the judge, since Christmas. It was March and Tom could smell spring in the Louisiana air as he made his way to the Judge's house. As he walked down the sidewalk he thought about his long relationship with the judge. The judge had been responsible for encouraging him to enter politics so long ago and the judge's support had been unwavering through the years. The judge had no children and he treated Tom like his only son. Although he had talked with the judge a few times over the last couple months he had not been by to see him because of his busy schedule. Now that congress was in recess for the week he would spend his time at home among the people he loved and take the opportunity to visit the judge.

During one of their phone conversations in early February he noticed the judge seemed in much better spirits than before Christmas. He asked the judge about his health.

"Please tell me you didn't think that I would leave you before you got to be President."

Tom worried that the next time he would see the judge would be at his funeral, but now the judge was once again dreaming about him becoming the President. This had also been his dream, but in recent years he had all but given up on achieving it.

He thought about how he was becoming increasingly disheartened with his dream of making a real impact on this world. As he turned the corner to walk down the judge's street he remembered himself as an eager young man, full of dreams about a better world, and his plans to be a part of making that happen. The judge had taken this young, energetic, idealistic man and groomed him to be a politician that had the skills to go with the idealism. Had it not been for the judge, Tom would have probably burned out many years ago. As the senator now approached 50 he was beginning to give up on the dreams of a young man. Many of his colleagues felt this way also. They were tired of being full-time fundraisers and part time public servants. Many had left politics altogether, while some had become independents, a few had even joined the Centrust Party.

There will be none of this negativity today, Tom thought, as he made his way up the walk to the judge's front porch. It was the front porch where the two men had spent so much time discussing life, politics, and the future. Tom hadn't even knocked on the door when the judge swung it open and stood before him grinning.

"Well, hello there Senator! I was beginning to wonder if you were ever going to make it over here to see me." He quickly stepped aside so Tom could enter the house.

Tom could not believe his eyes! The judge had put on at least 25 lbs. since he saw him at Christmas. He had heard the judge had made an amazing recovery, but standing before him was the man he knew ten years ago.

"Don't just stand there with your mouth open, come on in," the judge said. "Would you like some coffee Tom?"

"That would be great," Tom said trying to control the look of amazement on his face.

He stood there in the foyer dumbfounded. The whole scene took on a surreal quality.

The judge was still talking to him from the kitchen, but he couldn't make out the words. What's going on here? He thought. Something's happening, this feels strange. He looked up to notice the judge's wife Kathy smiling at him from the couch in the living room. She walked over and touched him on the arm and he came back to reality.

"Hello Tom, it's nice to see you again."

"What happened to the judge?" Tom asked.

She just smiled again and shrugged her shoulders.

The judge came back into the foyer.

"What do you say we head out on to the porch for a chat?"

"Sounds good. It's nice to see you again Kathy," Tom said.

No sooner had their seats hit their chairs than the judge started asking questions.

"So, how are things in Washington?"

"Well, there have been some new twists lately," Tom said.

"Are you referring to the war on terrorism?"

"Yeah, that's one of the them," Tom said.

"Before the terrorist attacks, reform was in the forefront."

"That would be the other one," Tom said.

He knew the judge loved to talk about such things, but he was eager to leave Washington behind.

"I'm sorry Tom, I know you're taking a break and need to remove yourself from Washington for a while."

"What happened Judge? No offense, but my wife told me you were on your deathbed."

The judge wanted more than anything in the world at that moment to tell his friend about the prophecy he received, but he knew he couldn't. Not yet anyway. He also wondered how Tom felt about it, and how he could casually bring it up in conversation.

The judge thought it would be all right to tell Tom that he made a decision in a dream to live longer, and after making this decision his health began to improve immediately. He was just about to explain this, when his friend broke the silence.

"Have you heard about this prophecy circulating the Internet?" The judge nearly fell off his chair. He knew about the prophecy circulating the Internet; it was the same one word for word he had received by courier. It was impossible however for him to control the look of amazement on his face. Tom was looking towards the street; he turned to meet eyes with the judge.

"What, what's up Judge?"

The judge knew that Tom knew him too well for him to be able to pull the wool over his eyes, so he hoped that half the truth would do.

"Yes I've heard of it," the judge said. "As a matter of fact it was after hearing of this prophecy that my health improved. It was the strangest thing Tom, in a dream I had, I decided to live longer. Immediately after this dream my health began to improve." It appeared from the look on Tom's face that half the truth would suffice, and the judge was relieved.

Tom slid all the way back into his chair let out a deep sigh. "For some time now, I've been gravely concerned, judge. My party is no longer the party it was when I began my career." Tom paused for a moment and stared out at the street again. "Everyone, myself included seems to be solely concerned about staying in office and getting re-elected. The really terrible thing is that this has become an acceptable practice."

The judge put his hand on his friend's shoulder. "Don't be so hard on yourself Tom."

"Judge it just takes so much money." Tom had a look of deep sadness, as their eyes met again. "It takes so much money to stay in office, and to run a campaign. So much of my time is spent just trying to raise money. Sometimes I just feel...I mean what's the use?" Tom paused and he could feel the despair growing within him.

"I've been thinking about a lot of things lately and one example I keep coming back to is that 30 years ago oil production peaked in this country. At that time my son was not even born yet. Now he has a son of his own, and we are more dependent on fossil fuels for energy then we were then. In the last 30 years what has been done to develop alternative fuels? I realize that many people haven't wanted to spend more money in developing alternative fuels over this time period. But, isn't it our job as elected officials to come forward with the truth and tell the people about the importance of making these tough decisions?

Think of it Judge. If we weren't so dependent on oil from the Middle East we could play a completely different role in seeking peace in that region of the world. As long as this dependency continues our intent will always be questionable. We are polluting our planet, spiraling toward economic devastation, and are unable to promote peace all because we are too fearful of making changes before the final hour." He let out a deep sigh and slumped back into his chair.

The judge sat silently while Tom watched people walking up and down the street. When he felt the time was right he broke the silence. "You're right Tom. Throughout human history, whenever a few have had control of a strategic resource that everyone else needs, it has been a recipe for disaster. In this case we're talking about oil, but I think the greater issue here is people's fear of change. You know from being a politician that there are a lot of powerful people who are desperate to keep things the way they are, no matter what the consequences may be," the judge said.

He looked Tom right in the eyes and smiled.

"What do you plan to do about it Tom?"

"I just don't know Judge, I just don't know. Maybe it would be better for me to leave Washington. I mean, be free of its obligations so I could speak the truth about this and many others issues. It's not that I haven't been truthful, it's just that my colleagues and I, because of our fear, have avoided being completely candid with our constituents."

Tom paused and shot his mentor a crooked smile. "I have to hand it to the Centrust Party. They have come out and stated the facts as they see them. Their founder, Scott Stahl has the luck of the Irish and their press secretary; Helen Shultz, boy she's a sharp cookie. The public really seemed to be responding favorably to them. I'm telling you Judge, before the World Trade Center tragedy, and the war on terrorism, both parties were worried."

The judge noticed a light in his friend's eyes as he talked about the Centrust Party, and he silently hoped that Tom would rise to the occasion, as much for his sake as for that of the country's. Tom sensed there was something going on.

"What's going on Judge?"

"I was just thinking that if this prophecy is true it might be just the thing that is needed to get people moving in the right direction again, on so many of these crucial subjects."

"Maybe it is. If that doesn't work I don't know what will" Tom said.

"Well, Judge I've got to get going. It sure has been nice to see you." He stood up to leave "I'm overjoyed that you're going to be with us a little longer." They shook hands and Tom made his way down the front stoop.

"Like I said Tom, I had to stay around long enough to see

you become President."

"Goodbye old friend, I'll see you later." Tom shook his head and smiled. *He just never gives up on that one,* he thought as he walked back down the street.

Uzziah could feel the eyes of the store's clerk on his back as he stood nervously in front of the freezer shifting his weight back and forth from one foot to the other. He was about to purchase his second soft drink since he arrived at the small trading post 45 minutes earlier. As he walked back to the counter to pay for his soft drink a couple of patrons seemed to be eyeing him with suspicion, except for a rather tall Indian man wearing a cowboy hat and dark sunglasses who smiled at him before exiting the store. The woman at the cash register asked him if he was lost or he needed help. "No thank you," he replied. He couldn't blame them for their suspicions; he was the only white person there and probably within miles.

His mind was working overtime now. He kept telling himself he was nuts to be here in the first place. What the hell was he doing at a trading post in Mountain Home Utah anyway? His rabbi had told him he needed to go there to help save the world.

When Uzziah heard this for the first time he thought his rabbi had really gone off the deep end. He sat alone with his thoughts on the walkway in front of the trading post. He had tried a thousand times on the journey west from New York to Utah to talk himself out of coming, but to no avail.

His rabbi was a mystic and for that reason Uzziah sought him as his teacher, because Uzziah wished to become a rabbi in the Kabbalic tradition also. He had refused to take this journey in the beginning. Only after his rabbi insisted, and threatened to no longer be his teacher did he finally relent, and agree to come.

His rabbi had a vision in which he saw Uzziah as a member of some kind of council that would pray and meditate to bring about a global shift in consciousness.

"This shift in consciousness just might save the world," his rabbi told him. "You should be honored to have been chosen to be a member of it."

Maybe so, the young man thought as he sat waiting, *but what am I going to do now? I don't think these people will let me sit here forever, while I wait for God only knows who to show up.*

Talking Bird dashed through the front door of Joseph's home. "There's a young fella hanging around down at the trading post looking like he's lost." He stopped to catch his breath. "He looks Jewish. Maybe he's here because of you guys. One of you had better get over their, cause folks down there aren't necessarily friendly when it comes to strangers."

"What does Jewish look like?" Father Morales asked.

"He's a short fella with a New York accent and he's wearing a yamaka."

"Excellent, "Joseph said. "We've been expecting someone."

"Well why didn't you let me in on it?" Talking Bird said.

"We have to let some things remain a secret," Father Morales said. He smiled at Talking Bird and patted him on the shoulder as he and Joseph made their way out the door to head for the trading post.

Uzziah sat on the edge of the concrete porch in front of the trading post watching an old pickup truck barrel down the road. As it turned into the gravel parking lot it swerved throwing rocks. *Were did they learn to drive?* The young man wondered. The pickup truck came to an abrupt stop in front of the trading post near where he was sitting. Its doors swung open and an old Indian man about six feet tall and a smaller man who looked to be South American and perhaps 50 got out of the truck and headed towards him. His heart was pounding in his throat as he realized that until this moment he hadn't really believed that his rabbi's vision was true. He realized that until now he thought he would show up in Utah to appease his rabbi, and then travel back to New York explaining that he was unable to make contact with anyone.

He stood up as the two approached him. When they were in front of him the smaller man spoke first.

"How are you doing there young man?" Father Morales said.

"Well, I guess I'm Ok," Uzziah said. "I've had a long drive and I needed a rest—

"Let me get right to the point young man," Joseph said. "Are you here to be a member of a council?" Uzziah almost fainted.

"Whoa," Father Morales said, moving quickly to catch the young man.

"Are you all right?" The priest asked. Joseph let out a chuckle.

The two men spoke to Uzziah in the parking lot for couple of minutes to assure him that they were the reason he was here and then told him to follow them back to Joseph's home.

On the short drive from the trading post Uzziah's mind was reeling with questions. *How long would he be here? Were there only three of them, or are there others? Why did they have to meet so far out in the middle of nowhere? How had his rabbi known to send him here? What was their purpose? Who are these two guys and why do they need me? Most importantly had they heard of the prophecy, and did they believe it was true?*

The pickup truck pulled into the drive of a property that had two manufactured homes on it. Uzziah told himself not to be rude, and bombard these men with all his questions in the first two minutes of their conversation. Joseph and Father Morales exited the pickup truck and motioned for Uzziah to follow. The three men walked up the wooden stairs and into Joseph's home.

Joesph asked Uzziah to sit down at the kitchen table, and

then sat down himself directly across from him. Father Morales broke the uneasy silence. "Can I get you something to drink young man, perhaps a glass of water."

"That would be great, thank you," Uzziah said.

Father Morales sat down at the table with them and looked at Joseph. With a gleam in his eye the old Indian looked at Uzziah . "I'm sure you have many questions, why don't we start there." Uzziah choked and almost had to spit out his water when Joseph said this. After catching his breath he thought, how did he know that?

"What exactly are we doing here?" Uzziah asked.

Father Morales looked puzzled. "Do you not know why you are here?"

"My rabbi told me what he knew, but now that I'm here I would like to hear it directly from you." Joseph looked deeply into the young man's eyes long enough for Uzziah to become uncomfortable.

"A time of great transition is coming. Many people are starting to wake up and realize that the pursuit of material things and wealth as a first priority does not lead to happiness. Many men and women have forgotten about their spirit and their need to nurture it first and foremost. Man's spirit cannot be nurtured with wealth or material objects. It is not that material things and wealth are bad; it's just that spirit is not fed in this manner; it never has been and never will be. What one feeds grows, what one neglects dies. Fortunately the spirit of man is one with his creator, and therefore it can never die."

Joseph searched his mind for a few moments for the right words, and Uzziah thought that he appeared to be listening to something that he himself could not hear. "The human race could continue on this course of destruction until we remember how to properly feed our spirit. Unfortunately our population growth and the rate at which we are consuming the earth's resources has brought us too quickly to a point of great imbalance."

At this point Uzziah's eyes lit up and he couldn't contain himself any longer.

"You guys have heard of the prophecy, haven't you?"

"Heard of it!" Joseph lunged forward and pointed his thumb at Father Morales.

"This man sitting next to you received it." Uzziah's mouth fell open and Joseph let out a roar of laughter.

Father Morales leaned over and patted Uzziah on his shoulder. "Don't worry young man that's the reason we're here. To save the earth."

"Well that makes me feel a whole lot better," Uzziah said. "Just exactly how are one old Indian, a priest, and a Jew supposed to save the world?"

"Ah, Ha!" Joseph said. "You have forgotten about the power of your spirit, and that is why your rabbi sent you here."

Father Morales looked at Uzziah with confidence. "You have a teachers love and energy. Your rabbi knew this, and that is why he selected you to come. Many teachers of all faiths and races will be needed to teach about the forgotten power of the spirit."

"When I read the prophecy on the Internet...I mean, I just didn't want to believe it was true, but somehow in my heart I knew it was," Uzziah said. He lowered his head to stare at the table. He gathered himself and slowly returned his gaze to the two men.

"Now you're telling me that I'm sitting here with the man who actually received the prophecy."

"Hey, I've received prophecies before too," Joseph said. He smiled at the priest and Father Morales couldn't help but let out a laugh.

Uzziah couldn't believe it, they were talking about the possibility of an asteroid destroying the earth, and these two still found time for humor.

"That's because we take our work seriously but not ourselves." Father Morales replied to Uzziah's unspoken thought.

Oh shit! Uzziah thought. *They are like the rabbi, I will have to watch my thoughts.*

"Don't worry we will teach you how to do that too," Joseph said. Father Morales let out another laugh.

"What do you say we have something to eat now?" Joseph said "You must be hungry after such a long drive. We'll have dinner and relax. Tomorrow when you're rested we can talk about getting started and what else needs to be done."

The three men enjoyed dinner and some idle conversation mostly about Uzziah's life and studies. Father Morales and the Joseph showed Uzziah to his room. After their conversation he wasn't surprised to see the room had been prepared for a visitor. At this point Uzziah could have no idea that he would come to call this place home.

As Uzziah lay awake in this strange place, in a strange bed, he struggled to make sense of it all. Here he was, almost all the way on the other side of the country, staying with people he didn't even know. And if that wasn't enough, he also found out that the prophecy was true. Not only was it true, but somehow he was to play a part in making sure the earth's conditions would be met as spelled out in the prophecy. *That's one hell of a day* he thought. Sleep understandably, didn't come easily that night, however when he did sleep, his dreams were vivid and lucid.

Uzziah had heard about this type of dreaming before from his rabbi, but he had never experienced it.

"You will know that it is a mystic dream when you are the commander of the dream, a conscious participant rather than a powerless passenger," his rabbi told him. Uzziah craved these experiences, and at times had become impatient.

"These gifts and experiences will come when you are ready for them and most likely when you least expect them," his rabbi told him

In the beginning of Uzziah's dream he saw a new presidential candidate. Without thinking he knew that this candidate belonged to the Centrust Party. He recognized the man at the podium. This will make waves, he thought. As soon as he wondered who the man's running mate would be, the running mate appeared next to the candidate. Uzziah realized his thought had led to him seeing the running mate. When she appeared next to the presidential candidate, Uzziah burst out laughing and his laughter rumbled through his dream. The people in power now are not going to like this. Along with this thought he saw and felt how threatened they would become.

Instantly Uzziah became overwhelmed with an urgency to do something to help these candidates. He could see all at once how important the next presidential election would be, and realized that the shift might not actually happen.

The prophecy was true!

A massive shift in consciousness was needed if life as we know it was going to continue on this planet. This shift must happen, he thought.

"What will you do Uzziah?" A voice that came from everywhere asked him.

"I will do anything!" Uzziah cried out. He fell to his knees weeping with his head in his hands.

"I will do anything!" He shouted. "I will do anything!" He woke up in a strange bed, in a strange place.

Father Morales poked his head through the doorway. "I trust you've been having pleasant dreams Uzziah?" He let Uzziah feel his warm smile and kind eyes, and then proceeded down the hallway towards the kitchen. Joseph was not far behind him, he walked into the room and stood at the foot of the young man's bed. He was grinning from ear to ear. "Are you sure you'll do anything?" Uzziah knew his rabbi was a powerful man, yet he had never shown at least to Uzziah, powers such as these men had. He had only been here one night, and already these men were able to read his thoughts and visit his dreams. Uzziah lay there in bed for a few minutes wondering just what he'd gotten himself into. After he collected himself he got up and joined the two men in the kitchen.

When Uzziah made it to the kitchen the two men were already seated having coffee. Joseph poured him a cup and asked him to sit down.

"We need to discuss in detail what we're doing here Uzziah," Father Morales said. "If after we explain to you what our purpose is, should you decide to leave, we will understand—

"However," Joseph said. "You must vow to tell no one where we are or what we're doing.

Uzziah thought the two men sounded like an old married couple finishing each others sentences.

"Even considering breaking this vow could create an instant karmic response…should I continue?" Father Morales said.

"Most definitely," Uzziah said. He was amazed he answered the question without hesitation.

"Over the next couple of years," Father Morales said. "The size of our group will grow dramatically, both here in Mountain Home and around the world. At our location, all races, religions, and political affiliations will be represented. You have read the prophecy from the Internet and we've told you that I am the one who received it."

Father Morales paused for a moment, and looked deep into Uzziah's eye's. "Our destiny is to hold space through prayer and meditation to bring about the shift you dreamt of last night."

Joseph smiled at Uzziah. "We will all sit in ceremony together. This is a requirement of taking your seat on this council. However, not one person will be asked to abandon their faith. Quite to the contrary. Each one of us will become a conduit of consciousness for people in our respective faiths."

The three of them sat in silence for a few moments.

"Uzziah, you must now decide. Is being a member of this council and a conduit to those in your faith something you agreed to do before you were even born?" Father Morales asked.

Uzziah sat there stunned for what seemed an eternity. Then he heard what almost sounded like a ringing in his ears, but he knew it wasn't. It was more like a vibration. All at once he remembered himself as spirit before he was born, and he indeed agreed to be here a long time ago. He remembered the ending of this very day that was still yet to come. He looked at Father Morales and Joseph, and everything became black around the edges. He could no longer stay seated and when he tried to stand up everything went black altogether and he fell to the kitchen floor.

"He hasn't been here a full day and he has passed out twice already," Father Morales said. "You'd better get him a glass of water."

The young man looked up to see Father Morales patting him on the cheek. As soon as his eyes came into focus he could see the old Indian standing above him.

"So is that a yes, or a no young man?" Joseph said. He was grinning from ear to ear again. All three of the men had a laugh as Uzziah sat back down at the table.

"It was the strangest experience I have ever had, indeed I remembered agreeing to do this before I was born. The answer is yes I will stay, and do that which I eagerly agreed to be a part of so long ago."

"Remember," Father Morales said.

"Every race and every religion will be represented here."

"I know," Uzziah said, "I remember."

"One way leads to diamonds, one way leads to gold,

another leads you only to everything you're told.

In your heart you wonder which of these is true,

the road that leads to nowhere, the roads that leads to you.

Will you find the answer in all you say and do?

Will you find the answers in you?"

Enya

Chapter 11—The Candidate

It had been a long hot summer in coastal Louisiana and Senator LeClaire was glad to see it come to a close. He cherished every minute he spent with the judge over the summer, but fall was coming and that meant changes were on the horizon. He also spent much of the summer pondering his future and getting back in touch with who he was, and what he hoped to accomplish in this lifetime. This had not been an easy summer for him, because he was unable to hide from the truth any longer.

During the long summer nights he spent with the judge on the front porch of the judge's home, some strange twist or shift in his consciousness occurred. He had the wisdom and the political savvy that only years of experience could bring, yet somehow he had regained the faith and fire that only a young man has when he strikes out to make his mark in this world. The faith and fire had made him a little uncomfortable in his own skin, something he had not felt in quite some time.

He embraced this feeling, because it made him feel alive again. The young man's fire in his belly urged him to face the reality of what was going on in this country and the world.

Simply putting in his time and just doing his job was no longer an option for him.

He had been walking down the beach, and now he found himself alone staring out into the gulf waters and listening to the waves lap upon the shore. The last hint of a beautiful sunset faded in the western sky as he sat down to contemplate his situation further. The newfound passion that had ignited within him made watching the events of recent months intolerable. In addition to the passion, he had also regained a young man's faith. It had been so long since he had felt this that he had forgotten what it felt like. It was a blind faith, the kind that is unavailable to a man that has denied his dreams and allowed life to dictate its terms. This brought with it the inspiration that he could and should do something about the problems currently faced by the world.

Tom lay down on his back in the sand and watched the stars as they appeared in the evening sky. His mind drifted to thoughts of the prophecy, which by now had been heard by many people. He wondered, as he looked at the stars, if there really was an asteroid headed for Earth. If so he believed that the government knew about it, and he understood why they wouldn't say anything. The realization that the prophecy was true methodically engulfed him like the pull of the tide and this led to a fear that almost ached. Just then a divine breeze blew over him, chilling his body and bringing with it the insight that even if the asteroid did hit the earth everything would still be all right.

He stayed with this thought for a few moments. After sitting up he took in a deep breath, and let it out slowly.

"It's time for this old boy to shake things up a little," he said out loud as he looked out at the sea. He stood up and headed back down the beach to where he had left his family to be alone for his walk, tingling with a feeling that his life was going to get exciting once again.

It was a Sunday morning in early October, one month from the congressional elections and a little over two years from the next presidential election. Scott arrived at the Centrust Party headquarters to meet Jack, and of all things, to stuff envelopes. Financially the party had been operating on a shoestring, and everyone was pitching in, doing what they could to keep it alive. Scott intentionally arrived 45 minutes before Jack, so he could have some time alone to think. He made the coffee, and sat down on one of the secondhand chairs at a long table that faced the front door.

A little more than a year had elapsed since the environmental conference in Las Vegas. Many times Scott feared that the Centrust Party would cease to exist. Global terrorism and the war in the Middle East were now in the forefront of everyone's minds. These issues were very important, but unfortunately they put reform on the back burner.

His thought turned to the prophecy. *If the prophecy is true the clock is ticking and we need to act now!*

The Centrust Party had candidates running in November in a few senatorial and congressional elections, but with the exception of the senator from Vermont none seemed to have a snowballs chance in hell of winning.

The governor from Minnesota had been a godsend. Even though he had decided not to run for re-election he provided the Centrust Party with a lot of publicity they wouldn't have received otherwise.

He took a couple of gulps from his coffee, and thought about those first few months after the election of the president. Scott realized at the time, that the party's notoriety, and all the attention they were getting would naturally fade, but this didn't make it any easier to accept. The party's early success had been a boon, fueled by the excitement of something that had never happened in American politics before. It would be only natural for it to fade from the limelight after the controversy about the election died down.

Scott became irritated. He realized he had been feeling sorry for himself, and few things bothered him more than self-pity. The odds against the Centrust Party becoming successful were astronomically high and he knew this when he started. Scott was standing in front of the table with his back to the door holding onto this thought when Jack arrived.

"Good morning Scott, how's it going this morning?" He stood a couple of feet inside the office doorway waiting for Scott to turnaround. This was the way Jack was. He did very little unconsciously, and this included greeting someone he had greeted a thousand times before. This was one of the qualities Scott appreciated in Jack.

"I'm good Jack. How are you?" Jack glanced down at the floor and shuffled his feet a little bit. This let Scott know that he was uncomfortable with him being less than truthful.

"I'll be a lot better once I get a cup of that coffee," Jack said. He walked over to the coffee pot and as he made his coffee he began to whistle one of the sacred songs he so often whistled.

After stirring his coffee he joined his friend at the table. They sat down together to finish their coffee before they started work when Scott came clean.

"Actually, before you arrived, I was wallowing a bit in self-pity about our progress over the past several months." There were a couple of moments of silence as Jack nodded his head in acknowledgement.

"Don't be so hard on yourself Scott." Scott realized as he looked into his friends eyes that they were extremely bright. Jack was almost always bright and sometimes it made Scott feel uncomfortable, today however, Jack was brighter than usual. His smile suggested that he knew something that Scott didn't.

Scott didn't know what he would have done the past several months without this friendship. Jack had always been there for him, and he required nothing in return. Jack's response was always, "Don't worry yourself Scott, if I need something I'll ask." In the year and a half that Scott had known Jack he had never seen him worried, and couldn't recall ever having seen him tense.

He had however, seen him become serious and most notably this occurred when the two men would discuss the prophecy that appeared on the Internet. Both men believed major global changes were on the way, simply because the earth could no longer tolerate the treatment she received at the hands of mankind for much longer.

"Do you think we will wake up in time to save the earth?" Scott asked Jack once during one of their many conversations.

"It's not the earth I am concerned about," Jack said. "She will save herself. Will she hit the reset button on the human race? Now that's the question."

During these conversations Scott couldn't seem to keep fear from creeping over him like a thick black smoke. Jack on the other hand did not become fearful, just serious. The way Jack looked at these things helped Scott clear away the cloud of fear.

"Don't run from your fear Scott, turn and face it. Then embrace it, and let it teach you," Jack said to him once. Scott could feel the question he wanted to ask move up from his heart and into his throat only to get stuck there, like it had so many times before. He was afraid to ask Jack whether he believed the prophecy was true or not. Scott knew he just wasn't ready to hear the answer, and his friend being the man that he was, would never give anyone information they weren't ready for. So there they sat, the shaman, and the founder of the Centrust Party, stuffing envelopes on a Sunday morning in October.

Scott decided he was ready for an answer.

"Jack do you believe the prophecy is true?"

Jack laughed and shook his head. "I love the way you do that."

"Do what?"

"Start a conversation from out of nowhere," Jack said. He turned to look into the eyes of his friend, and determine if he was ready to hear the answer to the question he just asked. He looked deep into Scott's left eye for so long that Scott thought he might have to look away.

"I not only believe that it is true, but I know that it is," Jack said. He paused to take a sip of coffee.

"Do you remember when I referred to the senator's phone call in the natural food store that day we first met." Jack paused took a deep breath and let it out slowly. He appeared to be listening to a distant voice. Scott had seen Jack do this before, but never asked him about it either.

"Yes, I remember," Scott said.

"The people who have delivered this prophecy are some of the people who have been sent to help you. I knew about them before I even met you. I also knew about the asteroid beforehand."

Scott leaned back in his chair in silence. Jack got up to get himself another cup of coffee and let his friend take a minute to digest what he had just told him. When he returned to the table Scott hadn't moved a muscle.

"So you see my dear friend," Jack said. "You have never been alone at any time during this adventure over the last year and half. The wheels were in motion long before our current president even considered running for office. It takes the universe some time to work out things of this magnitude."

Scott cleared his throat. "What's a man supposed to do with information like that?"

"Hold it," Jack replied without hesitation.

"That's easy for you to say," Scott said. Jack put his hand on Scott's shoulder.

"Try to relax Scott, and remember you agreed to this a long time ago. You are not alone. There's an army behind you." Jack paused for a moment and then stated the obvious. "I'm sure you realize that you should be very careful who you share this information with."

Jack returned to the task at hand and began stuffing envelopes once again. When Scott didn't return to working in a couple of minutes he turned to him and said, "This is a very big day for you Scott, and for the Centrust Party. Don't refuse to be present in it, because I answered a question you already knew the answer to."

Scott didn't know what he felt at that moment, but Jack was right: he knew a long time ago that the prophecy was true. He just didn't have the courage to face it. After a couple more minutes of contemplation he returned to stuffing envelopes with his "well-connected" friend.

Tom LeClaire sat in a coffee shop across the street from his true destination in Phoenix that weekend. He had come here under the guise of visiting some old friends. After spending Friday evening and all day Saturday with his friends he sat there trying to shake off the fear, and come up with the courage to walk across the street and do what he came to do.

The fear he felt now surprised him somewhat, because the decision he made a couple of weeks ago was accompanied only by excitement. His fear was understandable because once he walked across the street his life would never be the same. *Enough with the melodrama* he thought as he gulped down his last swig of coffee. He tossed the cup in the garbage, and opened the door to walk out onto the sidewalk. He smiled as his thoughts told him it was not too late to change his mind. He walked into the street, and was about to cross when a truck whizzed by.

"C'mon Tom," he said out loud. "Pay attention or you won't even live long enough to get over there."

He ran across the street onto the driveway of the office building, took a hard right onto the sidewalk and was in front of the door. He reached down to open it when he noticed his palms were sweaty and it wasn't just because of another hundred-degree October day in Phoenix. The prominent senator with such a long distinguished career was about to abandon his party without notice and make a run for the presidency of the United States on a third party ticket.

Scott was in the backroom getting more supplies when the senator from Louisiana walked in. Jack stood up immediately, walked around the table, and greeted the senator with a smile.

The senator began to introduce himself. "Hi, I'm Tom LeClaire from—

"Oh, I know who you are senator, and I know where you're from. Allow me to introduce myself. My name is Jack Anderson. Would you like to sit down?" He motioned to a chair in front of the table with its back to the door.

"Thank you."

"Would you like a cup of coffee?" Jack said.

"That would nice. Thank you."

Jack was pouring the senator a cup of coffee when Scott returned from the storage room. He froze in the doorway with his arms full and his mouth open when he saw the senator. Scott's mind raced through a thousand different reasons why this man could be here, but none of them were as exciting as the truth. Scott had talked with the senator about a couple of different issues over the last year and a half, but at no time did the senator give any indication that he would visit, or was at all interested in the Centrust Party. Scott set down his armful of boxes, and walked over to greet him.

"Hello Senator, I'm Scott Stahl, it's a pleasure to finally meet you in person."

"The pleasure is all mine Scott. I've been wanting to meet you for sometime."

"Well Thank you," Scott said.

Jack returned with Tom's coffee and sat down as calmly as if he was sitting down at his own kitchen table with an old friend.

After some small talk that only added to the uncomfortable feeling of this unexpected meeting, Tom got to the point of his visit. This made Jack smile, and Scott sit on the edge of his seat.

"As both of you know I have decided not to run for another term in the Senate next month," he said. "What you don't know, is that I've been deeply disturbed about a myriad of issues, and the lack of any real progress by our government in resolving them. I am no longer comfortable with our current pace of moving forward as a nation, not to mention as a species. For years now I have watched and waited as Washington whittles time away. Over the past couple of years there has been a churning inside of me that has left me with the sense that time is running out. I have tried to avoid this feeling, but every time I do it either brings me great pain, or I run right back into it. It is for this reason that I am here to inform you that I intend to seek the nomination of your party to run for President in the next election."

Tom sat back in his chair relieved. He felt as if he had released a burden he had been carrying his whole lifetime. Scott slumped back into his chair speechless.

Jack's grin widened. "Sometimes Senator we run away from, other times we run towards. What we find out is that it really doesn't matter which way we run. It is the movement that is important."

Tom smiled warmly at Jack and nodded in agreement. He felt more alive at that moment than he had in some time. It felt like an autumn so long ago when he left the judges porch as a young man to set out and make a difference in this world.

Scott couldn't believe his ears. This would undoubtedly raise the Centrust Party from the dead. He also found it hard to believe that his friend Jack would give the prominent senator spiritual advice after only meeting him five minutes earlier. This was Jack however, present and almost always comfortable in every moment.

The air was electric and full of energy. Each man had awareness that they were participants in a special moment in time. In this atmosphere the beginning of the special relationship between these three men was forged. Almost a full minute of silence ensued before they discussed what their next move would be.

"C'mon Scott that's not very nice. You should never tease me about something like that," Helen said.

"I am not kidding you Helen!" Scott shouted. "Jack is right here and if you don't believe me you can ask him. We sat here one hour ago and listened to Tom LeClaire tell us the reasons why he wants to seek the nomination as the presidential candidate for the Centrust Party."

Helen let out a shriek and you could hear her feet tapping as she was running in place. "Oh my God Scott this is unbelievable. I told you something great was going to happen didn't I," she said referring to Scott's recent battle with doubt.

"This is excellent! We are going to have to come up with the greatest media event ever to make this public." Helen caught herself and snapped off the question Scott had been waiting for.

"Who else knows about this?" She asked.

"You, me, Jack, the senator, and I would suppose his wife, and anyone else he has told, although I'm sure his list is very short," Scott said. He began laughing and Helen smiled on the other end of the line. She and Scott had gotten to know each other very well.

"It goes no further, I mean no leaks Scott," she said. "We want to capture all of the media's attention as we come in like a surprise storm out of nowhere."

"I will be telling Elizabeth," Scott said as Helen paused to take a breath.

"That's fine as long as you swear her to secrecy." Helen and Scott made arrangements for him and the others to come to California and brainstorm on a plan to bring Tom LeClaire's candidacy public.

After hanging up the phone Helen sat down on her couch to ponder what had just happened. She had really never lost faith completely yet, like Scott, she had her doubts. She just kept them to herself. Little did Helen know that there were so many people of true power behind them who never had any doubt. She continued to sit there for a few minutes in complete silence and let the days events sink in.

Her mind would not rest long however, and she began to think about what to do next. It was October and congressional elections were next month. She wondered if now would be the best time for their media event. Thanksgiving, Christmas, and New Years were not far off. These might be a better time to go public with their candidate.

Helen completely lost track of time as her mind mulled over what to do. Before she knew it she realized her phone call with Scott had ended over an hour ago.

One day turned into two days and Helen became anxious over not having a plan. Up until this point each idea for every major press conference had come easily to her. Except for its founding, this was by far the biggest event in the young party's history, and the answer to her problem was proving to be elusive. At the end of the second day she decided to call Scott, and ask him if he had any ideas.

"Why don't you call the senator," Scott said. "He's in Washington now, but I have his home phone number. You can call and leave a message for him to call you back, I'm sure he'll call as soon as possible."

"Thank you Scott that's exactly what I should do," Helen said.

Helen called Tom LeClaire's home the next morning, and after having a nice conversation with his wife Trish she left a message for him to call her. Helen was a bit nervous about her first business conversation with the senator. She was very concerned about making the most of his candidacy announcement, and she also wanted the relationship between her and Tom LeClaire to be comfortable. Her fears were completely alleviated when the senator returned her phone call that evening. She discussed her dilemma about struggling with the time frame for the news conference announcing his intentions. After a warm conversation he told her he would think about it for a few days and call her back. Helen hung up the phone relieved.

Tom LeClaire returned to Washington a new man, with a new lease on life after his meeting with Scott and Jack. As he went about his business he realized that the transition that was occurring in his life paralleled something he had read about major life changes. The author he was thinking about explained that our lives move in a particular direction based on the decisions that we make at critical times and then gain momentum tracking forward in that one direction. The author called this the momentum tunnel, and 98% of what happens in our lives occurs within this narrow tunnel because of the momentum our lives have taken on. Making significant changes in life are hard for most people because breaking out of this tunnel involves the risk of venturing into unfamiliar territory that is beyond what they believe is possible. Tom thought about how he dreamed about completely changing his life and his impact on this world.

As he walked to his office he smiled as he remembered almost word for word something that was written in this book.

"Every once in a while a great person comes along. This person does not believe he or she is any better or greater than any other person, this person, however, is aware of the greatness in every human being. When this person visualizes turning the momentum tunnel of their life he or she feels and sees how this will positively impact others. Doing so adds incredible power to their experience and helps that person to perceive dramatic change in life as being achievable. Being able to visualize and feel that the change has actually occurred is generally the last step before the dream starts to become a reality."

Tom realized that over the past year his life had involved shifting his own momentum tunnel. When he put what he had visualized into action, he began to feel like he was living in a dream. As he looked around the capital that day he saw a place full of possibilities and everything looked different even though he had been there for years.

Now, if we can turn the momentum tunnel of this country and the planet, then we will really be on to something.

Over the remainder of the week when he had the time, Tom thought about how to announce his candidacy and maximize the publicity. This would be something they could do only once and, like Helen, he wanted to get it right. On his weekend flight back to Louisiana his mind drifted to one of the conversations he had with the judge. He recalled talking about the progress that has been made over the last 30 years. His oldest son would be turning 30 soon and now had children of his own. This was the reason he was going to run for president to create a better world for his children's children.

His son's 30th birthday would be January the second and he would discuss holding the press conference on that day with Helen. They could alert the media a couple of days before Christmas and this would allow plenty of time for speculation and anticipation to grow. He wondered with everything else that was going on in the world, if the Centrust Party could grab the public's attention once again. This was no small concern to him.

But let's face it, he thought, *there is something greater at work here than just the Centrust Party and myself.*

The next day at home in Louisiana Tom called Helen Shultz to tell her about his idea for the timing of their announcement.

"Hello Helen, how are you doing this afternoon?"

"I'll be doing a lot better once we come up with a plan."

"Well, I wanted to run something by you that's been rattling around in my head."

"At least you've got something rattling around up there, my mind seems to be on vacation lately," Helen said.

"For quite sometime I've been concerned about leaving our children and their children a better life than the one we have, not only economically but environmentally. Our focus as a nation has always been on economics with concern about the environment only as an after thought."

"Yes you're right. Prioritize our own lifestyles at all costs," Helen said.

"Exactly, but I don't believe we have the time to turn a blind eye to how we are affecting the earth and it's ability to sustain life for too much longer. I don't see this as a take one and leave the other proposition. In other words I believe we can build an earth-friendly economy that can be sustained indefinitely, but we must start immediately."

"Your preaching to the choir here, senator," Helen said.

"What I propose we do is have the press conference on January second. It's my oldest son's birthday. He has a son of his own now and this is why I'm running, for my children's children and their children. I thought this could be the theme for my speech when I announce my candidacy."

"This idea has some potential and it's definitely consistent with the Party's founding principles," Helen said.

"I thought we could announce the press conference right before Christmas and this will leave plenty of time for speculation and anticipation to grow over the holidays."

"Now that's a great idea, I love keeping the press guessing. Maybe you could discuss this with Scott, he's been doing all of our speech writing and I'm sure he would love to work on your speech with you," Helen said.

"Ohhh…that's who it is," Tom said. "I've been wondering who's been writing your speeches. He's been doing a great job."

"Yes he has been," Helen said.

"That's just what I'm going to do. I've got to get going now. We'll talk soon and I look forward to getting to know you better."

"Thank you senator."

"Your welcome and would you please call me Tom?"

"Ok. Thank you Tom."

After returning from his Sunday afternoon visit with the judge. Tom called Scott and they talked for three hours. The two men became fast friends during this phone conversation. They discussed their passion for politics, this country, and people in general. Scott took notes during their conversation about the issues they both felt so passionately about and how to weave them into a speech that would arouse the passion of the voters. Both men left the conversation filled with excitement, and renewed hope for the future.

Over the next couple of months the founding members of the Centrust Party met with their new candidate three times at Helen Schultz's home in Los Angeles. This was selected as a meeting place to avoid media attention, and keep the upcoming announcement a surprise. Helen put everyone up at her house. As a result the group became an even tighter knit organization and everyone got a chance to get to know Tom personally. They hammered out the details for the upcoming speech and dreamed together about the kind of world they all wanted to leave for their children.

During his second visit to California, Tom had an interesting dream. In this dream he learned that Jack Anderson, Scott's friend whom he had met that first day at the Centrust Party headquarters, would become a very important person in his life.

"It is of the utmost importance that you keep him close to you," a voice told him in his dream.

The next morning Tom approached Scott. "Where is your friend who was with us at the headquarters that Sunday morning in October?"

"You mean Jack?" Scott said.

"Yes…is he employed by the party?"

Scott laughed. "Actually Tom, no one has really been employed by the party as of yet. We're all volunteers. Jack is a registered member of the party, and a close friend, but that's all."

"Is there any way for him to be with us, or could he be employed by the party so that we can keep him near us at all times?" This question got Scott's attention. He looked into the Tom's eyes for an answer to what this conversation was really about.

"What's going on Tom?"

"I really don't want to get into it right here, right now, but I was impressed with him that day in the office, and I would like him to be an integral part of this campaign."

Scott could see from the Tom's eyes that this was all the information he was going to get for the time being.

"Sure, I'll talk to the others and see what we can do about having Jack become our first campaign worker."

Scott spoke with the others later that month about bringing Jack into the campaign. They agreed without any reservations, because the list of things that needed to get done was growing and they desperately needed help. This was how Jack

Anderson became the first full time Centrust Party employee. When Scott called Jack to ask him if he would consider the position Jack didn't seem surprised at all, and accepted the position without hesitation.

"Oh people look among you it's there your hope must lie.
There's a seabird above you gliding in one place
like Jesus in the sky."

Jackson Browne

Chapter 12 — The Stage

Everything was in place and, three days before Christmas, the Centrust Party announced they would be holding a press conference at a mountain preserve park in Phoenix on January the second.

Just as Tom LeClaire had predicted, this led to a feeding frenzy of speculation over the holiday period. During this particular time there were no major news stories and the media had little to do but speculate on the upcoming press conference. "This is perfect," Helen remarked to Scott.

The big day came and a crowd of media personnel converged on the mountain park. The scene was picturesque except for the brown cloud of smog that obscured the view of the mountains on the other side of the city. To Scott's surprise Jack said he wouldn't be on the stage behind the candidate with the others that morning.

"I'll be out in the crowd mingling with them to get a feel for how they're receiving our message."

"Ok, if that's what you want," Scott said. He was somewhat puzzled.

A platform was set up so that the press could see Tom LeClaire and he could see the audience without the sun being in their eyes.

When the press saw Tom LeClaire walk onto the stage there was a frenzy of activity among them. Several got on their cell phones immediately to inform their superiors what they believed was about to happen. The sudden media response that resulted was more than anyone had expected.

Helen Schultz's stepped up to the microphone at the podium. "From the look on most of your faces I would say that we've done a good job of keeping the details of this press conference a surprise. So without further fanfare I will turn over the microphone to Tom LeClaire the former senator from Louisiana."

Tom walked confidently up to the podium, took a deep breath and started the prepared statement he and Scott had written together.

"I want to start today by thanking the founders of the Centrust Party for having a dream, and maintaining the focus necessary to make that dream a reality. For quite some time now I have been concerned about many of the challenges that confront us as a nation, and as a planet. To me the significance of this particular day is that exactly 30 years ago my first child was born. Now a grown man, my son has a son of his own and it is for my grandson's children's, children that I am announcing my intention to seek the nomination of the Centrust Party, to run for the presidency of the United States." At first the crowd went silent, and then there was a buzz of conversation. When this died down Tom continued.

"We live in the greatest country in the world, of this there can be no doubt. With greatness, however comes responsibility. The word responsibility has its root in the word response. It is time for us as a nation to respond to a call from the earth and from all its children. That call beckons us to reduce our impact on the earth and ensure our long-term survival.

When my son was born 30 years ago, we had an oil embargo. In the 30 years that have elapsed since then, America has become increasingly more dependent on foreign oil, and on burning fossil fuels for energy. Very little has been done in response to that warning 30 years ago. This has led to two unfortunate circumstances. The first is that our ever-increasing appetite for oil has dictated our foreign policy. Our dependence on foreign oil, at the very least, creates an air of impropriety when it comes to our foreign policy in dealing with oil-producing nations. What kind of world would we be living in if over the last 30 years a serious effort had been made to improve and promote public transportation and to develop alternative fuels to reduce this dependency? It is impossible to predict how much more effective we could have been in helping a region of the world that cannot seem to get a grip on lasting peace, if we weren't influencing their economics and politics so strongly.

Another unfortunate, and perhaps even more important byproduct of this country's energy policy, is the effects that burning fossil fuels have on our environment. My son now has a son of his own and his name is Seth. If we continue to unconsciously burn fossil fuels at such an accelerated pace, and set the standards of consumption that developing nations aspire to emulate, what kind of atmosphere will we be leaving Seth's children?"

Tom paused and looked around the audience making eye contact with various people, as if he was waiting for an answer to the question. Anyone could tell that this question was close to the hearts and minds of most of the people in attendance.

"In 1973, the year my son was born, many of you may remember the long gas lines. That year our government spent only $0.02 of every tax dollar on energy and the environment. Ten years later, as our dependency continued to grow, the federal government's spending grew to whopping $0.03 of every tax dollar for energy and the environment. In 1993, 20 years after the embargo, our spending for energy and the environment was back down to only $0.02 of every tax dollar collected. This year, 30 years later our nation will spend only $0.02 out of every tax dollar on energy and the environment. This trend is not going to lead to developing alternative renewable sources. Indeed, we know that alternatives are available, but we are just not pursuing them because of the influence of special interest and the federal government's unwillingness to guide us in the right direction.

The environmental community includes some world-renowned scientists who have been ringing the alarm bell for some time now. One thing they all seem to agree on is that we don't have another 30 years to debate on a course of action. Even if you don't believe the environmentalists, you have only to look out your own windows at the air quality in our major cities. This should provide the only proof you need."

All at once, the audience looked up at the brown cloud that obscured the view of the beautiful mountains on the other side of the valley. The air became electric, and many, who were of a sensitive nature, became aware that something special was going to happen.

"The next issue the Centrust Party has so boldly come out in favor of is the growing of industrial hemp. Today 95% of America's forest cover has already been depleted largely due to the fact that 50% of all wood that is harvested is chipped for paper. We could go on at length about the environmental effects of this country's, and the world's deforestation. Today I will mention three key benefits that our forests provide us. None of which we can do without. First, our forests produce oxygen for us to breathe. Second, they regulate our atmospheric process."

At this point, Tom paused for only a second to take a breath, when suddenly there was a huge clap of thunder that rumbled through the valley. This amazed all who were present, because there were only a few clouds in the sky, and none of them were thunderclouds.

After the sound of thunder died down, a large red tailed hawk circled above the stage and then landed on the top of a saguaro cactus directly behind where Tom stood at the podium. The audience was stunned.

Tom smiled warmly and continued: "Third, our forest's massive root systems prevent soil erosion. What will my son tell my grandson 30 years from now, when he wants to have children? That we were too afraid to restructure the paper industry because some people might lose their jobs? Or that some people might try to smoke the product we could have made paper out of and as a result of these things we continued to cut down the world's forests and throw them into a landfill.

The Centrust Party has also made campaign finance reform central to their party platform. There has been some legislation enacted recently that represents a step in the right direction, and I would like to thank the members of congress who worked so diligently to create it. We still have, however, a long way yet to go to eliminate the extraordinary influence of special interests in Washington. Eliminating the practice of adopting legislation that is favorable to the few instead of the many is essential if we are going to shift from an economy that will burn through the earth's remaining resources in the next 30 years to an economy that is truly sustainable. This shift is necessary to leave the kind of country and world to our grandchildren's children that we all dream of.

Special interest is also woven into the tax code in this country. In no area of our lives would we accept anything as inefficient and cumbersome as our tax code. No company in the world could stay in business if its business plan was as complicated as our tax system. Personally, none of us would choose to conduct our affairs in such an inefficient fashion. Why we have put up with this for so long could be a matter of discussion for another time. Should we continue to support the current tax code when doing so results in higher taxes for all of us? This is the question I pose to all you today! The Centrust Party has answered this question with a resounding, no! It has become obvious that a substantial tax cut could be afforded to us all by eliminating the current tax code and moving forward with simplicity. Now, it is time for action!

We propose and support a progressive flat tax with no deductions for individuals and an overhaul of the tax code for businesses and corporations that includes incentives to reduce our impact on the environment. I realize that adopting such reform is going to bring a lot of criticism from charities, and other organizations, but let me remind you all, that this would mean a lower tax burden for all of us. People do not give to charities solely for the tax deduction. Under this tax reformation, they would have more money to contribute to charities or anything else they choose to invest in. Those of us who are fortunate enough to own our own homes don't do so because of the tax deduction, we own our own homes because we prefer living in a home to the alternatives."

Tom took a deep breath and shook his head in bewilderment.

"The current tax code consists of 982,000 words detailing the income tax laws. Income tax regulations that provide guidance we all need to calculate our taxable income have grown to 5,947,000 words. The inefficiency is appalling, not to mention the amount of paper that is wasted. By far the most disturbing numbers of all come in the form of compliance costs. These are estimates, but nonetheless need to be heard.

In 2002, according to the tax foundation, a 65 year old independent organization dedicated to public education on taxes, the time required for business and nonprofit organizations to comply with our tax regulations was an estimated 5.8 billion man hours. This amounted to imposing a 20.4 cent tax compliance surcharge for every dollar the income tax system collected." Tom paused to let these numbers sink in.

"Imagine the resources a simple progressive flat tax could free up, and the result this would have on our economy!" He said with enthusiasm. "Also when compliance costs are examined by income level they are completely regressive. Lower income taxpayers pay more in compliance costs as a percentage of their income. The Centrust Party believes with great conviction that it is time to end this insanity and abolish the current tax code by putting into place a progressive flat tax with no deductions. This paves the way for deeper campaign finance reform as we eliminate the influence of special interests through a tax-advantaged system."

Tom paused for a long moment and looked around at his audience, as he did the red tail hawk stood up and spread its wings behind him. Scott was astonished as was everyone else in attendance.

Scott scanned the audience anxious to see the look on Jack's face, but he couldn't find him. *Well there are a lot of people here,* he thought, *maybe he's just standing behind someone else.*

Tom began to conclude his speech.

"We are setting out to create something new. A governmental culture that is no longer bound by special interests. One that is able to act responsibly and quickly to the needs of all its citizens and businesses alike. I am standing here today to announce my intention to become the next President of the United States of America, not for myself, not for the Centrust Party, but for my grandsons children, and your grandchildren's children. Thank you, and may God bless America."

There was a round of applause, and when it was over the hawk spread its giant wings and flew over the podium and the crowd towards the mountains behind them.

"We will now take a few questions." He pointed to Kate Seymore the reporter from CNN.

"Your speech makes it sound as if we are completely on the wrong track. Other than supporting your new party, what do you propose the common citizen do regarding the issues you spoke of?"

"As a nation we have made an incredible amount of progress as the freest society in the world. However, some of what we are doing doesn't make any sense for the long-term survival of the world we know today. According to the 2000 census there are over 287 million people living in this country, and over 6 billion on the planet. In America we consume far more than our share of the world's resources. What will happen to the earth as the world economy becomes more of a reality and the rest of the world emulates our lifestyles?"

Tom paused at this point, it almost appeared as if he was asking some higher power whether he should continue with this point or not. "I think we all know the answer if we are honest with ourselves. The earth cannot support 6 billion people engaged in the kind of uncontrolled consumerism that we exhibit in this country." This comment made Helen Shultz wiggle in her seat.

"There has however, been a shift starting in American consumerism. Some of our wealthiest citizens have been buying open land, and setting it aside as wilderness. Consumers are flocking to buy the few alternative fuel vehicles that are available, because they sense intuitively that this is the correct thing to do. Organic food sales are skyrocketing. Growing food organically is not only better for our health, but is also environmentally friendly. Vegetarianism is on the rise, especially among young adults. It is not by denying our consumerism that we change our current course, it is by embracing it. Each and every American has the power to shift our economy to one that can be the envy of the world not only economically, but environmentally as well by supporting earth friendly practices with their consumerism. Businesses and corporations will follow the consumer and give them what they want. This is how we envision America leading the world into a sustainable economy."

Helen let out a sigh of relief and sat back in her chair. Scott turned and smiled at her.

"So you see, it is through capitalism and consumer consciousness that we can have the most influence. The goal of all Americans throughout our history has been to leave a better world to our children. At the Centrust Party it is our utmost priority to leave a world to our children that is better, both environmentally and economically."

"Yes," Tom said as he acknowledged another reporter.

The reporter stood up and asked, "Did anyone in the Democratic Party know you were going to do this today? Also, why didn't you seek their nomination for the presidency?"

"The answer to your first question is no. I came to this decision by consulting only with my immediate family and my closest friends." Tom took a deep breath, and for the first time, Scott felt the pain that the senator felt in leaving the party that he had contributed so much to over the years. "In response to your second question, the reason I didn't seek the democratic nomination for President is because our two-party system has become so entangled with special interests that it is virtually impossible to tell them apart any longer. I believe that catering to so many special interests hampers the progress this country needs to make. I feel the only way for us to progress in a meaningful way is to speak directly to the hearts and minds of the American people. The Centrust Party, as you all know, will only take contributions from individuals within the current campaign finance laws. This allows us to speak directly to the hearts of the American people and engage in dialogue on that level to determine how we are to move forward as a country."

Tom took a few more questions and he told the reporters that they could find out where the Centrust Party stood on the myriad of other issues by visiting their web site. He also asked for the public's support monetarily, because without the resources of soft money the road to the party's success was going to be an uphill climb, financially. He did indicate that he believed the American people would come through with the support the Centrust Party needed to offer an alternative in the next presidential election.

Helen Shultz stepped forward and indicated that would be all the questions for now. As everyone was walking off the stage one reporter shouted a question to the candidate. "Mr. LeClaire, do you believe the prophecy is true? When He heard this question he stopped dead in his tracks, thought for a moment, turned around and walked back to the microphone.

"I believe we should act as if it is."

The event concluded with those words. Jack was waiting for the others at the limousine for the ride back to the party's headquarters in Tempe.

"There you are," Scott said. "Where have you been? I couldn't find you in the crowd."

"Oh, I've been around," Jack said shrugging his shoulders. After everyone had climbed into the limousine, and it was pulling away Scott turned to Jack.

"Incredible, that clap of thunder and its timing was unbelievable!"

"That it was," Jack replied as he gazed across at Tom LeClaire.

Helen couldn't wait to see the news coverage. The clap of thunder and the large hawk directly behind the candidate were the kinds of images that a promoter's dreams are made of. The news coverage was nothing short of phenomenal. Every station across the country showed video containing the clap of thunder, and some carried the speech in its entirety. Many included footage of Tom coming back to the podium to answer that final question. Even news programs in some other countries carried the story. The Centrust Party was not only back, but soon they would once again be in the hearts and minds of all Americans.

It had been almost one year since Michael Fisher the astronomy student from Boston University made his ill-fated discovery. The past year was filled with difficulties to say the least. He was no longer enrolled at the university and was more or less a prisoner at Lowell Observatory. Michael had been cleared by security to embark on the work that began with his discovery. However, the authorities were concerned about his ability to keep it secret. He kept in contact with his family and friends so as not to arouse suspicion. Michael convinced them that leaving school temporarily and staying on for another year of internship at the observatory was good for his career.

He was not allowed any unsupervised contact with the outside world. Even to the point of being accompanied when he went into town. His emails and any other kind of correspondence were also being monitored. Shortly after his discovery Michael slipped into a deep depression. At times he felt the secret was too much to bear. It was funny though, because to him, all the surveillance was unnecessary. He couldn't even imagine telling anyone about the asteroid. Sometimes he wished he didn't know about it at all.

A CIA staff psychiatrist was brought in to help him deal with keeping the secret. This psychiatrist had been responsible for counseling many members of the CIA who had been involved in various undesirable operations, leaving them scarred and with secrets to keep themselves. This psychiatrist was very helpful to Michael. He taught him how to keep a secret even from himself by living in the moment. At any time that Michael felt he needed it, this psychiatrist was made available for him to speak to. Through speaking to this man Michael was able to let go of his resentment of not being allowed to return to his normal life.

The only way that Michael was truly able to keep up with the outside world was through television. *Thank God for cable,* he thought. Growing up he had never been the type of child who spent much time in front of the television set but this changed dramatically during his time at the observatory just south of Flagstaff, Arizona. Daily he scoured news programs and any programming that had to do with science looking to see if news of the asteroid had gotten out. About two months ago there was a documentary on the Discovery Channel about how the prophecy that had been circulating the Internet was very similar to prophesies that where hundreds even thousands of years old.

This documentary detailed what was in the prophecy and also discussed people's growing interest in it. Michael almost fell off the couch when the narrator talked about the part of the prophecy in which an asteroid was forecast to eliminate 80% of the world's population if man didn't wake up and assume his true role as a caretaker of the planet. What troubled Michael the most was that the earth's requirements to avoid this cleansing were very simple, straightforward, and achievable.

In the last month various religious leaders had started to weigh in on the talk show circuit as to whether they thought the prophecy was authentic. Most of the leaders believed that if the prophecy were authentic it would have been brought forward by one of the major religious leaders. The few who believed in the prophecy's authenticity were ridiculed, and even labeled as quacks. Michael thought that this behavior was typical of people in power. They get a clear message to move forward or in a different direction, and the first order of business is always to argue about whether moving is necessary. He supposed that if they did determine the message was correct, the next step would be to argue over what to do about it. Unfortunately, when it came to this message there was no time to conduct business as usual.

Due to the earth's simple requirements Michael began to feel a growing responsibility to let people know. He would ask himself daily. *What can I do? I'm under almost constant surveillance.* He wondered how many other people knew about the secret and if they were they also put under wraps. Michael made a decision not to talk to the psychiatrist or anyone else about these thoughts.

One night, like so many others before, Michael had a terrible time falling asleep. After a lot of tossing and turning, he decided to pray. This posed a dilemma for him because he had never prayed before. He was raised in a household without strong spiritual beliefs. He was, however, desperate and willing to try almost anything. He took a deep breath and spoke out loud.

"Dear God. I do not know who you are and have never spoken with you before. In fact, up until this past year, I didn't even believe in your existence. I am sorry. Please forgive me. My burden has become more than I can bear. I wish to do my part. I feel this is the only way to lighten my load. I long to let others know that the prophecy is true, so that they can make their own decision on whether they want to fulfill the earth's requirements. I feel trapped and unable to do this. Please help me."

Michael took another deep breath and exhaled all the stress from his being, and fell into a deep, deep sleep.

Some time after falling asleep Michael begin to dream. An angel came to him in his room and beckoned him to follow her. He was afraid and unable to move.

"Do not be afraid," the angel said. "I have been summoned to bring you to a very special place." Michael allowed himself to go with the angel, and the next thing he knew they were in a beautiful forest. The angel told him to sit down on a fallen tree and wait. The forest was his favorite place on earth. He could smell the scent of pine, and hear the breeze rustling through the tops of the trees.

Michael became aware he was not alone; there was a presence other than the forest there with him. Shortly after he became aware of this, a brilliance appeared moving through the forest towards him and he was filled with awe. His mind could not describe its beauty and the way it made him feel in words. The brilliance stopped about 10 yards in front of him and spoke.

"My beloved son I have heard your prayer. You are never powerless. Indeed you have all the power that is in me." Michael began to weep and shake uncontrollably because he knew in that moment that it was true. " I have heard your prayer and I am here to answer it.

It is through your breath and the air that you connect to all of life. Who is to say where the breath of one ends and another begins? Who can say where the air of one of your countries ends and another begins? There are many people all over your world who know this. Even those who do not believe in this truth receive information unconsciously through your air.

Go from this place and learn to broadcast your message through the air. Those who have ears to hear will receive your message, and those who don't will be unable to deny the truth communicated by your intention. Broadcast your message of love through meditation and prayer."

With that, the presence began to move again, and a wave of all that is passed through Michael taking with it every fear and feeling of helplessness he had in him.

When he awoke it was morning already. He could still smell the scent of pine in his room. Michael arose that morning with a new sense of purpose ready to engage life.

Meditation was something he knew a little bit about; he had been involved in yoga and yogic breathing exercises his freshman year in college. Prayer was something he would learn more about. He set out that very morning to use the breathing exercises and the meditation technique he had learned a couple of years earlier to start broadcasting his message energetically. The message was that the prophecy was true, and it was time for mankind to do something about it.

This was the beginning of the time when people would start to realize, some consciously and some unconsciously, that the prophecy was authentic. Things continued to change, and the pace began to accelerate. Little acts of mercy for the earth and between human beings continued to multiply. Scores and scores of people began living by and talking about the ten fundamentals for global transformation. Supermarkets could not seem to keep organic food on their shelves and alternative fuel vehicles had to be back ordered. Land philanthropy, unheard of two years ago continued to grow. The Centrust Party had been raised from the dead and now had a viable candidate for the presidency. When Michael felt that he wasn't accomplishing anything by broadcasting his message, he would note these signs to himself and say, "It is through our breath, and the air that we are all connected."

Uzziah had been on the Indian reservation for several months now and his time there had brought him enormous spiritual growth. He knew now why his rabbi stressed the importance of seeing God in all of nature. This was the foundation of the mystical tradition of the Kabbalist. He also found out during his months there that this was the foundation of every mystical tradition on the planet.

Joseph told him, "The way to the Father is through the Mother. The Father's love for the Mother is where we are, and it is through the Mother that we start our journey back to the Father."

A pair of shamans from Peru, one male and one female, made their way to Mountain Home a couple of months back. They were not married and Uzziah was more than curious as to why the male shaman was not put in the room with him. Father Morales just smiled when Uzziah asked him about it. He felt a bit out of place at times because everyone else was so much older, but the elders would smile at him and tell him not to fret.

"Your time is coming young man," the old woman from Peru told him.

"A time is coming when all that is will teach you of your power, and lay it at your feet. When that time comes it will be entirely up to you to face your power, embody it, and hopefully live it through love." Uzziah was unsure of the meaning of this statement, but when the shaman told him this he felt incredible energy run through his body.

One night after dinner while the elders sat around the kitchen table having coffee and enjoying each other's company, Uzziah excused himself to go outside and pray. It was early April, and the air was cool and crisp. He watched every moment of a sunset from a place he often went to pray. After the sun went down he watched the stars appear one by one in the night sky. He began to look back on all that had transpired in his life over the last couple of years. This naturally led to thinking about everything that had been happening in the world. The war in Israel, America's war on terrorism, and mankind's continued destruction of the planet. He could feel hatred start to well up inside of him and this disturbed him deeply. He had been working on releasing this negative energy, but just couldn't seem to let it go.

Several times Uzziah thought of asking the others for help, but something had stopped him. He knew deep down inside that this was his reluctance to let go of the chains that bound him. He felt that his spiritual growth had stalled during the past couple of months, and there was no hiding from himself the reason why. He began to pray with focused intensity.

His prayer opened his heart. After his heart became open he began the breathing exercise he was taught by his rabbi. He began meditating on the name of God. His rabbi taught him this as a means to induce trance. As he progressed through the name he began to feel lighter and lighter. When he made it to the end portion of the name, he fell into a trance. His mind's last thought was that he would fall off the boulder he was sitting on, yet he somehow maintained an upright position.

Uzziah was surrounded and enveloped by a white light. A realization came over him that he was everything there ever was. He didn't know how long he was in this space because there was no time there. He had the clear experience that being everything is also being nothing. This produced a longing that he could not describe. Then there was movement. It was created out of the all-knowing longing that comes from being everything. The movement produced a flood of beauty, the beauty of knowing oneself through the entirety of creation. Uzziah experienced what is the most hypnotic, intoxicating state of being known to mankind. He realized he had a choice to make as to whether he was going to return from this mesmerizing state or not.

Uzziah felt himself getting stuck in the sweetness of this beauty. Angels came and told him that it was time to come back. The angels were in a different place than he was, they were at his body on the rock. They began to gently nudge his body and lovingly encourage to return.

Slowly and not so surely Uzziah returned from that sticky sweet space. When he came back into his body he fell off the boulder onto the ground and gazed up into the stars. He had now experienced what before he had only known intellectually the separation between God and man was just an illusion. Uzziah began to weep. He wept because his heart was now fully open and full of love and truth. His heart went out to all those that didn't know this truth and this led him to a deep sadness in his soul. At that moment he heard the voice of the Father and he immediately rolled over and hid his face in the ground.

"My beloved son. Cry only in joy because of the path I have laid out before you."

Uzziah longed to look up into the face of the Father, but he knew that he wasn't ready yet.

"It is time for forgiveness; forgiveness of yourself and of others. Its power will free you from everything that binds you. Then and only then will you be ready to walk the path that I have laid out before you."

There was a long pause as tears continued down Uzziah's face making mud in the dirt he laid in. The presence was still there and he knew not to roll over.

The voice, that incredible voice that brought with it knowledge of everything in each utterance spoke one more time.

"Forgiveness my beloved son, forgiveness."

Uzziah didn't know and didn't care how long he lay in the dirt before collecting himself. He sat on his boulder staring up at the stars after getting up off the ground. Slowly he walked back to what he now called home wondering what he would say to the others about the shape he was in. His face was covered with dirt and mud. When he opened the sliding glass door on the back porch to go into the house he realized everyone had long since gone to bed.

The next morning Uzziah awoke still vibrating from his experience the night before. He got dressed and went into the kitchen to join the others for breakfast. They all smiled warmly at him and he could feel and see the love they were sending him. It was beautiful and made Uzziah completely grateful. The group ate breakfast together as was their custom.

After breakfast the group was sitting in the family room chatting and enjoying each other's company, when Talking Bird burst through the front door just as he had months earlier to announce Uzziah's arrival.

"A group of Muslims arrived at the trading post in a van," he said, "and they left one member of the group behind."

He put his hands on his knees and breathed deeply to catch his breath. " You can't miss him he's a young fellow wearing one of those round hats."

"It's called a kufi," Father Morales said as he stood up.

"Let's go," Joseph said to Father Morales. The two men grabbed their jackets and followed Talking Bird out the door to greet the new arrival. After they left the old woman from Peru turned to Uzziah smiled at him and nodded.

When Joseph, Talking Bird, and Father Morales arrived at the trading post, the young man who was dressed in a long gown was standing patiently in front of the trading post with his hands folded in front of him. He looked very out of place yet not at all uncomfortable. After some brief introductions it was apparent that the young man had not been left behind by mistake, but was here to become a member of the group. Joseph, Father Morales, and the new arrival rode in the front seat of the old pickup truck while Talking Bird rode in the back for the short drive back to Joseph's home.

Moments after making their way through the door of the Joseph's home the young man whose name was Reshad, was introduced to the rest of the group. Reshad had a quiet, almost reserved presence about him. The older members of the group immediately saw an energy of untrust, but they welcomed him with the love that comes from having an open heart. The group learned during their initial conversation that the young man's mother was a Palestinian, and his father was Egyptian. He was an apprentice studying under a renowned Sufi mystic. Reshad like Uzziah, was told to come here by his teacher who had received the message on the wind. Reshad told them of his hesitancy to do so. His teacher however, all but insisted that he come.

"Your traveling to Mountain Home and taking your seat among the others could quite possibly be the most important service you can offer in this lifetime."

In response to Reshad's hesitancy his teacher said, "This is all I can tell you about it. You must go and find out the rest for yourself, if you choose to do so."

The group continued to chat for another half hour. When Joseph got up to show Reshad to his room, Uzziah knew whom the extra bed in his room had been saved for all this time. There was something between the two young men that they both became aware of that first day. Uzziah sensed that this energy was not sourced from either one of them.

That evening after dinner Joseph and Father Morales called the young Sufi into the kitchen for a conversation. This conversation went much like the one they had with Uzziah, fainting excluded. Reshad explained to the two elders that for him to walk the Sufi way was to walk the path of service. He was then entrusted with a secret that his teacher already knew, which was that the prophecy was true and that the universe had assembled this group to help mankind through this time. Reshad went numb all over when he heard the words that his heart knew where the truth.

Over the next few weeks the two young men got to know one another. They began to talk about the mystic traditions they each belonged to. They both knew of the similarities between their paths, and they also knew that in the thirteenth century Sufi and Kabbalah mystics even studied together. Reshad and Uzziah were getting a first hand experience of how many similarities there were in their two different traditions. They would talk long into the night about the hard yet beautiful path of service that the mystic walks. During their entire first three weeks together they were both aware of this energy present between them. Each man knew that the source of this energy did not come from either of them. They didn't mention it to each other, it was just there.

One of the duties the group had taken on was to keep abreast of events in the outside world through the news media, and the Internet. They would take this information and ask Spirit to guide them in prayer. This was not an easy task, for what they saw would make their hearts heavy. Prayer and meditation would bring back the peace and understanding that can only come from divine will. One afternoon in particular, just a couple of days before the full moon ceremony, was hard on the two young men of the group.

The war in the Middle East between the Israelis and Palestinians was heating up again with no solution sight. This particular afternoon was worse than usual. A pregnant Palestinian woman was shot and in some strange twist of random chaos. That same day, a pregnant Israeli woman was also shot. Reshad and Uzziah became distraught. A dark cloud of despair blanketed the group like a thundercloud that cannot pass around a mountain and the elders of the group allowed it to remain. Not much was said that day between any of the group. Even Talking Bird was quiet.

The next morning after breakfast Father Morales called Uzziah and Reshad into the kitchen for council where Joseph was sitting waiting for them. Father Morales motioned for them to sit down, and then he took his seat at the table where an open Bible lay.

"We are all distraught from time to time over many of the things that are happening in the world today. You two young men have a very special role in God's plan for this time. The thought of this plan fills my heart with humility and gratitude," Father Morales said.

Father Morales stopped to take a deep breath, his jaw quivered and a single tear ran down his face. Joseph put his hand on Father Morales's right shoulder and he regained composure.

"You are both on a mystical path, Reshad you are studying the way of the Sufi, and Uzziah you are studying the Kabbalah. Therefore, we will use the Bible for this teaching that I have been instructed to give you. As you both know this is the book of my tradition." He looked down and read from the sixth chapter of Matthew.

"But when you pray, go into your room and shut the door and pray to your Father who is in secret; and your Father who sees in secret will reward you."

Father Morales then went to the book of Luke and read from the beginning of the 21st chapter.

"He looked up and saw the rich putting their gifts into the treasury; and he saw a poor widow put in two copper coins. And he said, truly I tell you, this poor widow has put in more than all of them; for they all contributed out of their abundance, but she out of her poverty put into all the living that she had."

Joseph and Father Morales looked at both of the young men and Father Morales asked. "What do you two suppose is the meaning of the Scriptures I just read?"

After a period of silence that was uncomfortable for the two young men Uzziah spoke first. "The teaching is about how hard it is for the wealthy to give from the heart."

"The Scripture's are also about how the path of service is to be done in secret. The widow gave all she had to give and this is also being of service," Reshad added.

"Although both answers could be interpreted as correct. You are looking at the surface of the teaching," Joseph said.

Father Morales added. "Why should a person pray in secret? Rather, what happens when we pray in secret in the presence of our Father only?"

"Could the church not do more with the larger offerings from the wealthy people's gifts?" Joseph asked. "Couldn't they accomplish more in the work for God with these larger offerings than with the two copper coins?"

Joseph paused and looked at both young men. "Are the gifts from the rich people not appreciated, and put to good use? How could the widow have put in more than all of them?"

Father Morales had a look of excitement on his face. "We want you two to spend the day together, discussing the deeper meaning of these Scriptures."

"We also want you to breathe and meditate together, and come back to us before dinner and we will discuss what you have learned between now and then." Joseph said. He smiled and winked at Father Morales.

Reshad and Uzziah went back to the room looking rather puzzled. They decided to pack a lunch and head up to the mountain to spend their day together and find the deeper meaning of the scriptures. Both men walked together in silence mulling over the words of the Scriptures. Neither man had any idea how important each of their roles would become. They left the pain of everything that was going on in the world back in the television set at Joseph's home. They spent the day together with open hearts and minds. This allowed them to become of one heart and one mind, just as each of their teachers had spoken of before they came to Mountain Home, Utah. After a beautiful day together they walked down the path filled with humility. Together the one heart and one mind of all that is had given them the answer they sought.

Before dinner Reshad and Uzziah took their seats at the table in front of the two older men as they had earlier that morning. Joseph motioned with his two hands outward for one of them to speak. Uzziah motioned with his hand to Reshad to offer him the honor of answering the question.

"We believe what you are trying to convey to us through the Scriptures is…" He paused and took a deep breath, and Father Morales smiled.

"The Scriptures are about intention. When our intent is pure we have all the power of the almighty that Jesus spoke about. With no one else around to know how or what we pray for our pure intention is assured. Pure intention unlocks the power of heaven and earth. This impeccable intention is most easily reached in secret between just ourselves and the one being we call God."

Reshad motioned for Uzziah to speak. "When the widow gave all that she had to give, she unlocked all the power of pure intention. Therefore her gift, which appears by this worlds standards to be smaller than all the other gifts, becomes greater because it has all the power of God behind it. When we have offered all that we have to God from our hearts as the widow did, all the power of the universe is behind us. This only happens as we continue to give everything we have to him in service."

Both Father Morales and Joseph had huge smiles on their faces. Uzziah and Reshad were relieved that they passed the test they couldn't know at this time how important it was. They could feel the love from both of the older men coming to them from their smiling faces and open hearts.

"Tomorrow night is the wesak moon," Joseph said breaking the silence. "People of consciousness all over the planet gather together under the same moon to transmit energy that emanates

from the very heart of God. This energy is transmitted for the
enlightenment of all mankind. We will be in ceremony together
tomorrow night at the fire. Determine using the knowledge you
were so graciously given today to decide what you wish, or
rather what the Great Spirit would wish for you to transmit."

"Very good Joseph," Father Morales said.

"It was good, wasn't it?" He smiled widely at Father
Morales.

The two young men walked away from the table to consider
what they would bring to the ceremony tomorrow night. They
talked about many things that evening, but not about what
they would bring to the fire ceremony the next evening. The
following morning without consulting one another they both
decided separately to fast for the day. Nothing was said by the
four elders when the two young men didn't show up for breakfast that morning, because their hearts were full of joy and
excitement for what was going to take place that evening.

Evening came, and the six members of the council and
Talking Bird headed up the mountain to the sacred location for
their ceremony.

The moon was so powerfully bright and the mountain at
their backs held its energy. Joseph worked the fire while the
group sang, and chanted. The four elders had made their offerings and motioned for Uzziah and Reshad to come forward to
the fire. The two young men moved slowly forward and knelt
down in front of the fire and the four elders joined hands to
hold space behind them. Their ceremony had created a vortex
unlike any Uzziah had felt before. It was so powerful he thought
for a moment that he might have to remove himself from in
front of the fire. He regained his composure and prayed.

"Great Father, I come to you with an open heart of forgiveness. It is my intention to forgive all people who have
harmed me. I also forgive all karmic debt that is owed me from
this lifetime, and all my lifetimes unless to do so would disrupt

another beings path. If you would allow me, I also wish to stand in for all the people of my faith and my race, and forgive all who have hurt the Israeli people. Thank you for bringing me here to do this."

Simultaneously Reshad was praying. "I forgive all karmic obligations from anyone to myself, unless to do so would injure them or others. I know there is only you, the one being, and I rededicate my life to the path of service this evening. If you would allow it of your servant, I wish to stand in for all the Palestinian people, my people, and forgive everyone who has ever harmed us. Thank you for allowing me to hear the call to the path of service."

The chanting of the elders was in perfect unison, and both Reshad and Uzziah could see they were all enveloped in a pillar of energy attached to the moon. This energy rang in their ears and when it peeked both young men blew their intent with their breath into their offerings. Their offerings became translucent and filled with so much energy that neither man could hold the offering in their hands any longer so they simultaneously placed them in the fire. With their offering came a whorl of fire and there was a release of energy unlike any of them had ever seen or felt before.

People of consciousness all over the world felt these acts of forgiveness by these two young men. After the energy subsided, all that was left was the glow of the moon, the mountain, and the group at the fire; they closed their ceremony and headed down the mountain.

The two young men were enthused and they wished to discuss the experience with the elders. On the way down the path the female shaman pulled them both aside.

"The word secret has its origin in the word sacred. Keep the sacred events of this evening secret within your hearts and this will lead to true humility. To even speak about what happened on that hill this evening could reduce its power."

Four or five days had passed since the fire ceremony. Reshad and Uzziah were sitting on the couch talking when Joseph walked into the room and turned on the television. He changed the channel to CNN and stood to the side so the two men could see the program. There was a news alert pertaining to the Palestinian and Israeli conflict. Apparently the terms of a cease-fire had been agreed upon. Joseph looked at Uzziah and Reshad with a smile on his face, turned and looked back at the news story, turned back to them and said.

"You can do almost anything in this world, if you let others take the credit for it." He turned off the television and walked back out of the room.

The world was a different place after people of consciousness all over the planet met that night under the wesak moon. Tom LeClaire was nominated to run for President on the Centrust Party ticket, and at his suggestion they waited to see who would show up to take the vice presidential nomination. The Democratic Party, after a bitter battle, nominated the same candidate who ran in the last election. With the unlikely exception of the Centrust Party candidate, the next presidential election would be a rematch between the two previous candidates.

Others were hearing the call to join those in Mountain Home, and began making the pilgrimage. People of consciousness from all walks of life, and all different faiths, realized the importance of all these coinciding events and their numbers grew as the time drew close.

"Great Spirit grant me vision that I may not go wrong,
and find myself in prison of things I have not done.
Teach me the secret that I might see.
Fill my heart with compassion to love my enemy."

Red Thunder

Chapter 13 — The Attack

A poll taken right after Tom LeClaire abandoned the Democratic Party and announced his intention to become the Centrust Party candidate asked a group of registered voters if they would consider voting for the third party candidate 50% said yes. From that point on Robert Kelton and Andrew Knight knew they had a problem, Knight however took it personally. His advisors were the only reason he didn't challenge Tom LeClaire to a debate before he even won his own party's nomination.

Since the completion of the primaries election polls were absolutely useless. One would have the race in a three- way tie. Another would show the incumbent winning easily, presumably because of the introduction of another major party. Knight felt he could deal with the Green party. However, adding the Centrust Party wild card to the mix, made him nervous. He felt his opportunity was slipping away again before he even had a chance to get started. Something needed to be done to turn the tide of public opinion away from the Centrust Party and back to his candidacy. Knight and his advisers felt that the only way to win the election was to destroy the Centrust Party's candidate first, and then turn their sites on the incumbent.

Almost immediately after the primary process had come to a close, and before the respective parties could even have their conventions, Knight challenged Tom LeClaire and Robert Kelton to a debate. Tom LeClaire, Scott, and Jack happened to be together at the Centrust party headquarters when Knight held his press conference to lay out the challenge.

"We've really got him sweating now Tom," Scott said without turning his attention from the television.

"I believe you're right," Tom said.

"He knows your candidacy is a real problem for him, but should we debate this early? That's the question," Scott said.

"I've known him a long time, and I would bet that he's counting on the president to turn down this challenge, so that he can go one on one with me...What do you think Jack?"

There was no reply. Tom and Scott turned their attention from the press conference to see Jack sitting by himself on a chair about six feet away staring off into space.

"Jack, are you with us here? What do you think about this debate challenge?" Jack stood up walked over to them and said.

"Your right, there's no way the incumbent will debate this soon, if ever. His press secretary will indicate later today that the president is too busy with America's business to debate at this time, especially when the parties haven't even held their conventions yet."

Jack paused and thought for a moment. "I think we should accept the challenge to debate before his people come to their senses, and he changes his mind. Your candidacy has him consumed with fear. We should be able to use this to our advantage."

The three men figured a conference call was in order, and ducked into a separate office to get away from the noise of the campaign workers.

"Hello Sam this is Scott—

"Did you see the press conference?" Sam asked.

"Yes we saw it, and that's why we're calling. Let me put you on hold and patch Helen in."

"Okay, Sam, Helen I've got Tom and Jack here with me, and we were just discussing the debate challenge," Scott said.

"Hello Helen, hello Sam."

"Hi Tom."

"Hi guys," Jack said.

"Hello Jack."

"I would like everyone to weigh in on the debate challenge. Jack thinks we should accept before our opponent comes to his senses and changes his mind," Tom said.

He turned to Jack with a smile. "Thank you for the vote of confidence Jack."

"No problem Tom," Jack replied.

"It's awful early for a debate. What do we have to gain by debating now? Thanks to the enormous amount of individual contributions, we have plenty of money," Sam said.

"Plenty of money for now, but wait until the advertising really gets cranked up," Helen said.

"You got me there," Sam said.

"Knight has everything to gain and almost nothing to lose by debating us so early. I think perhaps we should stall him. You know, make him really nervous," Scott said.

"Helen's right. His pockets are a lot deeper than ours. We need to remember that, and use every chance we can to stay in the limelight. I could see the sense of desperation in his face at the press conference. He needs to debate us as soon as possible," Tom said.

"I believe this debate is going to be our biggest publicity boon yet," Jack said

"Imagine that," Sam said.

"He is so desperate to eliminate us as an opponent, and I believe if we are coy we can negotiate almost anything we want, including the debate location," Jack said.

"The debate location?" Helen asked.

"Yes, it has to be somewhere outside. I have somewhere specific in mind," Jack said.

"Well the great outdoors has been good to us so far," Scott said.

"Then it's settled, we will accept the challenge to debate. We're going to need every bit of free publicity we can get our hands on to finish this campaign," Tom said.

"Helen will you take care of the negotiations?" Tom asked.

"I'd be glad to."

"Remember Helen—

"I know Jack, the debate location, don't worry I'll get it," Helen said.

Later that afternoon at a White House press briefing, a reporter asked the president's press secretary if he would accept the challenge to debate.

He replied. "The President is currently too busy with America's business to debate at this time, especially when the parties haven't even held their conventions yet."

It only took a month for the debate to be scheduled. Helen had quite effectively negotiated not only the debate location, but also to ensure that a variety of issues central to their candidate's campaign would be discussed. Among these were, tax reform, campaign finance reform, and a new emphasis on the environmental and energy policies of the government. The debate would be held at Dead Horse Point State Park in Utah. The two candidates would be positioned so the audience would have the breathtaking view of the canyon below as a backdrop.

Knight would approach this with a ferocity unlike any of his previous debates. He had a reputation for being a "pit bull" when it came to debating. Tom LeClaire had almost no debating reputation to speak of. For this reason Knight was over confident.

Scott, Elizabeth, Jack, Sam Jameson, Jeff Kline, and Tom LeClaire converged on the home of Helen Shultz the week before the debate to discuss strategy and rehearse.

Scott and Sam had spent the previous two weeks finding all Knight's vulnerabilities when it came to the issues they would be discussing. They were planning ways to fend off the pit bull's attacks, and counter attack his record to make him look bad.

The past few years of being attacked, personally ridiculed, and audited had hardened Scott's heart somewhat, and he seemed to have forgotten one of the reasons he started the party in the first place. This really didn't feel right to some of the group, and that afternoon while the candidate was downtown making a speech Jack suggested an alternative.

"A major reason for our popularity is because we have proposed so many common sense ways of doing things differently. If we attack the other candidate we will no longer be different, we will be common," He looked around the room at his companions.

"To attack, or even to defend oneself in fear, is to admit to ourselves that we have something to defend, or that we believe in attack as a solution."

"Are you suggesting that we don't defend ourselves, because Knight is obviously going to attack us," Sam Jameson said.

"He will also attack Tom's voting record. This will make his own record fair game, and believe me his has plenty of holes in it!" Scott added.

"What I'm saying is that I have been sitting here listening to you plan an attack on another human being, and as I do so, you all sound like every other politician I've ever seen. Is that what has brought us to this point?" Jack said

"Just what exactly are you proposing?" Scott said.

"The moment we attack the other candidate we are telling America that we are vulnerable. If we don't attack and stick to creating something new, we will not get lured into defending and attacking the rest of the campaign.

The reason we have received so much support up until now is because Americans are sick of this, and want something different. If we give them something different, I believe we will continue to ride and build on the current tide of public opinion that is currently in our favor," Jack said.

For the first time in the young party's history there was a division on how to move forward. Scott, Sam, and Jeff Kline relished the opportunity to fight during the debate. Jack and Elizabeth believed attacking was not the way to go, while Helen was on the fence and openly discussing both methods. The debate was not heated, but the group was stuck, and Scott feared they would waste too much of the time they had set aside to prepare in disagreement. When Tom LeClaire returned he found his group in a quandary for the first time. They talked late into the night about which way to proceed without coming to a solution that evening.

That night both Tom LeClaire and Scott had a dream. In their dream they saw into the hearts of the American people and felt how discouraged they had become. The American people no longer trusted the political process. In addition to this, they had no hope that their government could respond to the needs of everyday people in a timely fashion. Both men could feel the sadness of the American heart, and it was overwhelming.

"What can we do?" They asked.

"Do things differently!" A voice replied.

This was the only reminder that Scott needed; he would, however, get many more.

The next morning the group took breakfast in virtual silence. There was an air of anxiety. After breakfast Tom assembled the group and said. "I would like to weigh in on the question at hand."

"Last night I had a dream where I saw into the hearts of the American people and how discouraged they have become." Scott's face went white, and Jack smiled.

"In my dream I saw what I already knew. The American people no longer trust politicians in this country. I also saw that every day Americans no longer have any hope that their government has any true interest in responding to their needs." He paused as he thought for a moment, and Scott almost fell off his chair.

Tom had just, word for word described the exact same dream he had.

"For us to get caught in a downward spiral, of attack and defend, and attack again," he continued, "would halt the momentum of our campaign. We have come this far because the American heart is broken, and needs something different. The word trust is a part of our party's name, and people do not trust someone who is constantly attacking other people. When we attack we are saying that we believe we can be attacked. This puts us on the defensive, and people also do not trust someone who is defensive.

Therefore I propose, that at this debate we make this a campaign issue in my closing comments. Our democratic opponent is not accustomed to campaigning without attacking his opponents, and trying to instill even more fear in the hearts of the American people. It is the only way he knows. If we make this a campaign issue and he continues to campaign in this fashion, he will lose a lot of his already weakening support. This puts him between a rock and a hard place. If he tries to remake himself into something he is not, we will have to trust that the American people will see through him."

The group was amazed at the wisdom of what Tom had said, and everyone was in agreement about approaching the debate in the same spirit in which the Centrust Party was founded. The group spent the remainder of the evening rehearsing Tom, and discussing the possibilities for America if their party's platform was implemented.

That night before Tom and Scott went into Helen's den to write up some note cards, and put the closing comments down on paper, Scott had a moment where he could talk to Jack alone.

"I had the exact same dream as Tom last night!" He said.

"I know, isn't that great?" Jack replied.

The day of the debate came and it was a beautiful calm day in southeastern Utah. There were two podiums set up right out on the point, so that with the exception of a few boulders, behind the Centrust candidate the backdrop was the Utah Canyonlands. More people than had probably ever been to that point before at one time, were there to see the candidates square off. News media from all over the world, supporters for both candidates, as well as a medicine man and a priest from Mountain Home, Utah were in attendance. Father Morales and Joseph were there to bestow their blessings on the Centrust party.

Everyone from the Centrust Party except for Jack was on the edge of their seats. This included Tom LeClaire; he was very concerned, and wanted more than anything to do his best. The debate opened up with a question to Tom LeClaire about campaign finance reform to which he replied.

"Legislation has been enacted recently for campaign finance reform. It is a step in the right direction, but it still leaves plenty of room for influence by special interest groups. Our campaign as you all probably know by now, will not take any block donations from any special interest groups. We are only accepting donations from individuals up to $2000.00, which is the current limit under campaign finance law. At the Centrust Party we believe the elimination of extraordinary influence by special interests will free the intelligent people who we have elected to do the job that they were put in office for.

One of the major problems facing your legislators today is the amount of money they need to raise to run a campaign in order to stay in office. I know this because I was one of the senators for the state of Louisiana for many years. If most Americans knew how much of their legislator's time and energy was spent raising money and kowtowing to the special interest groups, they would make it politically impossible for congress and the president not to completely overhaul the system.

Campaign finance reform must fit within our constitution, and there we have a bit of a problem. The constitution requires free press. Those with money to spend can run ads in support of their candidate, or attack their candidate's opponent while the rest of America struggles to find a voice. We propose legislation that gives the other candidates equal television time to respond to the accusations that are usually made in this type of ad. With a new law such as this, individuals would still have the freedom of press, yet an under funded candidate would have equal television coverage to state his or her position. Networks would have to provide equal free airtime to the other candidates in the race. This would discourage the smear type advertising that is done by wealthy individuals, corporations and the Democratic and Republican Parties with their soft money."

This took Knight completely by surprise. To this day no one had seriously proposed something of this nature. Free airtime had been discussed before, and dismissed because of its cost to the networks. This idea did not call for completely free airtime; it did however offer a common sense way of leveling the playing field.

Knight stuttered and stammered in reply before he not so eloquently changed the subject. His response was not much of a rebuttal at all. This set the tone for the remainder of the debate.

The next question was to Knight about tax reform. He lit into the Centrust Party's progressive flat tax claiming it was a plan that would penalize charitable organizations. "I don't think what the American people want is to hurt their charities." He said in a tone like he was talking to second graders.

He then changed the subject by attacking Tom LeClaire for his voting record on tax issues while he was a senator. Tom LeClaire could feel his blood start to boil as Knight continued his assault.

Then he heard Jack's words, "don't attack Tom, don't attack."

When it was his turn to reply, Tom took a deep breath and responded as he looked straight into the eyes of Andrew Knight.

"I am not going to spend our time here today, or the time of the American people defending my voting record to you. I am however going to give the American people the truth as my party and I see it. This is why I joined the Centrust Party, because above all else they were going to give the American people the truth."

He then turned to the audience and said. "If anyone out there wants me to explain why I voted a certain way in the Senate over the last fifteen years you are more than welcome to contact my office, and I will gladly discuss my reasons for voting the way I did."

As Tom LeClaire was talking to the audience, an eagle circled overhead. When he had finished the giant bird landed on the boulders behind him. The audience was awestruck.

"Oh my God it's a golden eagle," Scott said. He turned to look at Jack who wasn't next to him any longer. Scott then noticed that there were dark clouds developing about 20 miles away at the other end of the canyon.

"Uh- oh," he said under his breath.

Knight found this hard to compete with and frustration began welling inside him. Tom LeClaire had disarmed his opponent by not reacting to his attacks, but that would not stop Knight from pursuing this tactic.

During a question about environmental issues, an issue that was close to the heart of Andrew Knight, he tried to convince the audience that Tom LeClaire was a Johnny come lately environmentalist, who had not voted on the side of the environment many times in the Senate. When Knight did this there was a crack of lightning and a huge clap of thunder that rumbled through the canyon to their location like a runaway freight train. It made it hard to hear his declaration.

The dark, ominous clouds moved into the middle of the canyon as the debate wore on. The strange thing was that there were no clouds or storms anywhere else. Never once throughout the course of the debate was the voice of Tom LeClaire obscured. The voice of Knight was not obscured unless he went on the attack. Knight made this correlation during the course of the debate, but towards the end of the debate he felt the need to go back on the attack again. The more he tried to attack the worse it got and during one such attack the thunder got so loud you couldn't hear him say a word. He became furious.

With all the commotion the golden eagle never left its perch behind the Centrust Party candidate. The plan to destroy Tom LeClaire's credibility completely backfired and resulted in a surge of public support for the Centrust Party.

The press recalled the clap of thunder and the hawk in Phoenix when Tom LeClaire's candidacy was announced, and later reported, in jest, that perhaps Mother Nature was weighing in on the side of the Centrust Party.

That afternoon the White House staff took a break to watch the debate, and became hysterical about Knight's predicament. Later they wouldn't find the weather amusing.

The clincher came with Tom LeClaire's closing comments in which he effectively took attacking one's opponent off the table for the rest of the campaign.

"The way a person gets elected to public office in this country is by either taking credit for their accomplishments, or by attacking their opponent for his mistakes. Most campaigns up until now have done both. Our campaign will not be run this way, and I will tell you why. There are many brilliant minds with good hearts out there in America today that would love nothing more than to serve their country. They won't however subject themselves and their families to the kind of vicious attacks that have become part of the American political process.

We are all human beings and we all make mistakes. Bashing people for their mistakes breeds resentment and inactivity. The time of resentment and inactivity needs to come to an end. We all live in a smaller world with a global economy and our government has to be able to respond quickly to the needs of the people and the earth. We need to move forward in a timely fashion with environmental and energy policies that make sense so that we can leave a world as beautiful as the scene you see behind me to our children's, children and their children.

Let the brilliant minds of our time come forward to serve the public, and help us all come up with a sustainable way to extend the American dream to every American, and to whomever else may want to share it, without fear of being crucified for making a mistake."

On the drive back to Mountain Home Father Morales turned to Joseph and remarked. "Nice job with the thunder clouds, Joseph."

"I thought you might enjoy that, but I would have never done it if I wasn't asked to and I had some help out there today from the eagle," Joeseph replied.

"I noticed," The priest said.

The group at Mountain Home was filled with excitement as the priest and the medicine man returned from their trip. There was much laughter and joy for all the publicity the Centrust party was getting, and new hope for all they could achieve.

Jessica Thomas, the EPA administrator sat at her office desk with the door closed staring blankly out the window. She turned and looked around her office asking herself out loud, "what am I doing here?" She had suspected for quite a while now that she had been wasting her time. Lately, however this thought had become a feeling that settled into the core of her being.

Jessica Thomas, knew in her heart that the prophecy was true. Publicly the administration was dismissing it as nonsense that was floating around the Internet. She found it interesting that the same prophecy had been reported to come from prophets of many different faiths.

She had noticed a change in the president's demeanor, and also other members of his administration who would have to be aware of such things. Her intuition told her that there were preparations being made behind the scenes. For her it was easy to see in the president's eyes, that over the last year and a half he was carrying a burden unlike any he had carried previously.

She came back to the question she'd asked herself moments earlier. What was she doing here? She should be spending time with her family, and not working long hours running the EPA, which wasn't fulfilling the requirements of the prophecy anyway. She wondered if the president regretted some of his decisions regarding the environment. Since his election he had abandoned the Kyoto treaty, pushed through legislation to drill for oil and gas in a wildlife preserve and repealed environmental standards that protect the nation's waters and forests. She felt completely hopeless. For the first time in her adult life she made a decision to give up on ambition.

Where had it led her anyway; alone and in her office still at work at 9:00 pm?

In a long awaited moment of complete clarity, and embodiment of what she really wanted, she tendered her resignation. She would go to the White House tomorrow and deliver it to the president personally. In her resignation she recommended that the deputy director of the EPA be promoted to administrator.

In closing she wrote: "It is with great sorrow that I leave this administration without accomplishing what I set out to do. In light of the developments over the last year and a half, I desire to spend as much time with my family as possible. The world we live in today is not just different from the one three years ago, there are fundamental core changes happening. To date many of these have been painful. Therefore, until I am directed on the course I should take in facilitating these changes, I wish to spend as much time with my family as possible."

The president was not happy when he received her resignation the following day. The now former administrator could see into his heart, and realized that he knew the prophecy was true.

One week after the infamous debate and five days after her resignation. Jessica Thomas sat in the kitchen of her Connecticut home sipping her morning coffee and feeling completely at peace. She noticed there was a reporter interviewing the Centrust party candidate on her television set, so she decided to turn up the volume and see what he had to say.

The reporter asked. "If you are asking people not to judge you based on your previous voting record, how should people determine if you should be the next president of the United States?"

Tom LeClaire thought for a moment and replied. "Judge, that is an interesting word to describe whether people should support us or not. I would like to ask the American people to look at what has taken place within the Centrust Party. Its founder, Scott Stahl, gave up his business to found the party. I gave up my career as a senator and left my party to seek their nomination. As a matter of fact everyone involved with the Centrust Party has put aside their lives as they knew them, to create something new. The Centrust Party was born and has continued to grow from the energy created when people put their lives on the line for the greater good of mankind. This is the criterion that I would hope the American people will, as you put it, judge us by."

Jessica Thomas almost dropped her cup of coffee when she heard this. She remembered in an instant something she had forgotten. A dream, in which she was told that what was needed in Washington to lead the world forward, was the sacrifice of ego, and a balance between the feminine and masculine energy. In that dream she saw that everything and nothing was up to us. Our decisions collectively would determine our fate. She was shown a fork in the path of mankind and was allowed to see the result of either path.

She began to shake as she remembered seeing the results of mankind taking the easy path. She recalled how in her dream a voice asked. "What will you do to help mankind take the right path?"

She repeated her answer in the dream aloud that morning as she sat in a daze in front of the television. "I will do anything...I will do anything!" She couldn't even recall when she had this dream, but it was as vivid as if it happened last night.

The reporter finished the interview with the question that would change her life and the lives of many others forever. "Are you getting close to making your decision on a running mate, and if so, who might that be?"

"There are many people in the private and public sector who are qualified, and whom I would be honored to have as my running mate. We've decided to give this issue a little time, and believe that the perfect running mate will come forward," Tom LeClaire said.

That evening Jessica told her husband everything. She said that she believed the prophecy was true, recounted her dream and the commitment she made in it. She told him about the sacrifices made by everyone involved with the Centrust Party, and how she believed that sacrifice was necessary before real change could take place. "You are my partner." She told him. "This decision involves you as much as me. Therefore I'm asking for your permission to submit my name for consideration to be the vice presidential candidate for the Centrust Party."

Without hesitation her husband answered. "What are you waiting for? Get going."

Two more people were now making a sacrifice. Jessica Thomas was giving up her new freedom, and her husband was putting everyone else's needs ahead of his own by supporting his wife's decision to serve. She booked a red eye flight that night to Los Angeles. She didn't even know if Helen Shultz was home, but she wanted to move quickly to insure that she didn't talk herself out of the decision she had made.

That evening in Mountain Home, Utah the members of the group assembled for ceremony. Their group had grown considerably since the wesak moon. A Hindu woman from India who traveled the world giving people hugs had joined them. The love that poured forth from this woman was over-powering. The group now numbered twelve, and every major faith was represented.

At their ceremony Joseph nudged Father Morales.

"Brother, look deep into the fire. Can you see them?"

Father Morales gazed deep into the fire and saw the prominent republican woman joining Tom LeClaire at the podium. *Oh boy! This is going to upset a lot of people.* With this thought two very powerful men appeared behind the candidates. Both Father Morales and Joseph recognized them.

Suddenly the whole group was gazing into the fire and saw the same vision, the joining of the masculine and feminine to ascend to the most powerful position in the world. Each member committed their support and their lives to bringing this vision into reality.

The next day before the extraordinary events of the debate even had a chance to fade from the public's attention, a software giant familiar to everyone held a press conference. He turned the political arena upside down, when he announced that the two networks that he owned, would voluntarily comply with the campaign finance reform that the Centrust Party candidate proposed in the debate. If any candidate or any candidate's supporters ran ads attacking their opponent on his networks they would offer equal airtime for the opposing candidate to respond.

The following day the media mogul who had been buying as much open land and forest property he could get his hands on indicated his broadcasting companies would be doing the same. These two men of power coming forward and committing their resources to ending attack and smear-type advertising in politics would make it the equivalent of political suicide for the two big parties to use soft money to attack the Centrust party candidate.

After arriving in California Jessica Thomas was not surprised to find Helen Shultz in town. They didn't really discuss the reason for her visit over the phone. Jessica told Helen she needed to talk to her in person as soon as possible. Helen told her that the others would be coming into town that evening after a couple of days of campaigning in the all important state of California.

"Why don't you come by this afternoon around 2:00 pm," Helen said.

She tried to hide the excitement in her voice.

Jessica's palms were sweaty and she couldn't seem to avoid an incredible feeling of anticipation during the 45-minute drive through L.A. traffic. When Helen opened the door the former administrator was pale with anxiety.

"Don't worry, everything will be fine," Helen said

"Let's get you inside before someone spots you."

"With all the publicity the Centrust party has been receiving I don't think anyone even remembers I resigned my office." Jessica said. The two women took a seat on the couch in Helen's family room in the back of her house.

"Would you like some tea, Jessica?" Helen asked.

"That would be great," Jessica replied, "Thank you."

"The polls sure have been unpredictable recently. I can't recall a time when such large percentage swings happened from one day to the next," Jessica said.

"It sure keeps our opponents guessing. They can't figure out if their coming or going, or if they have been there already," Helen said.

Jessica let out an uncomfortable laugh.

"I believe the polls indicate that Americans are seriously considering an alternative," Helen said. She brought a tray with their tea and set it down on the coffee table, and sat down.

Helen couldn't take the suspense any longer and decided to pop the question.

"I guess this leads us to the purpose of your visit," Helen said. She gazed into Jessica's eyes and smiled.

Jessica took a deep breath and said. "I would like to put my name in the ring for the vice presidency." After the words left her mouth she let out a big sigh of relief.

"Wow!" Helen said.

"I believed that's why you were here, and I guess I could have let you off the hook a little earlier. It's just so incredible to hear you say it."

Helen got up to retrieve her cell phone and called Tom LeClaire immediately. Tom and Scott were busy so Jack answered the phone.

"You'll never guess whom I have here with me right now!"

"Jessica Thomas, the former EPA Administrator," Jack replied.

"Some day you're going to have to tell me how you do that Jack."

"Ancient Chinese secret Helen. I'll let Tom know, and we'll see you this evening."

Tom, Scott and Jack arrived at Helen's home at around 9:00 pm that evening. They brought a trail of reporters with them.

"I almost had a whole day of peace, and you guys have to ruin it, don't you?" Helen said.

"They're looking for Mrs. Thomas," Tom replied.

"At every stop we made today we were questioned about the vice presidency," Scott added. A somewhat uncomfortable silence fell over the room.

After what seemed an eternity Jessica Thomas opened her mouth and she couldn't believe what came out.

"I had a dream." She put her hand over her mouth and looked noticeably shaken.

"That's Ok," Tom said.

"We've all been having those dreams for quite some time. Please tell us yours."

Jessica told them her whole story. The reason for her resignation, that instant when she remembered the dream, her realization about the prophecy, and the feeling of helplessness that had overcome her in her position as EPA administrator over the last year and a half.

The group listened intensely, and seemed to hang on every word. After she was finished Tom LeClaire said.

"Mrs. Thomas would you accept my invitation to become my running mate to be the next vice president of the United States."

"Only if you call me Jessica." A single tear ran down her face, and the Centrust Party ticket was now complete.

The group decided to announce Jessica's candidacy at the same location where Tom LeClaire announced his. Helen believed they could get everything together and have the press conference in two days.

Later that evening Jessica got her first chance to speak with Jack. She felt an incredible peace in his presence, and believed there was something very special about him. Jessica was puzzled about one thing however, and that was why with all the press coverage the Centrust Party was receiving, she had never noticed him before. She meant to ask Jack about this, but it slipped her mind.

The stage was set once again for a press conference at a mountain preserve in the southwestern United States. There was an air of incredible excitement and anticipation by the press, and the American people. Jack had called Ben and asked him to meet him at the press conference, and later for dinner so the two men could catch up. Jack had been traveling extensively and had not seen his dear friend for quite some time.

When the two candidates got out of their limousine and walked up to the podium there was a gasp from the press corps. The Centrust Party had once again succeeded in surprising them. Jack had excused himself from the group to be with his friend Ben in the crowd. He told Scott he would meet up with him the following morning to resume their campaign schedule.

While Tom LeClaire was announcing his choice of Jessica Thomas for his vice presidential running mate, there were two hawks circling low overhead. These two magnificent birds were circling low enough for the cameras to pick them up while both candidates got a chance to speak.

Some members of the press made fun of this, saying that the Centrust Party had the animal kingdom on their side, and it was a shame they couldn't vote. Others took it much more seriously, proclaiming this and the other events that had happened were some kind of sign. People of knowledge in America, and all over the world didn't need to be told. They knew that the hawks brought with them vision, and an overall view of what needed to happen.

This day sent the political community in America reeling. Not only had a prominent democratic senator left his party to run for president on the Centrust Party ticket, but also a well-respected republican woman with a long distinguished career in public service had joined him.

"I imagine they're probably going to take the gloves off now," Jessica remarked to Tom LeClaire after the press conferences was over.

"Let's hope so," he replied.

After the press conference Jack left with Ben, and the two men drove to a little town north of Phoenix to their favorite cowboy restaurant. During the drive Jack filled Ben in on everything that had happened in the campaign up to that point. They laughed and joked just like old times before any of this had started.

Ben was happy to get a chance to spend time with his old friend. Jack was aware however, that there was something bothering him. It wasn't on the surface, but just below. He thought he might take a look, and see what was bothering his friend, but when he asked about it, Spirit told him.

"No, do not look."

Jack and Ben talked as they enjoyed their dinner together.

"There was another one of us there Ben," Jack said referring to the debate.

"I was busy and didn't get a chance to spot him, but I had the sense that he was an elder. Very powerful! I believe that he's a leader of one of the many groups that is supporting us."

"Very interesting," Ben said. "I have spent some time journeying, and I'm telling you, there's an incredible amount of power behind you guys. Every day after work I turn on the news to see what you've been up to, and also what this power has been up to. It's very exciting to say the least. It feels to me like the energy of every person's prayers who has ever prayed for the earth, peace, and a better life for their children is behind you all at once."

"That's a mouthful," Jack said.

Ben drove Jack home after dinner. He parked the car in front of Jack's house and said.

"I love you brother, and I'm very proud of you. You're doing a great job."

"Well, I love you too Ben. I'll see you soon," Jack said.

He reached to open the car door.

Ben leaned over and gave Jack a heartfelt embrace, an embrace where he held on a little longer, and a little tighter than usual. When the door closed and Jack walked up to his house Ben waved and said.

"Goodbye friend."

No longer having to keep a secret from his friend, and no longer wanting to keep the secret even from himself, Ben wept the whole drive home. He sat outside alone on his porch before entering the house, because he didn't want to upset his wife Patricia. Ben couldn't even remember the last time he cried, and if he had ever wept so completely.

Ah, when to the heart of man
Was it ever less than a treason
To go with the drift of things,
To yield with a grace to reason,
And bow and accept the end
Of a love or a season?

Robert Frost

Chapter 14 — The Shaman

The group in Mountain home Utah was now reaching out through prayer and meditation to groups like itself that had sprung up all over America and the world. Their group had great power, because of its unique combination of so many different faiths. Each member was able to reach out through prayer and meditation and speak to the millions of people in their respective faiths. Even though almost no one knew that the group even existed, they were largely responsible for the wave of new consciousness spreading across America.

Summertime campaigning was not friendly to Robert Kelton or Andrew Knight. Several campaign appearances were canceled or delayed because of the weather. If their campaign stops were not canceled because of vicious thunderstorms, they would arrive only to be greeted by one of the summers stifling heat waves. Even Air Force One was grounded on a couple of occasions because of the weather. All of this increased the Centrust Party's popularity and added to their notoriety.

With six weeks left until Election Day both Kelton's and Knight's frustration reached a boiling point. Up until this time both parties had refrained from the kind of brutal attacks on their opponents that had become commonplace in American politics. They had done so, because they were afraid of the political backlash that might happen as a result of this kind of campaigning. With six weeks left however, they had become desperate. Both Kelton and Knight went after Tom LeClaire and Jessica Thomas, and attacked with a viciousness that was unparalleled in American politics.

This of course backfired. The Centrust party was running out of money and if it had not been for the voluntary cooperation by some of the networks to provide free air-time to address these attacks, the Centrust Party couldn't have done any advertising at all. When it became apparent to Kelton and Knight that all they were doing with their attacks was helping the under funded party, they took off the gloves and squared off against each other. With there being very little free advertising available, the Centrust Party needed to pull another miracle out of the hat.

The software giant and his philanthropist wife had been watching these events closely. They had felt in their hearts for some time that America needed a change; a common sense approach to the environment and tax policy, among other things. One night as the couple relaxed in their Seattle home discussing these things, and the Centrust Party's financial woes, she came up with an idea that would rock the opposing campaigns and ensure that the Centrust Party would still be in the race come election day.

The following day the software giant held a press conference to detail an employee bonus program. All of his American employees could come forward who wished to support the Centrust Party financially, and receive up to $2000.00 in bonus to donate to the campaign. In accordance with the Centrust Party's wishes it would be up to each individual's conscience to use the money as they said they intended to. No employee would be checked up on to see if they actually donated the money.

This event of course led to another feeding frenzy by the media. Some of its members were trying to figure out how much money the software giant would be giving away, while others were wondering if this was just another way for a powerful businessman to influence an American politician. All of this resulted in more publicity for the Centrust Party. Robert Kelton was flabbergasted! How could the Centrust Party have gained so much support from business? It was unexplainable. The Centrust Party was once again saved by another miracle.

"Let's hope it's not the last miracle." Tom LeClaire was reported to have said regarding these events.

One afternoon Knight was taking a break from the campaign trail in his hotel room. He actually had something to be happy about. Congress had just passed a law that prevented the news media from releasing the results of their exit polling on Election Day until the polls close in California. The president indicated he would sign the bill into law before the next election.

One of Knight's aides entered his hotel room with a file in her hand.

"Sir, I have something here I think you'll find very interesting," the aide said as she sat down in a chair next to him.

"What is it?" He asked without removing his gaze from the television.

"There is a member of the Centrust Party campaign who has a very interesting story." Knight sat up in his chair and turned to face her, she now had his undivided attention. She pulled a picture of Tom LeClaire, Scott and Jack from the file. "This is him right here," she said as she pointed to Jack.

"That's strange, I've never noticed him before." Knight looked puzzled. "With all the media attention and publicity the

Centrust Party has gotten, how come I haven't noticed him before? A better question would be, how come <u>we</u> have never noticed him before?"

He looked to her for an explanation and his eyes included an unspoken statement. *You mean to tell me we have all these people on the payroll, and no one has noticed this man yet?*

The aide took a deep breath. "That is part of his story sir. Our detectives never even recalled seeing him. It wasn't until we got his name, Jack Anderson, that we were able to find anything out about him—

"Now that we've discovered him, what is it about him?"

"He is a shaman," she said.

"A shaman?" He looked away as he searched his memory. "That's a pagan, or an earth worshiper!" He grinned widely.

"Another aide has been curious about these people all her life and has done an extensive amount of research on the subject of shamanism. She told me that one of the practices of shamanism is invisibility. She says that if he is a master shaman, he could be right in front of us and we would never notice him unless he wanted us to."

He became even more excited and let out a big laugh. "Oh, this is great stuff, the party of visibility has a member of its campaign engaging in the pagan practice of invisibility."

"It gets better than that sir," she said. "Master shamans have been reported to exercise control over the weather, and other natural forces, including animals." Knight made the connection and he became enraged.

He looked back over the campaign and remembered each instance where the Centrust Party grabbed so much publicity from the timely appearance of claps of thunder, magnificent birds overhead, and sunshine. He grew angrier, and angrier.

He stood up and almost screamed. "You mean to tell me that all the problems we've had with the weather could be due to this…this…shaman character?"

He regained control of himself and sat back down somewhat calmed, with fire in his eyes. "Please, by all means continue."

"Our other aide highly doubted that one shaman, even a master shaman could be responsible for everything that's happened. Until now this man, Jack Anderson has chosen to remain invisible, this takes incredible focus of his attention. Therefore it is very doubtful that this one shaman alone could have done all these things," she said.

"We've got to find out everything we can about this Jack Anderson," he said. "Who else knows about this?"

"There is the detective, myself, and of course you. The other aide's name is Judy. She asked why I was asking so many questions about shamans, but I was able to avoid answering the question directly by changing the subject," she said.

"Very good Elaine," he said. She smiled acknowledging her own efforts. "We must keep it that way. Tell the detective to find out everything about this man, and swear him to secrecy. Find out if Judy can be trusted and if she can I want her to travel with me for a day or two, so I can learn more about this. We must keep this a secret, and we have to be very careful here, because every form of attack on the Centrust Party to date, has backfired. If we're going to leak this, our timing must be perfect."

The aide left Knight's room to perform the duties he laid out, leaving a copy of the file with him. He felt that this information coming to him was too good to be true, and he would struggle over the coming weeks on when to use it.

Robert Kelton became increasingly frustrated about some of his support from the business community going to the Centrust Party. He had enjoyed an approval rating that up until his presidency was almost unprecedented. His administration had effectively waged a war on terrorism, and yet he always felt like he was playing catch up or reacting to what was happening with the Centrust Party. Privately he was regretting the decisions he made regarding environmental policy, because it had become one of the key issues of the campaign.

After a meeting with his campaign strategists, during which they estimated that the Centrust Party was pulling 65% of its support from people who usually voted democratic, he decided to go on the offensive against Tom LeClaire and Jessica Thomas.

The Republican Party began to run a series of ads proclaiming how many people would be put out of work in the logging, and paper industry if American farmers began to grow industrial hemp. The ad proclaimed that American forests were healthy and capable of providing paper indefinitely under the management of the Forest Service. They also claimed according to experts in the DEA that it would be impossible to control marijuana growth in this country if industrial hemp became legal for farmers to grow.

After the Republican Party and Kelton began attacking the Centrust Party, the livestock industry decided to follow suit. They began to run ads of their own attacking the Centrust Party's affiliation with vegetarianism and Planet Save. This smear campaign did its best to paint the Centrust Party as an ultra left wing party rather than one that was centrist as it proclaimed to be.

The weeks leading up to the last week of the campaign were the most challenging for the Centrust Party. Their attackers ran as few ads as possible on the network stations that were supporting the campaign finance reform that the Centrust Party had proposed. Their campaign team worked 20 hours a day to present their case to the American people. They used the response ad time they received from the friendly broadcasting companies, but this wasn't enough. They were forced to respond by running ads of their own, not attacking their opponents or defending their positions, but simply stating them and explaining what they believed were the benefits of following their strategy for America. All this advertising was draining the Centrust Party's campaign coffers. During this period, no interviews were refused in an attempt to bring their case directly to the American people.

The Centrust Party ran a long and a short version of two different ads. The first presented the environmental and health benefits of a plant-based diet to the American people. The ad explained that in 1988, based on the ever-increasing amount of nutrition research the USDA decided to redraw its food chart. The Physicians Committee for Responsible Medicine asked the USDA to replace the "Basic Four" food guide with their "New Four Food Groups", all of them plant based. Just prior to the release of this new food guide the meat and dairy industries got wind of the change. These industry representatives attacked the current USDA secretary and the secretary postponed the release of the food guide. One year and nearly one million dollars later, the food guide pyramid was released with only minor changes.

This advertisement was about visibility, and letting Americans make choices in their lives based on knowing the facts. This is just one example the ad explained, of special interests affecting the information that the public receives from the government. Continuing to allow the same governmental agency to be responsible for educating Americans about healthy eating, while also promoting industry interests is a conflict of interest that at the very least; results in incorrect information.

The second campaign advertisement explained why the Centrust Party supported growing industrial hemp for paper, instead of using wood pulp. The United States consumes twice as much wood as any other industrialized nation. There are over 6 billion people on the planet today; only 287 million of them live in the United States. They asked the question: "What will be the damage to the world's forests, our global climate, and the 6 billion inhabitants of earth if the rest of the countries of the world seek to become industrialized and emulate the consumption patterns of the United States?

The government's refusal to use industrial hemp fiber for paper pulp is once again the result of special interests exceptional influence over the last century. Almost 50% of all trees that are harvested are chipped for paper pulp mills. As the world economy continues to grow the demand for paper coupled with the world's dwindling forests will force an alternative more likely sooner than later. In the meantime, while American farmers are forbidden from growing a crop that will produce two to three times more income per acre than wheat. At the same time American manufacturers are allowed to import industrial hemp from China and other nations to manufacture hemp products, resulting in the loss of possible jobs for Americans.

The ad explained that the Centrust Party did not wish to cause harm to the American paper industry, however the world is changing, due to its burgeoning population. America has always had a heritage of change. Now more than ever we need to embrace that heritage, for the good of all Americans, their children, and their children's children. We need to do this instead of doing what is profitable in the short term for a few special interest groups.

Both campaign advertisements directed Americans to visit the Centrust Party web site. The web site presented many facts pertaining to the environment, America's energy needs, tax structure, and dozens of other issues never published by a political campaign before. The web site also laid out the facts about why America needed to develop alternative sources of fuel. The volume of web site traffic and the ever-increasing amount of information put on the web site by the party, kept Jeff Kline and the people at New World Web Design working day and night to respond to America's growing hunger for the truth.

Rolling into the last week of the campaign, the election polls had become somewhat more consistent, and most had the candidates in a three-way tie. Five days before Election Day the Centrust party campaign converged on Los Angeles for a campaign rally and a day of rest, to be followed by a whirlwind tour of twelve important states over a four-day period.

*"Between the silence of the mountains and the crashing of the sea
there lies a land I once lived in and she's waiting there for me.
But in the gray of the morning my mind becomes confused
between the dead and the sleeping
and the road that I must choose."*

The Moody Blues

Chapter 15—The Decision

With most election polls predicting a three-way tie Andrew Knight saw his dreams of becoming president slipping through his hands once again. He made the decision to leak the information he had compiled about Jack's unorthodox form of spirituality. He had a democratic campaign worker leak to the press that Jack was a shaman and hoped that America's mostly Christian population would reject the candidate who was so closely associated with him.

Millions of Americans from all walks of life, and thousands of people who belonged to one environmental group or another arrived in Los Angeles for the biggest campaign rally of the season. These Americans had come to show their support for the Centrust Party's vision of building a sustainable economy for America and the world for generations to come.

Many of these people couldn't even explain why they had come; they just felt that they had to be a part of creating something new. The behind the scenes work done by the group in Mountain Home, Utah and groups like it that had cropped up all over the world awakened the yearning for something better within the hearts of the people. These Americans cast off the blanket of apathy and came out to support the Centrust Party.

The Los Angeles police department was overwhelmed by the number of people converging on their city. The secret service agents assigned to the Centrust Party candidates were doing their best, but they knew that securing a situation this large was all but impossible.

Nonetheless the Centrust Party moved ahead with the rally, which would include a speech from Tom LeClaire, Jessica Thomas and Scott Stahl along with some well-known celebrities who were supporting the Centrust Party. Scott, Jack, Helen, Sam, and the candidates enjoyed a nice lunch together after a relaxing morning, and then got in the limousine for the drive to the Los Angeles coliseum where the rally would be held.

During the hour-long drive the candidates were reviewing their speeches, so Scott began to reflect on the last four years of his life. He pulled out an old deposit envelope from his wallet on which he had written his dreams for a better America. His thoughts moved from the founding of the Centrust Party, meeting Helen and the others, to the senator from Louisiana's nomination as their candidate. Constant throughout all these experiences that had so drastically changed his life was the camaraderie, companionship, and support from his friend Jack Anderson. Jack had always been there for him over the last four years, and had never asked for anything in return.

Scott looked up at Jack who smiled and winked at him.

"Today is our big day Scott."

"I know, and I want to thank you," Scott said.

"For what?"

"You were always there when I doubted. You wouldn't let me give up."

"Your very welcome my friend," Jack said. "Thank you for getting the whole thing started, and pushing the big stone uphill by yourself when necessary." Scott thought how this was typical of Jack's manner; he never felt the need to take credit for anything and that the world needs more men and women like this.

"Oh, there are plenty of us out there. All these people coming to Los Angeles today is proof of that," Jack said in response to Scott's unspoken thought.

"After this is all over your going to have to tell me how you do that," Scott said shaking his head.

"It's a deal."

The limousine was only two blocks from the coliseum when Jack had a vision. Someone had slipped through and Jack could see there was danger in his pocket. He leaned over to say something to the candidates and the secret service when there was a thundering " Nooo don't!" in his head.

Jack quietly leaned back into his seat and closed his eyes. As he watched the man walking, he listened to the voice of Spirit.

"If you tell them now the secret service will call off the whole rally. They have been looking for an excuse to do so and remember they have political preferences also. If you don't tell them, there is still an alternative." Jack was then shown the result of either choice instantaneously. He made his decision, opened his eyes and waited quietly.

Traffic near the coliseum was completely congested. There were throngs of people everywhere. The driveway where the limousine was supposed to enter into a secured underground garage, was inexplicably blocked off, and there were people lining the sidewalks on both sides of the street.

"Well, it looks like we're going to have the opportunity to meet some people and shake some hands," Tom said.

"I don't think that's a good idea sir," one of the secret service agents said.

"These people have come here to see us and it doesn't look like their going to get inside the coliseum. This may be their only chance to meet us," Jessica said.

"That may be so, but it will be impossible for us to secure this situation," another member of secret service said.

"I can see the ramp to the underground garage from here. We'll just walk towards it and shake hands along the way. Ten minutes tops," Tom said.

"Ok if you insist, but at least let us get out and look things over a bit. I still don't think it's a good idea."

Tom looked right at the secret service supervisor. "Your objection is noted. Thank you."

The secret service entourage exited their vehicles to the sidewalk about a block from the entrance, to check things out while everyone else waited in the limousine. The supervising secret service agent asked the police officers present to clear the ramp down to the garage. After about ten minutes they returned and told the candidates and the others they could exit the limousine.

The people lining the sidewalk were so happy to see their candidates that they converged on them from both sides of the street. Among them was the man Jack had just seen in his vision.

Jack's vision became a reality as he spotted the man he had seen a few minutes earlier. The man walked up casually and called out, "Senator."

As Tom turned around with a smile on his face to shake the man's hand, he pulled the gun out of his pocket. In a flash, Jack stepped in front of Tom and was shot in the heart.

The secret service grabbed the man but one more shot was squeezed off catching Scott Stahl in the face. The candidates were covered under a swarm of secret service personnel, and then shuffled into the limousine. The driver began honking his

horn and slowly pushing his way through the crowd. The Los
Angeles police had cleared the ramp to the underground garage
and the decision was made to go into the garage for the time
being.

Jack felt more love for everyone and all things at that
moment than he had ever known. The ancestors who were
familiar to him joined him and without any resistance he left
with them. He knew the way, because he had been there before,
and he continued without hesitation or remorse into the light.

Scott saw Jack with the ancestors and longed to join him
but could not.

"You must stay my son, it is not time for you yet," he
was told. Scott watched Jack depart and wondered how one
person could love so much as to consciously accept death for
the benefit of everyone else.

Ben had taken the afternoon off to watch the rally and he
had begun to snooze as he waited for the candidate's speeches.
He received the news about Jack exactly as he had received it
four years earlier. He was awakened as a tear ran down his face.
He shut off the television, grabbed the car keys, and jumped
into his car to race over to Jack's house to be with Susan when
she received the news.

While the candidates waited in the secured underground
garage Helen Schultz and Sam Jameson remained on the
sidewalk next to Scott and Jack. Both of them were sobbing
uncontrollably. Jack was gone, there was no doubt, but Scott
was clinging to life. They knelt on the sidewalk in the blood
of their brothers while the gunman was arrested and their

supporters stood there in silent disbelief. An ambulance took both men away, and Sam rode with them to the hospital, while Helen made her way to the garage.

When Helen walked up Tom LeClaire and Jessica Thomas were standing there crying surrounded by a ring of secret service personnel. She sat down on a parking divider and continued sobbing. After about fifteen minutes of trying to come to grips with what had happened a conversation ensued about what to do next. For only the second time in her life Helen could not come up with a plan, and she thought she might be in shock.

"Perhaps we should call off the speeches and join Sam at the hospital," Tom said.

Jessica Thomas was able to look beyond her own personal heartache. "What would Scott and Jack wish for us to do at this moment? Thousands of people are waiting inside for us to speak about our vision for America, a vision that has become their vision also." She paused for a moment and both Helen and Tom were looking at her and nodding in agreement.

"If we don't go ahead with our speeches, no matter how difficult that may be for us to do, we will be letting down all the people that have gathered here today, including Scott and Jack."

"You're right," Tom replied.

An agent interrupted their conversation. "With all due respect there is no way you can go ahead with your speeches. This situation is out of control! We should have never let you leave the safety of the limousine—

"If there was any way I could change that decision I would," Tom said. He put his head in his hands.

Jessica walked over and stood toe to toe with the agent. "Listen to the size of that crowd inside, if we told them that there was an assassination attempt there would be panic and more people could be injured. You call someone and get whatever help you need. Hell, call in the National Guard if you like.

We'll delay our speeches, but we won't cancel them and that's final. Do you understand me?"

Jessica wheeled around and walked over to where Helen was sitting, she crouched down, hugged her and said. "Helen, would you mind going to the hospital and keeping us abreast of Scott's condition, while Tom and I go ahead with our speeches? We will meet you at the hospital as soon as we're finished."

"Ok Jessica, I can do that," Helen said through her tears.

Helen left for the hospital and the two candidates were escorted to the stage, but not before the secret service tightened security considerably. They actually called in the L.A swat team along with as many police officers as the department could spare. Jessica and Tom waited for their turn to speak and with all the courage they could muster, more than they had ever had to call on before, they both delivered the most heartfelt messages of their lives. Afterwards they were rushed off to the hospital to join Sam and Helen at Scott's side. Elizabeth had been notified and was awaiting a flight from Phoenix to LA.

The Centrust Party was once again receiving all of the media attention, however, this time one of them had made the ultimate sacrifice for it. That afternoon the majority of Americans forgot that there were two other parties running for office also. The group huddled in the hallway outside Scott's intensive care unit to wait for Elizabeth to arrive from Phoenix, and to contemplate if they were even capable of continuing the campaign.

Elizabeth arrived and broke down into tears again as she met the group and they all hugged one another. She entered Scott's room and sat on his bed next to him holding his hand. Before her lay, her lover, her best friend, the father of her children, and the man who had continually supported her as she redefined whom she was throughout her life.

Elizabeth stepped outside into the hallway to speak with her husband's doctor who had arrived to give her his prognosis.

"Your husband was shot in the right side of the face, and there is a 22 caliber slug lodged in his cheek bone. The prognosis for removing the slug and repairing his facial structure is very good because of the small caliber and grazing nature of the shot." The doctor paused and took a deep breath before continuing. "The problem is that after being shot he must have fallen backwards and struck the back of his head. The impact resulted in a small fracture in his skull and the trauma is causing his brain to swell. As a result he has fallen into a coma."

Elizabeth gasped. "When do you think he will come out of the coma?"

"That is impossible to say at this point," the doctor replied, "and until the brain swelling subsides and he stabilizes we cannot operate. We should know more within the next 12 to 24 hours."

"Thank you, doctor," Elizabeth said.

The doctor returned to Scott's room and Elizabeth turned to the group. "I was wondering if you all would accompany me to the hospital's chapel?"

"Of course we will," Helen replied and the others nodded in agreement.

Tom, Jessica, Helen and Sam walked Elizabeth to the chapel. When they were in front of the chapel entrance Elizabeth turned to them. "This is something I have to do alone, would you please wait for me here." Tom opened the door and Elizabeth disappeared inside.

She took a seat in the back of the chapel and did her best to quiet her mind. After slowing her breathing she remembered her dream in which a million points of light sent energy down upon her husband. She remembered a long conversation that she and Scott had a year and a half ago before he walked away from his business to make the Centrust Party vision a reality. Now he was in a coma and might lose his life for that vision. Elizabeth knew that the group outside the door was waiting for her to tell them it was all right to continue with the campaign as scheduled. As she made the decision to do this, she believed her husband would recover somehow.

Elizabeth exited the chapel to address the exhausted group. "If my husband was conscious you all know that he would insist that you get on with your business. Since he cannot speak I will speak for him. Thank you so much, all of you, for being here for me and Scott, but you have a job to do that is much more important than anyone of us is individually. Please continue with that job. I will stay with Scott and notify you all immediately if his condition changes."

Tom, Jessica, Helen, and Sam said their goodbyes to Elizabeth and left for Helen's house for the evening. They would regroup, prepare a statement for the press and resume the campaign the next morning. The press was waiting outside the hospital with questions about Scott's condition. They also wanted to know who Jack was.

News trucks were also camped outside of Helen's home and after arriving there the group prepared a statement, which Helen read to the press from her front yard.

Jack's ultimate sacrifice had removed him from obscurity and into the spotlight. Members of the media were scrambling to become the first to tell his story. Realizing that he made a mistake Andrew Knight tried to stop his plan to leak the story about Jack's practice of shamanism, but it was too late. A democratic worker located in Illinois had leaked the story that morning and it was already making its way across the country. This made Knight appear to be the kind of person who would even try to capitalize on another person's death for his own political gain. He spent the remainder of his campaign in damage control hoping that Jack Anderson would not become a martyr.

The city of Los Angeles had gone from celebration to mourning in a matter of a few hours. The religious leaders of all faiths came forward with statements condemning the shooting and the hatred that was behind it. It was a statement given by the cardinal of the Los Angeles's diocese that would prove to be the most interesting. At the end of his statement he called for three days of prayer and fasting starting the next day at noon. Later he would not be able to recall why he added the suggestion of fasting to his statement.

The group in Mountain Home, Utah and others like it around the world were amazed and very grateful for the cardinals call to fast and pray. At noon, three days before America would elect their next president, something extraordinary happened that has not been witnessed in our modern age. Without consulting one another people of consciousness went into ceremony and fasted for three days straight with a single purpose. Indigenous peoples across the planet kept their fires burning and their dances going. Native Americans from every tribe in the country, danced, sang, chanted, and fasted for three days as an act of prayer for the healing of the American soul. Some of the elders of these tribes even abstained from drinking water during their fasts.

The day after Jack was killed and Scott was shot was the beginning of the three days of chaos in America. Early November was unusually warm across the central states and two weather fronts collided resulting in numerous unseasonable tornadoes. The people of California and the state of Washington lived under the constant threat of an enormous earthquake and experienced almost continuous tremors. That night unexplainable rolling blackouts occurred in most major American cities. Some people thought that the blackouts were the result of terrorism, however, the natural events could not be explained so easily.

It was at the end of the first day of chaos that the controversy over Jack's practice of shamanism reached its peak. Conspiracy theories circulated that many shamans had banded together to use the weather to scare the American people into voting for the Centrust Party. Knight and Kelton alike insinuated that, at the very least, the weather had been used against their campaigns.

People were scared and unpredictable and the polling that day was completely unreliable. There were interviews taken on the streets asking people what they thought about Jack's affiliation with the Centrust Party. One man remarked,

"I have heard about these people, they worship the earth and animals, they practice sorcery and can control the weather. Some of them can become invisible and even change into animals." This was a great story and every news station in America ran it and some of the news stations played the interview over and over again.

The Centrust Party had a real problem on their hands, and they met in one of their Miami hotel rooms, by candlelight, that evening to discuss if there was anything they could do about it.

"We've got to do something about this immediately, otherwise we might as well throw in the towel. I've never seen any politician overcome anything close to this kind of bad publicity before," Helen said.

"If Jack were here he would know just how to handle this," Sam remarked.

"Well he's not, and we've got to come up with something fast," Jessica said.

"We didn't come this far to throw in the towel. I think we should tell the truth," Tom said.

"Tell the truth?" Jessica said.

"I think we should step forward in Jack's defense and explain his vision for America and the world," Tom said.

After much consideration the group decided to spend the remainder of their limited funds on an advertisement of sorts. The following day Tom would deliver a statement explaining to America who Jack was, what he was really about, and why they were so blessed to have had him as a friend, and a member of their campaign. They would buy as much television time as possible and play this statement over and over again on many different stations throughout America. Tom and Jessica would split up the next day and give interviews to the major news corporations, answering all their questions. They would all chip in their own funds to finish the campaign.

The second day of chaos in America brought the worst combination of weather patterns ever recorded. There were more tornadoes, torrential downpours, and dust storms across the southwest, the tremors in California and Washington were driving their residents to the breaking point. Christians, Jews, Muslims, and people of every faith continued to join together in prayer and fasting for the healing of the earth.

Tom, Jessica, Helen, and Sam worked late into the night and early in the morning on their prepared statement. Early in the morning on the second day of chaos they entered a Miami studio to record it. After recording the statement Sam remained behind in Miami to book the television time and coordinate interviews, while Tom, Jessica, and Helen continued the two days of campaigning that were left.

At around noon on the second day of chaos Tom LeClaire hit the airwaves with his prepared statement and people stopped what they were doing to watch him say:

"The last couple of days have been extremely chaotic and stressful for all Americans. For us at the Centrust Party they have been heartbreaking. We have lost a devoted friend and another lies in a Los Angeles hospital in a coma. It has been our campaign policy not to defend ourselves against any attack, because this only serves to focus on the attack, and not on the issues that face us today, in the here and now. My beloved friend Jack Anderson is no longer with us, and therefore I feel I must come forward and tell you all what he was about.

It is true, as reported, that Jack was a shaman. As for

all the other conspiracy theories that have been floating around and have been propagated by fear, I can tell you that they are absolutely false.

I asked Jack once, "What is a shaman?" He replied without hesitation that a shaman is a servant. "A servant of whom?" I asked. His answer was "the community." Jack's community was all of us, all of us at the Centrust Party and all of you who are watching or listening today.

The shaman, he told me, was first and foremost a servant. That was Jack. A servant to the community, and the vision or dream he held in his heart for that community. I allowed this vision to become my vision. Actually it had been there all along, Jack just helped awaken it inside me.

This vision included an America that was no longer run by fear and where the interests of a few no longer dictated policy, a vision of a sustainable economy for America and the world; an economy that would not only leave a better life for our children, and their children's children, but one that would leave a better environment to the generations to come.

Jack also held a vision of peace. Where people could leave their fear behind them as he had done, and no longer look outside themselves to blame others for all that was happening to them or in the world around them. In the beginning of our campaign it was Jack who convinced us all not to attack our opponents. "To attack," he said, "is to believe that you can be attacked." The fact that I am here today, still in this presidential race, is an indicator of how profound this truth is, and that it works." Up until this point Tom's expression had been somewhat somber. This last statement brought his eyes to life.

"Jack Anderson believed so much in this vision for America that he dedicated his time and ultimately his life to this campaign. When he realized that his vision was in jeopardy, he sacrificed all he had left to give. He gave his life here on earth to save mine, and this allowed his vision for America to live on through me. There's nothing that I could have done to earn such an honor.

The reason for Jack's invisibility, as the press has dubbed it, was not because he had anything to hide. It was because he didn't want his presence to detract from America focusing on his dream. If he ever did make it thunder, rain, or call a hawk to our campaign stops it would have only been to increase America's focus on that vision.

It is important, I believe, as we work through these days of chaos to pay attention. With all the tornadoes, flooding, dust storms, and earthquakes, not one person has been killed. The unexplainable blackouts have not led to rioting and looting, and none of the tremors have resulted in massive earthquakes.

Throughout my campaign I have been repeatedly asked whether I believe the prophecy is true. To date I have not answered this question directly, and I will not answer it here today. I ask instead for each of you to look into your hearts at what is going on in America during this time of chaos and then ask yourselves if you believe that the prophecy is true.

When each and every one of you enter the voting booths the day after tomorrow, I ask you to think about your children, and their children and vote in a manner that would serve them best.

May God bless America and each and every American. Thank you."

The third day of chaos would prove to be the most challenging of all. The soul of the country ached and this spread to the body, mind and spirit of each American, because of this one election analyst predicted the lowest turnout ever for a presidential election.

Sam Jameson negotiated the best purchases of television time ever in his career, however it was a long statement and was very costly to run. By 5:00 PM that evening the Centrust Party had spent what little remained of their funds. This time the news media would be the unlikely avenue for yet another Centrust Party miracle. The candidate had addressed the three days of chaos and the prophecy in his statement, and this made his statement news worthy. The statement was run in its entirety on many news programs across the country and Knight and Kelton cried foul.

That night in a brilliant interview given on the Larry Stein Live show, Jessica Thomas explained that if the other two candidates had addressed the three days of chaos and the prophecy, their statements would have been equally newsworthy.

Towards the end of the interview Larry asked Jessica. "What is the most significant detail that sets your candidacy apart from the others."

She paused for a moment looking for the answer, her eyes brightened and she said, "Sacrifice. Everyone involved with the Centrust Party has sacrificed their livelihoods, and even their safety to create something new."

On the dawn of Election Day the tremors ceased, and the weather cleared across America. The soul of the country had been cleansed, and a peace settled over the hearts of every American. It was the kind of peace that only comes after complete despair gives way to a total surrender.

In Mountain Home, Utah the fast was broken at 12:00 pm on Election Day. They held a feast of thanksgiving to the Creator, for bringing them together to do this work as their way of breaking the fast.

The world watched and waited as Americans went into voting booths across the country. The Centrust Party campaigned until about 4:00 pm on the east coast, and then each member flew back to Phoenix to their hotel to wait for the results. The media was prevented from using exit polls to call the results in each state until the polls had closed in California. Therefore when they arrived at their hotel in Phoenix it was impossible for them to know what the outcome might be.

At about 8:00 pm on the east coast the election precincts began reporting. In the beginning it seemed as if all three candidates were running neck and neck. By 9:00 pm however, enough precincts had reported to get a feel for what was going on. It appeared that in the states that would normally vote democratic, the Centrust Party had won about 60% of the votes. Tom, Jessica, Helen, Sam, and Jeff Kline sat in silence in their hotel room as the election results were reported. The room had a dream like quality to it.

At 7:00 pm on the west coast members of the media began stating the obvious. It was apparent that the Centrust Party would win in an unprecedented landslide. Apparently America felt it was time to create something new.

In Scott's private hospital room with the secret service outside the door, Elizabeth held her husband's hand and wept as she watched the results. She wasn't paying attention as Scott blinked his eyes and opened them. He squeezed her hand and she looked down at him. He was trying to say something, but his throat was too dry. She drew her face close to him and turned so her ear could hear him whispering.

"Did we get it done?" Were his first words.

Around the world the different observatories reported to their respective governments that the asteroid had apparently disappeared. All of the astronomer's were frantically searching the heavens for an explanation. What had caused this change to occur? Had it perhaps exploded, or could it have been deflected? No explanation would be found.

The group in Mountain Home would all make preparations to return back to their individual homes. Uzziah and Reshad would weep when they parted company. Father Morales would return to his beloved El Salvador. Joseph the medicine man would continue to teach children and young people of all color how to walk the medicine way, so that it could continue.

That evening Ben and his wife Patricia stood in front of their television watching the election results. Patricia went over to Ben and put her arms around his waist.

"Oh my God Ben this is going to change everything!" Ben closed his eyes and he could no longer see the red burning ball of fire that was the asteroid. As he watched another state go to the Centrust Party he said thoughtfully.

"I suppose it will."

"It's not the earth I am concerned about. She will save herself. Will she hit the reset button on the human race? Now that's the question."

Jack Anderson

"You may say that I'm a dreamer, but I'm not the only one. Perhaps someday you will join us and the world will live as one."

John Lennon

Epilogue

I sat alone in the center of a candle lit room with three other shamans. Two of us were men, and two were women, a perfect balance of the masculine and the feminine. It was our only night off during a weeklong workshop and the four of us showed up to engage in a journeying exercise.

Journeying is a shamanic practice of accessing different realms or traveling along the time continuum. We were there to practice vision and dreaming. That's right, practice. To those of us that this comes naturally, it still takes practice.

At one point during our exercise my spirit floated down from above the clouds. When I reached the clouds they parted and in an instant I knew where I was. It was Bryce Canyon Utah.

For those of you who have never had the most fortunate experience of visiting there I will do my best to describe it. This is not an easy task for I have seen few pictures that have been able to capture its beauty. From the side of a massive plateau a canyon formed that contains thousands upon thousands of spires in every shade of red, orange, yellow and purple. These spires are called hoodoos and they stand up several hundred feet from the canyon floor like colorful columns in a magical palace. Where there are not hoodoos, washes, or hiking paths there are pine trees. To see, feel and smell the sunrise and sunset on Bryce Canyon is an experience I don't believe anyone should miss.

I have been blessed with the opportunity to visit this magical place several times, but one time sticks out in my mind as the most special. It was eleven years ago and I was with my son who was eight years old at the time. We passed our time hiking the canyon together on a beautiful summer day. I can still hear his walking stick tapping the ground with each step he made, as we weaved our way around the hoodoos and pine trees.

So here I am eleven years later my spirit parting the clouds above the same canyon. I float down and take a seat on one of the log benches that are placed along the miles of hiking trails. After some time, a man about thirty and a young boy approach walking the path next to where I am seated. The boy is not really walking though; his walk could be described as something that was more like a bouncing motion. He is filled with that incredibly beautiful little boy energy. His father is present and thoroughly enjoying his son's unbridled enthusiasm.

As they pass me I suddenly recognize them! The father is my son's unborn son and his son is my great grandson. I follow along behind them, my heart filled with joy. The father is telling his son how his grandfather (my son) and his great-grandfather (me) hiked these same trails when grandpa was a little boy.

They stopped to gaze at one of the colorful monoliths standing above the canyon floor and the father said, "Imagine that son, grandpa and his daddy probably admired this same hoodoo forty five years ago and might have even hiked this same path."

When I told a friend of mine about this vision, he got it immediately. His eyes lit up and he said, "You mean it's still there? You're telling me that Bryce Canyon is still there."

"Yea Ken, it's still there," I replied

From time to time when I get to thinking negatively about where our current course as a species is taking us, I go back to this vision and send it energy. Knowing that every time I do this the odds are increased that this vision will become a reality.

As we all wander, walk, stumble or evolve our way through this most precarious time in human history, I believe it is of the utmost importance that we realize that dreaming and exercising our vision of the future, is how we create the world we live in. During this time of environmental destruction, economic upheaval, war, hunger and terrorism, many of us believe it is crucial to hold a vision of peace and prosperity for all life. A vision where the human race honors the earth and considers environmental care taking both a privilege and a responsibility.

Dream with me, won't you?

John English

January 2003

There are several books that have had a significant impact on who I am today as a person. Below is a list of a few that I would recommend.

Conscious Evolution: *Awakening the Power of our Social Potential,* by Barbara Marx Hubbard   ISBN #1-57731-016-0

Conversations with God Book 1: *An Uncommon Dialogue,* by Neale Donald Walsch   ISBN #0-399-14278-9

The Course of Miracles: *Text – Workbook For Students – Manual For Teachers,* by The Foundation for Inner Peace ISBN #0-9606388-2-2

Dance of the Four Winds: *Secrets of the Inca Medicine Wheel,* by Alberto Villoldo, Ph.D., and Erik Jendrescn ISBN #0-89281-514-0

The Food Revolution: *How Your Diet Can Help Save Your Life and Our World,* by John Robbins   ISBN #1-57324-702-2

Ishmael: *An Adventure of the Mind and Spirit,* by Daniel Quinn   ISBN #0-553-37540-7

The Last Hours of Ancient Sunlight: *Waking up to Personal and Global Transformation,* by Thom Hartmann ISBN #0-609-80529-0

The Power of Now: *A Guide to Spiritual Enlightenment,* by Eckhart Tolle   ISBN # 1-57731-152-3

The Prophet's Way: *Touching the Power of Life,* by Thom Hartmann   ISBN # 0-9655-7280-3

Shaman, Healer, Sage: *How to Heal Yourself and Others with the Energy Medicine of the Americas,* by Alberto Villoldo, Ph.D ISBN #0-609-60544-5

Steps to Freedom: *Discourses on the Alchemy of the Heart,* by Reshad Feild   ISBN # 0-939660-04-0

The World is as You Dream it: *Shamanic Teachings from the Amazon and Andes,* by John Perkins   ISBN #0-89281-459-4

John English first recognized the human capacity to dream one's life destiny into being approximately fifteen years ago. Over the next twelve years he would use this skill to direct his path in life. About three years ago he began to feel a strong desire to be of greater service to his fellow human beings and the planet. This led him to adopt the experiential path of shamanism. He is a writer, small businessman and a shamanic healer who studied with Alberto Villoldo, Ph.D., of The Four Winds Society. This is his first book. John and his family live in Phoenix, Arizona.